SHADOWED DOORSTEP

BOOK 1 – THE SHADOWED FILES

VIKKI COROWA

ISBN: 979-8-90057-139-3 - Ebook

ISBN: 979-8-90057-140-9 - Paperback

Namarca, Amariah, Jarell and Shanae

"Thank you for believing in me and encouraging me to take this first step in penning my first novel. You believed in me when I didn't believe in myself, and for this I am very grateful."

The light shines in the darkness, and the darkness has not overcome it.

JOHN 1:5 NIV

CHAPTER 1

Jules had always been challenged with direction, and today, she was downright bad at it. And all because her doctor had said she was having twins. She looked at the scanned image for the umpteenth time, and there staring back at her were two faces in the 3-D image.

Lost in thought and wandering the quiet tree-lined walkway in Upper Coomera, Jules dodged the odd exercise enthusiast while pondering her life. She breathed in a deep lungful of crisp air as she studied the afternoon sun, which would make any artist drool over its crisscross of pink and orange, sometimes distinct and other times a blur of melded colour splashed across the cloud-splattered sky.

As she rounded a corner of a building, her steps faltered when a sound from a cane-weaved basket on the pavement caught her attention. She inched towards it. Her heart raced as her mind registered what she thought she'd heard.

Jules bent and opened the lid of the oval-shaped basket. Almost hidden by thick black wavy hair, two big brown eyes stared back at her. "No way." Jules straightened to her full height of five feet nothing and dragged her eyes away from the ones watching her to look up the street.

No one.

She looked behind her.

No one.

She stared back at the bundle in front of her. She mumbled to herself to get it together, then took another glance around the street.

Who gets out of their vehicle and starts walking? Clearly, I do. Dumb. Dumb idea.

Where was she? She had no clue.

The baby began screaming, pulling her from her silent rebuke. And, as if on cue, as Jules leaned in, the baby's arms stretched out uncontrollably, begging to be picked up.

"You certainly are gorgeous," whispered Jules. Scrunching her nose at the whiff of a dirty nappy, Jules cooed as she lifted the baby into her arms.

Hunkering down in the shadows, sweat droplets formed on her forehead as Liz observed the woman snuggle the soft bundle into her arms.

A woman was not meant to find the basket.

Alex was.

Despite the wind whipping across her face and the chill in the air, Liz felt anything but chilled. She was downright perspiring. She gnawed on her bottom lip as her heart raced and her fingers twisted into a gazillion knots. She waited, watching and hoping the woman would do the right thing and take 'Little Butterfly' somewhere safe.

The street was eerily quiet. Liz watched as the woman took a step and looked around. She virtually pirouetted on the spot, scanning the shop fronts and beyond.

Taking a few steps backwards, Liz disappeared into the shadows.

She couldn't watch anymore.

⁂

Jules waited for someone to show themselves while she rocked the baby back and forth, but no one did. She took a tentative step, then two. She walked some more.

She patted the front of her pants pockets. Then her jacket. No phone.

She groaned. "What am I to do?" Throwing her head back, she let it dangle for a moment as she stared up at the departing sun.

How could she be lacking in self-awareness? She looked around to get her bearings.

There were shops, trees, very few cars, but no people.

How could she be a good mum and be directionally challenged? Her unborn babies' lives depended on her to know where she was going, to get them to and from home safely. Like this baby's life depended on her.

Pray came the answer.

Standing still, she bowed her head and focused on the brown-eyed girl snuggling into her jacket. "*Dear Lord, you know I need help—*"

"Um, excuse me, do you and your baby need help?"

Jules' eyes flew open as her head flung upwards to see a man standing a few feet away from her.

She took a step back. "I think God just answered my prayer in record time," she blurted out.

But the man said nothing else. He folded his arms across his chest and looked at her, then at the bundle in her arms.

With the sun setting behind him and his Akubra hat pulled so far down, the dark shadows made it hard for Jules to decipher his facial features. His faded jeans fit his tall, solid frame perfectly, and the flannel shirt he wore was pushed to his elbows. His worn boots were dusted with a sprinkling of water from somewhere because she sure hadn't felt rain.

She finished perusing him and looked up to see his lips hadn't budged one iota.

So he was of the silent kind. She'd soon fix that.

She shifted her weight to her other foot and flicked her eyes downwards away from his piercing gaze. "I know this may sound strange, but I found this baby. She was on the doorstep outside The Coomera Marketplace."

Jules waited for the farmer to reply, but when he said nothing, she couldn't help herself. "Do you speak?" she asked, shoving the baby towards him.

Instead, he shuffled his dirty boots and narrowed his look at her.

It was one of pure disbelief.

"I am serious. I found this baby on the doorstep."

She could almost hear him saying, "As if." His mouth pinched to a thin line, but still he said nothing.

The baby began to cry, and Jules jiggled her in her arms as the wind picked up around them, whipping her hair across her face.

Juggling both babe and plucking at her hair to tame it with one hand, she puffed out a breath of air through swollen cheeks. She side-stepped the sun that had now blinded her straight as she changed position.

How many things could go so wrong in one instant?

Add to that her pregnant belly was giving her pains, and this farmer-looking dude had not spoken more than one phrase since the beginning.

Swaying sideways and getting a bashful of sunrays at the wrong angle, Jules used her hand to shield her face as she panted. "I need to get this baby to a hospital…and I need to ring my husband." She puffed and dragged in a lungful of fumes as a loud car drove past and backfired, making her and the baby jump.

The baby began screaming.

"Shh, little one." Jules cooed. "Do you have a phone I could borrow, please… I left mine in my car, which is…" She spun around, flustered. She really didn't want to tell the stranger she had no clue where she'd left it.

"You mean you don't know where it is?"

"So, the man does speak?"

Okay, so she'd blurted out the last line without thinking and deserved his expression.

The farmer's mouth dropped open as he ran one suntanned hand down his short, trimmed beard, handing her his phone from his back pocket with the other. "Give me the baby while you make the call."

She passed over the baby, eyeing him with suspicion, and stepped back, glad to have the ache in her arms and back relieved.

"She looks like… It can't be…" Alex never finished his sentence as he corralled Jules, who still held the phone to her ear, towards his vehicle.

"Jay, I found a baby. Meet me at the hospital… No…I will tell you about it when I get there." She hung up the phone in a rush because the look on the man's face had her worried.

He placed the baby on her lap and buckled them both in. "We are going together to the hospital."

"Ah, no, we are not. What about my car?"

"How are you going to hold the baby and drive at the same time?" His raised eyebrow and hand waving didn't need to state the obvious.

He'd made his point.

"So, when do I get my car?" Jules was not letting this go.

"You can figure it out with your husband. It's obviously near here. We need to get this baby to the hospital ASAP."

"You don't look so good," Jules mumbled as he shut the door on the pair of them. She hadn't even finished talking when he rounded his side of the car.

No car seats. She hoped there would be no cops. It would be a bit hard to explain their way out of this one.

"What do you mean, I have to fill out a form for the baby?"

"Ma'am, to have your baby looked at by a doctor, we need your details, the baby's details, and your Medicare number," replied the nurse at the front counter.

"For Pete's sake..."

"Excuse me, who's Pete?" asked the naive, now annoying, nurse.

"No one is Pete. It's a saying." Jules heard the low chuckle beside her and flung a glare towards the farmer, who leant on his forearms beside her, clearly enjoying the moment. Brushing her hair back over her shoulder and turning to the nurse, Jules took another slow, deep breath before continuing. "As I was saying, I was out walking, and I stumbled over the basket with the baby inside." She flicked a thumb over her shoulder and continued. "This gentleman—"

"Alex. My name is Alex."

She pivoted her large abdomen his direction and ground through clenched teeth, "So he has a name, too."

"Of course I have a name, you never asked," Alex replied with a sparkle in his eye to the nurse who was now fully attentive to Alex, and rising to shake his hand.

Jules huffed. She never had her hand shaken. "Um, hello, I found the baby, and all he did was gawk at me holding the baby. I have the answers to your questions."

Alex's eyes glinted with humour, and the slight pull at the crease of his lips hinted he was taking pleasure in every minute of the interaction.

"Sir, can you confirm what the lady is saying?" interrupted a doctor who'd been standing nearby.

Alex nodded.

"Yes, apparently he can speak, Doc," answered Jules, turning to face the doctor. "He can tell you where—"

"Well, let the man speak," the doc said, and she saw that same glint and spark hit Alex's eyes and the same smirk tease the corner of his mouth.

So he was a smart aleck, too.

Nice.

She felt the heat in her cheeks.

"Jules. Jules. Are you okay?" Her husband rushed through the emergency room entrance and came to an abrupt halt. "Whoa, whose baby is that?"

"That is what we are trying to find out," said the doctor as she put her hands out to the baby.

Jules held on for a little longer than necessary before handing her over.

"Don't go anywhere. Please stay in the waiting room in case we need further information." The doctor strode off with the crying baby.

"You mean I have to sit here and wait some more?" Jules stared at the back of the departing doctor. Had that really happened? Had she really found a baby on the ground? Or was it all a nightmare?

"Honey, I'm talking to you."

Jules shook her head. She turned and stared at her husband.

"When you said 'baby', I left work immediately."

Jules grabbed her husband's forearm and dragged him towards the chairs. "I need to sit down before I start telling you what happened."

"Hang on a minute," her husband said, turning to face her. "Who is he?" Pointing to Alex with his head, the man put a protective arm around his wife as Alex stalked towards the chairs.

"That is Alex."

"What, Alex doesn't have a last name?" her husband asked, giving him a once-over.

"Portelli." Alex spun on his heel and put out his right hand.

"Jaymond Niko, Jules' husband."

Jules patted her husband's forearm, soothing the tension. "Most people call him Jay for short."

"What are you doing here with my wife? With a baby?" Jay's words were clipped.

"Finally," Jules muttered as she looked at her watch when the doors opened twenty minutes later and the female doctor strode back out without the baby, beside a police officer and another serious-looking person, her brother-in-law.

Why was Solomon at the hospital?

They were all ushered into a dark and sterile room. No colour, just off-white walls with one large desk and three chairs in the middle. Jules was offered a chair. The doctor sat on one, and Jay was offered the other. Solomon and the police officer remained standing near the door while Alex leaned against a hospital gurney.

Jules looked around at all their faces. There were no smiles, just concern etched in their eyes. Solomon was not looking at her either. Why was he not looking at her?

"There is no simple way to say this," the police officer began, "but it has come to our attention, Mrs Niko, the baby you found has a twin—"

"Come again?" Alex said.

"You don't think we had anything to do with it, do you?" Jules stammered, her eyes darting between Solomon, Jaymond and the police officer. Her heart rate peaked. She was going to faint.

"No, Mrs Niko. No one is accusing you of taking a baby, stealing a baby or whatever you are thinking," reassured the police officer. But he did shift his feet to angle his attention to Alex.

Jules noticed the farmer's previous olive complexion tinge a darker shade as his honey, light brown eyes zeroed in on the officer's face. The beefy farmer was bracing for some hard words.

"Mr and Mrs Niko, you can both leave. We need to talk further with Alex."

Her face blanched as she rose and left the room, with Jaymond pulling her close.

Holding her husband's hand for comfort, she whispered as they left, "I hope Alex is not in trouble."

"If he hasn't done anything wrong, he'll be alright."

"He seems such a lovely man."

Jay raised an eyebrow at his wife.

"What? Just an observation of my brief encounter. I can sense these things, you know," she answered as she waddled off beside him towards the entrance of the hospital.

"Alex, do you want to take a seat?" asked Constable Harvey.

"No, I prefer to stand." If he were about to be accused of baby snatching, he'd prefer to face it head-on. He watched the woman who had just turned his life upside down leave with her husband.

"Alex," Solomon interrupted his thoughts. "Take a seat, mate. This is rough, hearing it a second time in as many days."

Alex took the seat Jaymond had vacated and settled in as Solomon took the one to his right. The doc remained in her chair as Constable Harvey shut the door.

"We believe the other baby girl that you brought in yesterday, is this little girl's sister. We have run DNA tests and must wait for the results, but they look identical," the doctor said. "Solomon will have to do his reports for the Department of Child Safety, and the Child Protection and Investigation Unit will also become involved."

Alex needed water. He knew it the moment he'd laid eyes on the baby this evening, but to have it confirmed was on a whole new level. He found his voice. "So, what you're saying is, someone decided to drop off two babies at my marketplace, a day apart?" Unbelief laced his words.

His mind raced at the unthinkable. "Why? Why would a mother do that?" Alex shifted in his seat. He wanted to get out of there. "Am I accused of anything? Am I under arrest?" The thought suddenly hit him.

"No, not at present. You seem to be the random person chosen or the random location chosen," Constable Harvey said.

"But why?" Alex couldn't shake the feeling he had been watched, chosen, hand-picked by someone to leave their babies at his doorstep. He ran his hands up and down his face.

"That is for us to find out. A full investigation is underway. You may be required for further questioning, but for now, you are free to go," said Constable Harvey.

"But I have a few thoughts to add," he said. "I'd chosen to go out the roller door tonight. Had Jules not been there, that baby would have been left there all night."

The words hung in the sterile room as the doc, Solomon, and Constable Harvey weighed what he said.

A cold shiver ran down his spine at the thought of what could have happened to the baby.

"Well, let's be thankful Jules found herself walking the streets of Upper Coomera this evening," Solomon said, his voice pitchy.

"I agree," said the doctor, "otherwise this could have been a very different outcome for Baby Number Two."

"And someone could have been up for manslaughter," said Constable Harvey."

Alex gaped at the words. "Can I go? I need to get back to the farm." What he needed was a ride on his horse to unwind.

Guilt gnawed at Steph's conscience as she watched her friend take a long swig of water from a bottle and flop down onto the double-seat lounge chair opposite her. "So, how'd it go?" Steph shifted forward to the edge of the single chair in her friend's lounge room.

"Hang on. My head's pounding."

Steph waited as Liz massaged her temples and shifted the motion to above her eyebrows.

She could still feel her baby's little soft foreheads on her lips but knew over time that gentle caress would disappear. She squashed down the memory of that last kiss to each baby. It would only gnaw at her soul. Tears sprang to her eyes, and she swiped them away.

"So?" Steph asked again, pushing for an answer.

Something had gone wrong.

She could feel it.

"Little Butterfly Number Two took to its wings but in a different direction."

"What? How?" Panic hit her heart. She wasn't meant to care, but she did.

She'd given her babies up, and the plan had been nutted out and executed down to the timing of Alex being at the shop.

"Well, you know how Little Butterfly Number One was picked up by your person of choice; Little Butterfly Number Two was not."

"What do you mean she wasn't?" Steph asked, leaning her elbows on her knees.

"A pregnant woman found her in the basket."

Steph noticed the words 'pregnant woman' had been said quietly but chose to ignore them.

"Didn't you hang around and see what she did with her?"

"No. I couldn't."

"Why didn't you?"

"I would have walked out of those shadows and snatched Little Butterfly out of her arms," Liz ground between clenched teeth as she stood and shook her arms out.

"That's it. Enough with the names." Steph stood beside her, not bothering to hide the agitation in her voice.

Names mattered to her, and no one was naming her babies.

"Well, you never named them," Liz argued, "and I have to call them something other than it or her."

Steph glared at her friend. "You know how I feel about that."

Fiddling with her fingernails, Liz walked towards the window to stare out at the view that had always calmed her in the past. Mountains and valleys, filled with greenery, blue sky and fluffy clouds. "Fair enough. If you don't want to call them anything, then the brown-haired and brown-eyed babies are now safe in someone else's hands," she said with her back to Steph.

"Away from Rick," Steph muttered.

"You make it sound easy." Liz turned and faced her friend, propping one hand on her hip.

"I didn't ask for him to grab me and force himself on me." Steph's words rose as she stood squaring off with Liz, eye to eye. "You…you suggested I give them away." Steph spun on her heels and threw the pretty pink and white pillow she'd been clutching from her hands and stormed out of the room.

"Yes, but not like that." Liz bellowed after her.

Steph stopped in the hallway, retraced her steps, and in a tone that was calm and measured, she eyeballed her friend. "I never asked for them to be born. And now I must live with the fact that I gave them away. And you need to deal with what we have done."

And with that, she pivoted and walked out of the room, defeat, sadness and immense anger at what she'd been forced to do at the hands of fear.

CHAPTER 2

"Honey, I think I'm about to have the babies," panted Jules in between laboured breaths two evenings later. She sat propped up, leaning against the bedhead, pain squeezing her abdomen. The look in her eye sent her husband moving off the bed. "You may be a paramedic," she said in between breaths, "but have you ever delivered premature twins?"

A slow shake of his head and a quick change of clothes had them both moving out the door and towards the hospital in a matter of minutes.

Hours later, Jules heard words no woman in labour wants to hear. "Try not to scream, love," came the soft voice of a midwife. "Put your energy into pushing, not screaming."

The woman patted her hand, but Jules reefed it away. "Easy for you to say. You aren't the one trying to push a watermelon out," she ground out through gritted teeth as another contraction gripped her in its vice-like hold.

"Honey, she is only trying to help." Jules swung her upside-down smile at her husband, and her glare silenced the room.

He shrugged one shoulder.

"Don't go telling me how I should be. You aren't… Oww…" The sound dragged as another contraction intensified.

Sweat poured from her face as every part of her body ached, down to her tailbone. Pressure she had never felt before was bearing down on her. She thought her body was going to split in half vertically. The contraction eased, and she gulped in air.

"As I was saying, lovey, put your energy and focus here."

Pressure pulsed where the baby was meant to be coming out.

Jules gave the woman the most wicked eyes she could muster. She wanted to swat the woman's hand away that was between her legs.

But could she reach over her swollen abdomen and dislodge the woman's fingers? No way. Nada.

Deep down, Jules knew the midwife was trying her darndest to help, but the pain was unbearable, and she wanted to scream, but the woman was telling her not to.

Was the woman mad?

The squeezing built as a full-blown contraction hammered her stomach and back. Her screaming subsided as Jules did what the midwife instructed. Contractions came and went, and Jules puffed and panted, remaining focused, until finally, it was time to push.

"Oh my, the stinging." Jules dragged out the last syllable as the crowning of the first baby occurred. "What in the world…" The sentence was lost as the unbearable stinging overtook her perineum.

Tears fell from her eyes.

"Mr Niko, would you like to cut the cord of your first baby?"

"What? It's out?" Jules asked. Sweat poured down her face as she looked between her legs. Surely, she would have felt the baby slip out, but she hadn't. It had happened quickly. The birth and the squishy part had been a blur.

With tears streaming down his face, Jaymond cut the cord, and the baby was placed on her breasts. "He's beautiful, Jules."

She looked at her husband's eyes. He was in love as he gazed at the little bundle on her chest.

"Okay." It was the midwife again, speaking to her.

"Can you quit for a minute?" Jules asked.

Jaymond looked at her. She saw the shock in his eyes.

"It's alright. I'm used to mother's saying all sorts of things to me," the midwife chuckled.

Jules needed a breather. A time-out.

"You'll have a minute or two of breathing space, but when your body is ready, it will begin contracting again to move baby number two down through the birth canal. Jules, we don't want a contraction grabbing you while you're holding baby number one."

Jules looked up at Jaymond, who couldn't tear his eyes from his wife as he listened to the midwife. His deep chocolate-brown eyes oozed awe and wonder, love and admiration all wrapped up in that one gaze.

"Why don't we give him to your husband for a moment?" suggested the midwife.

"Okay," Jaymond answered.

"When the contractions start again, pass baby one over to the nurse, so you are ready for round two."

"Sounds like I'm in a boxing ring," Jules remarked. "I can feel another one coming. Don't I get a longer break between the two?" Jules asked.

Jaymond stared at his wife and gathered the soft, warm bundle, and passed him to the nurse.

"I wish we had control over that, but these natural births come as they are, and we just go with it," said the midwife.

Jules groaned.

"Now, remember what you did before. Focus on where the pressure is and put your energy there. Not into screaming."

Jules nodded at the midwife and bore down.

Several minutes later, a second boy was born into the world, and Jaymond sat beside his wife, unashamed of the tears coursing down his face as he held Kayden.

Jules watched Tyreece fuss at her breast, amazed at how small he was. They both would need to spend time in the neonatal intensive care unit in humidicribs, but right at that moment, the doctor and midwife were happy for her to try breastfeeding and giving them bonding skin time.

In another part of town, Steph lifted her hand to open the pub door, as a paper fluttered against her ankle and stayed there, begging to be read. She bent down and claimed it just as it had claimed her attention.

In the darkness of the night, she hadn't been able to make out its words, but the damp, dark hold of the pub dwelling fitted her spirits perfectly, so she stole a seat and as the stale cigarettes filled her nostrils she read words she'd never heard before, and it sparked a flame, a glimmer of hope in the darkness suffocating her.

She sat staring at the thin, ripped paper, questioning the meaning of the words. She didn't know who the words were talking about, but something deep in her soul forced her not to let go of the hope they spoke of.

As the sun peeked through the thin curtain, the following morning, she sat in her only lounge chair, contemplating her future. The chair represented her life – broken.

Too many wrong decisions.

Too many broken promises.

Too many shattered pieces of her heart scattered to the wrong men.

All she had left were fragments. How could they ever be pieced back together? With a broken heart came a broken spirit. One that others thought little of.

She sat staring at the paper like it was a sign from heaven.

With no desire to go out and no money, a day on the couch in front of her small TV seemed perfect. She closed her eyes and let herself drift off to sleep with the noise of the TV blurring in the background.

Rick's deep voice was loud in her ear as he screamed her name. "Steph, give me the money in your wallet. I know you have more."

"I have already given you everything I have." She tipped her wallet upside down to make her point.

He grabbed it off her and ripped it open, like somehow money would miraculously reappear in the centre bifold. "Where is it?" he growled as he threw her purse sideways, glaring at her with rage.

She knew better than to talk back. She had already received a wallop to the mouth for speaking when he had asked a question. "It was rhetorical," he'd said.

His speech slurred. His breath was a toxic mix of bourbon and Coke as he swayed in front of her.

She wished he'd stop yelling.

He grabbed a fistful of her hair and hauled her to the front door. "I give you money and you spend it on yourself," he'd ranted.

If he didn't spend it on alcohol, they would have more of it, she thought, but she wasn't game to voice that.

Steph had cowered in the corner of the front porch where he'd dragged her. The light met the darkness, casting a shadow on Rick's features as he shouted about her being useless while swaying on the doorstep.

She wanted to bolt but was too afraid to move. He slammed the door in her face, and she curled up in the cold shadows of the doorstep, waiting for him to let her back inside.

He never did.

A door banged shut, and she jumped, waking her from the deep sleep.

She rubbed her hands over her face and pinched her shoulders. Yes, she was awake and breathing.

She had been dreaming that nightmare again.

When would that dream stop haunting her? He never did let her in that night. She had nearly frozen to death in one of the coldest winters she'd ever felt, and Rick hadn't cared for her one bit.

She'd wished for death, but even death hadn't taken her.

She'd become a loner with her boyfriend as her sole companion.

Steph shuddered as she thought about her baby girls. What she did by leaving them abandoned on a doorstep was her choice. Liz never liked the idea, and as far as Steph could tell, she was still angry with her decision.

Liz had morals. Steph knew that. She'd come from a hardworking, educated family. Steph didn't even know where her family were. They'd all been separated in childhood because of her alcoholic parents and placed into the foster care system.

She only knew the details written on her birth certificate.

Samoan parentage. Stephanie Rose Sefo. It seemed ironic that her parents had given her such a pretty name. From as young as five years old, she remembered correcting her then-foster parents. "My name is Steph. Not Stephanie." She would not accept that anything beautiful could come from her life, even a pretty name.

But now, something had. Two beautiful baby girls had come from her body, and she had done the only thing she knew to do: remove them.

Steph knew by abandoning her babies, she'd forced them into the very system she hated. But she also knew, for them to be safe, they had to be free from her and Rick. She couldn't see any other way.

It had been her only choice. Hadn't it?

Steph flopped onto her back on her tiny couch.

Rick could never know.

The daily internal monologue tortured her soul.

No one knew she had twins except Liz. Rick had only recognised her pregnant belly but hadn't asked questions. She didn't tell him anything. All he wanted when he visited was money for drugs.

Steph inherently knew that she and the babies would be neglected or worse, beaten.

Everything went to Rick and his passions. A baby, make that two, could have pushed him to harm them. She couldn't live with that. She could barely survive the daily trauma, let alone take care of them.

A loud banging startled Steph, and she bolted upright.

"I know you're in there. Open the door before I bash it down."

Dread filled Steph to the depths of her being. Her hands shook. Her heart kicked into overdrive.

How could he have known I came back?

As if Rick had heard the unspoken words, his harsh retort came through the door, loud and angry. "You left your stupid jandals at the front door. They gave you away, you dumb woman."

Steph stared at the inch-thick piece of timber separating her from the man she dreaded.

The barrier hadn't softened his tone, and his voice rose the longer he stood outside. "I frequent here often enough to see when you'd show your face." Rick's voice changed. "Didn't you think I'd check up on you?"

Steph bit her nails as Rick's voice swooned on the other side. She jiggled her leg up and down as she stared at the door, but still she stood frozen in place. He would need to do a whole lot of sweet-talking to get her moving.

"Come on, baby. You know I didn't mean to sound angry. I miss you. Open the door so I can at least see you, and we can talk."

Shaking, Steph moved beside the door, listening to every word he said because in the end it was his charm that coaxed Steph into action like bait on a hook; she swallowed it, and he reeled her in.

"Come on, baby, I want to see your beautiful face. Our baby must be due soon."

Steph flinched at the mention of the word baby. Her palms grew sweaty, and she dragged them down her pants as Rick's voice grew edgy. Her babies were safe, and she knew if she didn't face Rick now, she would have to face him later. She breathed in deeply as she unlocked the door, stilling herself for what was to come.

"What the hang is wrong with you, girl?" His smoothness fled as he yanked her sideways to step inside. His eyes were wild with fury as he looked around the small unit. He stepped closer to her, and she inhaled a full whiff of foul liquor.

Steph took a footstep back.

Closing the gap, he stepped forward, leaning down into her face. "Why keep a man waiting? I don't care if your belly…" Rick's eyes traced from her face down her body, resting at her belly where the bump used to be. "What's going on here?" Grabbing her arm, he dragged her towards the bedroom.

His fingers pinched into her flesh as she fought to follow him. Steph remained silent as Rick flung her onto the bed, his rant now a one-sided angry exchange. "You'd be a no-good mother anyway, you know that…you never looked after me," he slurred his words together as he pulled his clothes off his body in uncontrolled movements.

She stayed quiet and pulled herself away from him when he struggled with his shirt buttons. She had snuck almost to the doorway when he grabbed her and slammed her back onto the bed, yelling, "If we had a baby, we wouldn't be able to make love."

If he thought this was love, he was way off base.

"You are mine, you know that, don't you? No one else can have you." Rick stroked her face and hair with his hand, and she steeled herself, refusing to shudder under his advances. Instead, she succumbed to what lay ahead. Too many times before she'd fought against him and had ended up worse for it. As she curled into a foetal position, waiting for what was to come, she let her mind drift to a peaceful place, separating her mind from her body.

❋

"Any idea why they picked your place?" Jeremy asked Alex as they sat around Jaymond's kitchen table, enjoying the brothers' Saturday morning coffee and breakfast ritual.

Staring at the eldest of the three Niko brothers, Alex answered, "Nah, not yet. It's like they, the mother or whoever, picked me."

"Why leave two babies at the same location, separate days apart, on the days you are known to take your produce to The Coomera Marketplace?" queried Solomon as he swirled the last of his coffee.

"True, and it occurred in the evening when the crowds weren't there," reminded Alex.

"So, what we have," concluded Jaymond, holding up one hand, making a point to count on his fingers, "is one, a person who knows you. Two, they know your routine. Three, they trust you to do the right thing." Jaymond sipped his coffee before continuing. "Four, they know you're reliable. And five, they know you take care of strays."

"That gives me the creeps," interjected Alex.

"Now we're getting somewhere," Jeremy added. "You're thinking like a cop, little brother."

"Can we look at your security camera footage?" Solomon asked as he stood to take his coffee mug to the sink. "I know it's not a part of my caseload, but I'm curious to see if a person who may be pregnant or not frequents your store."

Jeremy looked around at his brothers and rapped his knuckles on the table. "Off the clock, I'm happy to investigate, to make sure nothing is missed. These babies are Samoan, and that means our own are hurting, and I want to find out who they are."

"Amen to that, bro," chorused around the table.

"I think that'd be great," said Alex as he rose from his chair and began to clear the dishes from the table before stacking them in the dishwasher. "To have an answer as to why, and possibly who, would take a load off my mind."

"A stalker for a bloke. Yeesh." Solomon rubbed his hand at the back of his neck.

Alex stood upright at the dishwasher and turned to the younger brother. "Mate, come on. Seriously."

"Has anyone wondered why this kind of desperation has to exist in the world?" countered Jaymond.

Tracing a finger around the pattern on the bench top, Solomon voiced his thoughts. "I think it has to do with having free will. Man was given and will always be given the power to choose. That is called free will. That is God's Sovereignty at its highest level."

Everyone turned and looked at the softly spoken brother.

"What?" Feeling awkward about speaking his thoughts, Solomon escaped through the back door to join his sister-in-law and nephews in the backyard. His thick, wavy, black hair bounced as he exited the door.

Staring after his brother, Jaymond remarked, "Wow, that was powerful and insightful, to say the least."

"Agreed," added Jeremy.

Considering the sombre moment, Alex nodded to the remaining Niko brothers. "Thanks again for breakfast, I'd better get back to the farm and do some work." He walked down the hall towards the front door and let himself out.

Hearing the click of the front door close quietly, Jeremy turned and looked out the window at his brother holding little Tyreece.

An even bigger question than a missing mother lurked in the back of his mind.

He had always put the world's problems squarely on the shoulders of the Supreme Being. Blaming Him when things went wrong and acknowledging Him when things went well. If God was not in full control of everything that happened on this earth, then who was? Or was there more to it than that?

CHAPTER 3

Sitting on the couch, disheartened and hurting, Steph pondered the cycles of abusive patterns she'd fallen into and how the tricks of manipulation had worked on her time and again. Rick had made her think it was her fault that they had no money, that she'd spent too much on food, when all the while he'd been drinking it away.

He had made her feel special at the start, and he had treated her with kindness and love, but as the alcohol and drugs took hold, so had the paranoia that other men wanted her. Soon, she wasn't allowed out at all, to parties or social gatherings. The only outing was to buy groceries, and even that was timed. She was exhausted, and she'd had enough.

She hung her head in her hands and refused to cry. In a few days, she'd be gone from the only place Rick knew where to look for her. She'd remained hidden for the last few months of her pregnancy. Being able to hide the fact she'd given birth to twins meant the streets didn't know, which also meant Liz had kept her mouth shut.

Rick was losing his hold on her, at least in her mind.

"If he truly loved you, he wouldn't treat you this way." Liz's words echoed in Steph's mind.

Thinking of her friend brought a smile to her bruised face and busted lip. That girl had come back into her life at the perfect time, hiding her at her place until she'd given birth.

As Steph sat on the lounge chair that reeked of Rick, she remembered her conversation with Liz not long after her girls were born.

"I'll go back. It'll be all right. Rick hasn't been seen for months around town. He's probably gone."

Liz had disagreed. "I doubt it, my friend. Once a guy like him thinks he owns a girl, it doesn't matter how long you're gone. He'll come back. He'll find you."

"He may have changed," Steph had argued. She'd even defended him.

Now who sat in a sad and sorry state, wishing she'd been wrong? Hurt but not destroyed, Steph got up and cleaned the house, hoping to forget the mistakes she'd made. If only erasing the last few months of her life were as easy as wiping away the dirt and grime from dishes.

Not more than an hour later, she heard a bang on the front door again. This time, it took all her effort to stop her knees from buckling.

Only Rick and his mates visited her. And Liz. Well, that had only occurred once. That had been a miracle, and miracles didn't happen to the same person twice, did they?

Staring at the door, Steph's mind drifted back to an early childhood memory of when a foster mother had told her of a God who loved her and was a whisper of a prayer away. That briefest of visits to that home had shown her there was another way to live. One filled with hope and love. The memory brought a smile to her swollen lips.

She winced in pain.

Unfortunately, she hadn't stayed there long enough for hope to take root in her soul. She was quickly thrust into another house where the carer only had foster children for the sake of the money.

At that house, Steph decided, if there really was a God, He didn't want anything to do with her. He'd left her to fend for herself. He'd left her with parents who didn't want her, with parents who chose liquor over children.

She'd even gone to a foster care child's funeral once when she was younger. The little boy had died of leukemia. His parents had given him up because he was sick. She reasoned that if this God, who saw everything, as the preacher out front said, saw even the little sparrows fall to the ground, then He was obviously blind to them or didn't care enough about any of them in foster care, where they stayed, because that woman abused them. In that foster house, she had become an angry, hurt little girl who was mad at the world.

The banging at her front door grew louder, bringing her out of her daydreaming. This time, there was no yelling.

She began to breathe easier. Rick yelled if she didn't get to the door straight away.

Steph moved towards the front of the house, trying not to exacerbate the injuries to her already bruised knee. She peeked through the side curtain, which gave a view of the front porch.

Standing with a bag of groceries was her trusted and only faithful friend, Liz.

It seemed miracles did happen twice.

Being in two minds about opening the door, she paused with her hand on the doorknob. Either she would have to shield off questions of her apparent condition or go hungry for more days than she cared to remember.

Her hunger got the better of her and won out.

Steph cracked open her door to reveal a battered face.

Immediately, Liz's face went from shock to composure. Raising one hand with the bag of groceries and the other with a tray of takeaway cups, Liz offered, "Who's up for chocolate brownies, homemade, I might add, and a hot coffee?"

Steph could tell her friend was trying to shift the mood.

Shielding herself behind the door, Steph stepped back as Liz entered. She'd tidied up Rick's mess, but she couldn't hide the two broken chairs that sat neatly in the corner. Her room appeared decent, except for her hiding partially behind the door.

Liz briefed the room but didn't turn to her before stepping off in the direction of the kitchen. "I'll put the cold stuff away and the other things into your pantry. Then we'll sit and have coffee and brownies."

Steph said nothing. She watched the back of her friend disappear into the kitchen, her ponytail bouncing as she walked. If Liz noticed there wasn't any food in the fridge or pantry, she kept it to herself. If she noticed the broken chairs, she didn't say anything about them either.

Liz reappeared and plonked herself on the couch opposite, where Steph was still standing, hugging her stomach. "Okay, Steph, talk to me. You know you can."

Liz's compassion-filled eyes, quiet voice and gentle demeanour were her undoing. Vowing to herself only moments earlier that she wouldn't cry, tears leaked down her face. Rick wasn't worth weeping over, but here she was crying. Steph sucked in a deep breath, struggling to speak. She knew Rick wasn't even there, but she was afraid he would hear her accusations and see her tears.

Rick didn't do tears. Any challenge or show of weakness made him angry.

But she remembered he never used to be like that, and Steph clung to that, hoping he might change and love her again, that one day they could become a real family, along with the twin girls.

Her twin girls, who remained nameless, would have a father.

Fresh tears sparked, and she blinked them back. A lump formed in her throat. She would not cry. Any undoing would break her, and how could she escape if she broke into a million pieces?

She would have to gather up all those pieces and escape one by one.

Steph glanced at her friend's concerned hazel eyes and sat beside her, pain stabbing her knee. The love Liz oozed without even knowing it pricked her eyes with more tears. What was with all the crying?

Steph had learnt to be tough, but in front of her friend, that well-built stone wall had begun to crack.

"As you can see, Rick has been here. He saw my jandals at the front door and demanded I open to let him in."

"Why would you open the door, knowing what he might do?"

No judgment, only concern reflected in Liz's question.

"I knew if I didn't let him in, he'd be back, and I'd get it worse. I guessed facing him straight up rather than dragging it out would end better for me."

It hadn't.

It never did.

All his demands going unmet only ever ended badly for her.

At least she'd done one thing right. She'd taken her babies somewhere safe and far away from Rick. All she had to do was pull off her next steps and that involved leaving the dump of a dive she called home and leaving Rick.

"Steph, we're leaving together today. You're not staying here anymore. He'll come back, and it could be worse."

Her friend had read her mind, but she panicked. "I can't. Not today."

"And tell me one good reason why?"

"Rick doesn't know I've got to be out by the end of the week. I need to clean the house without Rick knowing so I can get my bond back. I need the money, Liz. I can't just walk away today. I just can't." Steph hated sounding so desperate, but she was desperate. Desperate to leave. Desperate for money.

Standing, Liz replied, "Okay, where do I start? It's not a big place."

It was more to herself than to Steph.

She set off in search of cleaning products, determined to get it done as quickly as possible. Steph followed in her wake, only with less bounce and a noticeable limp.

After several hours of work, Liz sat back on the lounge chair and looked at the apartment. "Right, we've nearly finished the walls. I'll come back tomorrow and finish the rest. At this rate, you'll be out the day after tomorrow, one day early," announced Liz, pleased with their efforts.

Sitting upright in bed, Steph strained to hear the scraping sound that had roused her from sleep. It was coming from her left. Quietly, she crept off her bed towards the window. The noise was getting louder. Whoever was on the other side of the window was not being quiet.

Peeking through the curtain, she saw Rick in the moonlight, screwdriver in hand, trying to break into the security screen. Thankfully, the old screens that popped out easily had been replaced recently with security screens.

Thank you, landlord.

Surprisingly, Rick wasn't hollering at her to let him in. He was swaying on his feet, but he was quiet. Maybe Rick wanted the element of surprise on his side. Pity he hadn't realised how loud the scraping noise was because the surprise factor was definitely wasted.

Steph watched in silence as he dropped the screwdriver and muttered something under his breath as he rummaged the ground searching for what he'd dropped. The moonlight wasn't enough to reveal his tool in the shadowy bushes. Coming up empty-handed, he left as quickly as he'd come.

But now sleep eluded her.

As Alex opened his back door and walked in, his phone chimed, alerting him to a missed call from Jeremy. His growling stomach had brought him in from the paddock in search of food, but en route to the fridge, he noticed his sister at the kitchen table with piles of papers spread around her. "Did you bring anything from home for lunch?"

Taking a sip of her tea, she shook her head and focused on what she was doing.

Alex stood at the fridge, staring at his food choices, feeling a pang of loss for his mother, who had passed away last spring. Her creative flair for cooking had made everything taste sweeter and richer. His stomach growled again in protest.

Alex, who was only twenty-eight, had begun running the farm, mostly alone, ever since his dad had handed him the reins a couple of years ago in pursuit of other business ventures. Alex gradually introduced new farming techniques, crops and produce to the Portelli farm.

He had no time to spend on cooking and made do with the basics he could whip up quickly.

As he searched through the leftovers, Alex wondered how his dad would feel about his changes. It was a new generation of farming with himself at the helm.

Unsatisfied with what he saw, he shut the fridge and looked over at his sister, who had a pen balanced between her lips. He trusted Kelly. He couldn't have asked for a better younger sister. They were so similar, it was scary. He relied on her accounting skills and business ethic to balance his outdoor labour.

"Any news on those babies found at the marketplace?" asked Kelly, standing to stretch.

"As a matter of fact, I missed a call from Jeremy. I am guessing he has news."

"Don't keep him waiting. Go and make the call while I hunt through your fridge and make us some lunch. Then you can fill me in while we eat."

Going to the cool of the back patio, Alex sat on one of his homemade timber stools. He ran his hand through his hair and wondered why he was nervous. In all honesty, the idea of a mother choosing his location to leave two babies had him worried, to say the least. Staring out across his backyard, Alex pondered the thought that it was not random, which sent chills up his spine.

He waited for Jeremy to answer as he watched the leaves blow across the green lawn.

"Howdy, Detective. Alex here," he answered when Jeremy picked up.

He heard a slight chuckle on the other end. He supposed Jeremy wasn't expecting such a formal greeting.

"Just showing respect where it's due."

"Thanks, Alex. Here's what I've got from the video footage. The first day you found the basket at the entrance to your shop was around six pm. What time do you normally go to the shop on a Monday night?"

"Six pm Monday."

"And what time on Tuesday night?"

"Around six-thirty pm on Tuesdays."

"How long do you hang around on any given night?"

Thinking about it, Alex stared out at the back paddock beyond his garden fence, drumming his fingers on the table. "Not long. It's a drop-off-and-go type setup. We have, say, four or five business owners drop off jams, chutneys, pies and cakes. I'd be gone within an hour of being there. Sometimes it's less. Why?"

"Well, the interesting thing is we have footage of a bicycle rider coming past five-thirty pm each night for a few weeks beforehand. We can't see much, but by their profile and bike, it appears to be the same person. I don't know where they go after that."

"But what's interesting about that? That might be their exercise route."

"Nothing in particular. However, on the two nights the babies were found, a bike rider was seen riding past five minutes before you arrived on both nights, holding a basket."

Alex sucked in air. "Seriously?"

"Yep. On each occasion, they quickly dismount, check inside the basket before placing it on the ground and ride off again."

"Can you see a face?"

"Unfortunately, the video quality isn't the best. It's too grainy to see a face. Plus, the person was wearing a hat pushed down with a helmet on, virtually covering their facial features."

"In other words, deliberately concealing their appearance." Alex huffed in frustration as he dragged a ragged hand down the side of his face.

"We assume it's a woman by the shape of the body and the long hair."

"And that's it?" Alex asked.

"Yep."

"So, nothing else to go on? No one wearing those clothes enters the shop on any day?" Alex probed, pushing for more information.

"Nope. It doesn't appear she shops there in those exercise clothes, but that would give her away, and she wouldn't want that," reasoned Jeremy.

"Thanks, mate, for telling me. It sounds like we've hit a dead end." Alex tapped his knuckles on the timber table where he perched.

"Since it doesn't fall under my jurisdiction, I can't do any more from an official investigation viewpoint, but we can still talk amongst our families in our community."

"Fair enough. Thanks for the update, Jeremy."

"Talk to you later, Alex."

Alex ended the call and sat looking out over the farm. A moment later, his sister slid open the screen door, bringing lunch, and Alex filled her in on what Jeremy had said and the patterns of their comings and goings. Finishing his wrap and downing the last of his apple juice, Alex stood, picking up the empty plates and glasses.

"That is kind of creepy, someone knows you that well, Alex."

"Yeah, it is. Anyway, thanks, sis, for fixing lunch. I'd better head back out and finish the slashing."

"Here, give me those," Kelly said, reaching for the plates and cups Alex had gathered.

"If I don't get back into the house before you leave, thanks for coming out today and doing the books. I'll see you next time you're out."

With a nod of his head and heavy feet, Alex retreated to the tractor. Normally, he could switch off while he mowed, but not since the babies had been found at the door of his Coomera Marketplace.

Instead of switching off, he had hours of thinking time, and he was becoming more drained with every passing day. He could feel it in his body.

Alex wasn't the type of guy who took an interest in babies. He had no problem admitting he was gentle with the calves and kids born on his farm. Even the odd chick that would stray from its mother he would gently place back under her. But human babies? He didn't have any experience. Didn't want to.

"You're looking good, Liz. It's only been several months since Jeff passed. How have you managed to transform yourself so well?" Steph was curious as she sat sipping water on the park bench.

She needed some of whatever Liz had.

"Part of that has to do with you and me exercising, like today. Going walking and catching up with a close friend from childhood has helped pull me out of despair."

"What's the other part?"

Liz turned to look her in the eyes. "God."

"What? How?" Steph stared back at her friend as her jaw dropped.

Liz sipped her water and looked out across the park at the other people walking and jogging along pathways that crisscrossed the large grassy area.

Steph watched, waiting for an answer.

Liz had taken on a distant stare, like she was going back in time, but abruptly, she stood and gathered up her bottle and keys, turning to Steph. "Ready? We'll head back, and I'll talk as we walk."

Steph rose and fell into step beside her friend.

"A couple of years ago, I fell pregnant. I hadn't quite hit twenty weeks, and I hadn't had a scan at that point. I was booked in, but the week of the scan, I experienced pain, like my insides were tearing." Liz paused for a long moment.

Steph placed a hand on her forearm. "You don't have to keep talking if you don't want to."

Liz's blonde hair bounced as she turned to face her, keeping step with Steph as she walked. She shook her head. "It's okay. I want to." Her strong voice defied the sadness in her eyes. "For Jeff and me, the joy of being parents quickly crumbled like a building collapsing in an earthquake. We were both believers, loving God, but that day, our foundation was rocked. Our desire and longing to be parents was stripped away when my babies tore away from my womb."

Spinning to stare at her friend, she gasped, "You just said 'babies'. Were you carrying twins?'

Nodding, Liz kept walking.

Silence ruled for a time before Steph could speak. Her mind raced as Liz picked up the pace, and Steph puffed to keep up. "I'm so sorry and now Jeff is gone, too."

"That day took a heavy toll on my body. By the time I got to the hospital, I was weak from the loss of blood. As I lost the babies, I went into shock and passed out. By the time I came to, I was lying in a hospital bed."

Steph didn't know what to say. Words seemed futile with such grief. She grabbed her friend's hand as they walked and squeezed it to reassure her she was listening.

"Jeff was sitting beside me, red-eyed, with his head resting back against the chair, watching me. He quietly waited until I asked him for the outcome. He explained that we had lost a baby boy and a girl, and that my womb had been damaged. It would heal over time, but falling pregnant would be harder."

Steph noticed her words held no emotion. They were empty, hollow, broken statements.

CHAPTER 4

Liz pondered her last statement. It had turned out to be true. They had tried having more children, but she hadn't conceived. Parenting children with Jeff would never happen, which was what Liz still had not come to terms with.

That deep despair had rocked her faith to the core. She never drank alcohol as a rule, but in her pain, she had reached out, not for chocolate, ice cream, chips or God, but for alcohol.

Which, in all honesty, still surprised her.

That one night after Jeff's death turned out to be an outcome that had her stumbling back into her old school friend's life. She took a glance at her friend beside her, who was singing along to some tune in her headphones.

She couldn't help but love her.

Steph had rescued her that night. Spending the following days after her hangover with Steph had helped her see that her life wasn't that bad. The healing to her heart had only come recently since she'd stopped blaming God for allowing her babies to die and for not stopping Jeff's accident.

She walked at a slow pace, dragging her feet the whole way back to Steph's unit, without talking.

Steph reached out to unlock her door and turned to her. "Why turn back to God now?"

Liz studied her friend's dark brown eyes. She could see openness, not the norm of a shielded look.

Steph wanted answers.

Liz could see someone searching behind those eyes. She sat down on the single step outside the front door, pondering the best way to respond. "Do you want the raw truth or an easy answer?"

"Truth."

Liz locked eyes with Steph. "Your pregnancy and the giving up of your babies caused mixed emotions in me." Could Liz be truthful with her friend and bare her heart? Her frankness would hurt her. She stared at the ground before her and picked up a dead leaf that blew across her path. She fiddled with it, weighing up how much to say.

Could she tell the woman who had abandoned her own babies on a doorstep what she so desperately longed for? Liz's eyes darted to Steph as she bent forward to untie her shoes. Multiple times, Liz had wanted to go to the authorities with both their names. She wanted Steph to be deemed unfit to parent.

Liz had been angry with her.

"Talk to me." Steph's voice was tender as she reached for her arm and sat down beside her on the front step.

How could someone have babies and then not want them? Liz's mind reeled.

She couldn't look at Steph. Her hands had to be busy. She fiddled with the dead leaf, crumbling it into pieces as the wind took control and blew the evidence away. She reached for another. "I had ridden off on my bike after you made the second delivery. I was bawling as I followed you, angry at you, angry at myself that I was allowing you to do such a cold and heartless thing." Her voice rose at the memory.

Her heart thrashed in her chest, like it would burst from its hidden spot. "The injustice of it all made me so angry. You chose not to keep your babies. I didn't have a choice..." Her last sentence was a whisper. Pausing to look at her friend, she couldn't hide the sadness in her tone. "I still want to go forward, Steph. You know that."

Steph turned and held her gaze. "You know we can't. Rick's family are powerful. They have never liked me because they knew of my upbringing, or lack of it. They know that I haven't made anything of my life."

Liz studied Steph's eyes. Her plea was mixed with fear. Raw. Real. Her heart ached for her friend. Liz couldn't keep looking at her. How was that possible? She wanted to stay angry at Steph. It would make going to the police easy. But it wasn't easy.

Nothing was that simple.

Liz forced herself to face her friend as Steph spoke. "If Rick were smart, he would keep his mouth shut about me being pregnant."

"Why was that better for him and you?"

"His family never wanted us together, to marry or to have kids. Apparently, Rick was going places before he met me. He had a good job, a loving family, but after I introduced him to the drug scene, I ruined him." Steph swiped at the tears running down her face. "He changed. He lost his job. I know he chose to keep using, but we were doing it together." She broke on the last word as remorse hit her afresh. A sob from somewhere deep inside her came out. "He wasn't like that." Her body shook as more tears broke forth.

Steph swallowed.

Liz waited, knowing there was more to come.

"See why you can't reveal the identity of the babies? My name will come out. They will realise who the children belong to, and I will never see them again."

"You aren't seeing them now. They're with strangers." Her tone was steady and measured.

Steph played with her water bottle, passing it from one hand to the other.

Liz watched her, mesmerised by the movement. "Wouldn't you want them with family instead of strangers? Maybe I should have looked after them. After all, I lost my two babies," Liz suggested after a beat of silence.

Tears pooled in Steph's eyes again. "Don't you think I've lost my two babies?"

"Yes, but you didn't have to."

Steph swung her head around, her eyes wild with fury. Her hair whipped Liz in the face as she stood. "Then you don't understand anything I have gone through to make that comment."

Liz was trying to understand her friend, but she was struggling. She stood and grabbed her friend's hand before she could race off. "Steph, I'm sorry."

Steph wiggled her hand out of her grip and hugged herself. "You don't think that every day I inwardly fight whether I did the right thing by handing them over?"

Liz wasn't gonna correct her on the 'handing them over' phrase because dumping them on a doorstep was not 'handing them over'. Instead, she chose a more diplomatic approach. "I know we went over all the possible scenarios, but I keep coming back to thinking, was there another way? And being with family, who I know would love them, would be way better than being with strangers."

She kept the conversation going on the tangent it was headed but paused to take a breath, hoping Steph would say something. And when she didn't, Liz took a gamble on her next statement.

Their dialogue could spiral downhill fast if what Liz said next wasn't received. "I figured you didn't think about them because you never mention them. It's like you gave birth and moved on like they didn't exist." Liz waited.

Her friend could bolt, and she'd go after her. They were in this together, and they were having this conversation, whether Steph liked it or not.

The whole saga Steph had dragged her into was like thick black road tar weighing her down.

Liz paced across the small front lawn to the timber fence overlooking the road. The grass crunched under her feet.

Dying. Fitting, like her soul.

Or so it seemed.

Steph had not tended her yard or watered her pot plants because it would look like someone was living there. She had hidden herself from Rick, like she had hidden her babies from the world.

The secret was destroying Liz from the inside. What she thought she'd overcome with her own losses had resurfaced at a different and at an all-consuming level. Liz swung around to face Steph. "I need to end this secret because I cannot keep living this lie, and I am pretty sure you can't either." Her speech wasn't cold, but it was void of kindness.

Crossing the short distance between them, Steph held her hands and spoke with a self-confidence Liz hadn't recognised before. "When I'm out of here and away from Rick, I'll think about going forward. But we cannot do it now. He is too volatile. I need you to trust me on this, Liz."

Taking a deep breath in again and holding it before breathing out, Liz stared into her friend's chocolate eyes. There was a determination that hadn't been there before. It was as if the strong-willed Steph she once knew was resurfacing.

Maybe, just maybe, her friend had thought this through. That the leaving of the babies hadn't been a hashed-out, thrown-together plan as Liz had previously thought. "Okay then." Her pitch wobbled as she forced her lips to move. "That's the plan, and I will hold you to it. You can stay with me as long as you need, and we'll work out how and when to go forward."

Steph wrapped her in a hug. Liz wanted no long-lasting feelings of resentment. She would have to work on it from her side.

"How about we finish the cleaning and packing, and I stay the night in case your unwanted visitor decides to make another house call?" Liz murmured in her ear.

Steph gave a brief nod, and the girls walked arm in arm inside the house.

Morning couldn't have come soon enough for Liz. She was inside grabbing the last couple of bags when an ear-piercing scream broke the silence. Steph had taken a bag out a minute before her, and it could only mean one thing.

Liz dropped the bags, ran outside and reached her vehicle at the same time Rick let a left hook connect with Steph's face.

"No," Liz yelled. She ran to stand in front of Steph's crumpled body. Her heart ramped up to overdrive as a shiny blade caught her attention in Rick's other hand. "Rick, put the knife down, now." Her words were slow but demanding.

His eyes were hollow. It was as if she were invisible to him.

He only had eyes for Steph.

Taking advantage of his distraction, she side-stepped and fumbled for something, anything, in the back of her ute, to use as a weapon to protect them both. Her hand landed on a cricket bat.

What?

"Thank you, Jimmy," she mumbled under her breath. He had obviously left it there when she took him to training two days ago. Relief flooded her at the simple voluntary task of taking a kid to cricket practice. It could now be the thing that saved her friend's life.

Saying a quick prayer heavenward, she gripped it, leaving her hand inside the tray, hidden.

Not wanting to make Rick more unpredictable than he already was, she kept her tone level. "Rick, come on, put the weapon down. You don't want to do this."

Steph's body lay motionless on the ground.

The rise and fall of her chest were the only thing calming Liz's frantic heart because if the blood on Steph's cheek and face was anything to go by, this woman had been critically hit.

How many times had he punched her? Had he already knifed her? Not wanting to be his next victim, Liz kept her eyes trained on him.

"She's not leaving me again. And you are not taking her from me. She is my girlfriend, and she owes me this." His tone was icy cold, haunting her, like his eyes. Rick waved a fifty-dollar note in the air with his free hand.

"Do you have to take the last of her money?" Liz growled, fighting back the desire to scream at him.

Rick smiled a sadistic grin.

A tremor waved over her body.

"See what happens" – he gestured to Steph lying on the ground with his knife-wielding hand – "when you don't give me what I want. Now, I will tell you again." His smile vanished. A hatred Liz had never seen before appeared on his face as he turned his hardened eyes on her. They were dark and lifeless. "Leave, before I hurt you, too."

Not moving, Liz stayed beside her ute, her hand on the bat. She wouldn't leave her friend to the evil controlling him. She screamed for someone to call 000. Maybe someone already had. But in this neighbourhood, people generally didn't intervene in anyone else's conflict. Most of the women in Steph's complex were all survivors of domestic violence, so stepping in to save the girl next door was out of the question.

"Leave," roared Rick as he stepped towards Liz.

She took a step back, but before she could move out of the way, he ran at her, wielding the knife. She winced as it sliced her left arm.

Somehow, she still held onto the bat and swung it at him as he barrelled her backwards towards the fence.

She connected at least once because she heard a thump and a yell of agony.

"Dear Jesus, help us!" she cried aloud.

Snarling at her like an animal, Rick mocked her. "It's only me and you, darlin'. I don't see Jesus anywhere."

"He's here."

With a strength she hadn't known, she pushed him off and ran the short distance to get her phone from inside on the kitchen bench.

Hoping he'd give up and run off, she saw him stagger over the boxes and head back around to Steph.

No. No. No.

She ran faster to collect her phone and punched in 000, waiting for it to connect. "Hello. I need an ambulance. My friend is hurt and lying still. I need the police because her boyfriend is here with a knife." Liz gave the address and hung up, pushing the phone into her back pocket this time.

Steph needed her, and she wasn't staying on the phone to talk as the operator had suggested.

"Get up, Steph. I told you, you couldn't leave me." Rick spat to the side of her body when she didn't respond. "I said, get up." He kicked at her hip and that was the last thing he did before Liz cracked him in the back of the leg with the bat.

He dropped, crying out in pain.

"Touch her again, and I will do the same thing to the other leg." Her body heaved as adrenaline surged through her. Blood roaring in her ears, almost deafening.

The sweet sound of sirens echoed in the distance, or were they closer? She couldn't tell. Rick struggled to get up. She wanted to hit him again so the cops could take him in, but she couldn't bring herself to hit a man who was already down.

She wasn't like Rick.

He raised himself and dashed off limping through the buildings on the other side of the road.

By the time the ambulance arrived, Liz was at Steph's side, feeling a weak pulse. Time stood still as the paramedics waited for the police to arrive to give them the all-clear that it was safe to enter the scene of the crime. Even her cries for help hadn't urged them into action. Watching like a spectator at a football match, Liz observed their quick manoeuvres. Practised and deliberate, they worked on her friend's lifeless body.

A man was standing in front of her speaking, but she didn't know what he was saying. His lips were moving and Liz forced herself to focus. The whir of the siren came back to her ears, and the flashing lights drew her attention back to where she was standing.

The paramedic had pressed a bandage to the gaping knife wound on her forearm.

"Hey, Mick," an ambulance officer yelled from in front of Liz. "We need to get this one to the hospital ASAP."

Liz turned her head from the chaos of red and blue lights on Steph's front lawn to read the name badge of the paramedic in front of her. "Jaymond, thank you. But I need to finish collecting the bags. I cannot come back here. I'm afraid her boyfriend will return and find me."

"Okay, let me talk to the police officer, and we'll figure something out."

Alex came out of his farm shed bellowing, "Kelly, I need to get to the hospital. They just rang."

She ran out the back door. "What's the matter?"

"Nothing." Confusion flicked across Alex's face as he met his sister on the lawn.

"Oh, don't do that to me," she breathed out. "With you hollering like that and mentioning the word hospital, I thought something bad had happened."

Alex put his arm on his sister's shoulder. "Sorry, I didn't mean to freak you out. I just received a phone call from the hospital about the baskets the babies were found in. They came from our farm—"

"What? How is that possible? Will it look like you were involved somehow?"

"I don't know about all the above. But I'm going in to get them and to find answers. Wanna come for a drive?"

"Sure, beats crunching numbers and filing papers."

CHAPTER 5

Liz sat sore, tired and lonely in the emergency room with the knife wound cleaned and sutured while waiting for her left wrist to be x-rayed. Hoping it wasn't broken from being thrown against the fence, Liz sat praying for her friend.

Steph had suffered multiple injuries and was now in surgery.

Tears threatened to fall from her eyes as she wondered how many times Steph had endured pain at the hands of Rick. What about the unseen scars and wounds? She knew the months ahead would be hard. They would both heal physically, but without some positive people around them, their mental and emotional health would wane.

She stared at her phone, wondering who to call. She'd only just returned to her old church after many months away. She and Jeff had been regulars once, even volunteering to help in the community shelter where she'd first met up with Steph since their old schoolyard days.

But when Jeff died, Liz stopped volunteering and now she sat in the hospital because of her re-encounter with Steph.

She wouldn't ring her family. Not yet anyway. She didn't want them to become a target of Rick's anger. He knew people who knew how to hurt people, and that sent chills down her spine.

As she closed her eyes and leaned her head against the hospital wall, she let out a gentle sigh.

No way would she blame Steph for this. Neither would she blame God as she once did when things didn't go her way. She had done that in the past, and it hadn't brought anything but more questions and misery.

She was convinced this was the work of pure evil in a human being. She'd been around the scene long enough to know that drugs and alcohol destroyed a person, contributing to their volatile actions. But she also knew Rick was to blame. He'd chosen to drink and use drugs, and, as a result, his darkness had overpowered the strength of two women. She shuddered at the thought of what could have happened if the police hadn't turned up.

Women and children were no match for a man's physical strength. They outmatched them every time.

A tear trickled from her eye, and she let it run down her face as she shook her head at the despair of it all.

Sitting all alone, Liz grasped the reality of Rick's potential to kill. She was scared. No, she was more than scared. She was petrified and knew they could no longer stay safe on their own. They needed other people who could protect them. But who?

"Excuse me, Liz Agius, we need to x-ray your wrist now," a nurse interrupted her as she approached her chair.

Liz forced her eyes open and felt giddy as she pulled her head away from the wall. Taking a deep breath to stem the nausea sweeping over her body, she looked up at the nurse, who stood a foot away.

"Have you had the bruise on your face looked at?" the nurse asked.

Liz swallowed the rising bile in her throat. "Yes, thank you. It may look painful, but your painkillers are working. I don't feel much pain."

"Hang on a minute."

Liz must have looked as bad as she felt because the nurse moved a few steps and collected a wheelchair from beside the nurse's station. "Hop in, and I'll wheel you to X-ray," she said with a smile.

If only Liz felt the same way. She suppressed a groan.

She was drifting off to sleep after her X-ray when her phone chimed. It was Liz's pastor. He had heard through a lady who saw Liz waiting in the emergency room. She texted him back, accepting his invitation to visit. He would arrive within the hour.

Someone cared. That was nice.

But who should she call? She'd already debated that. Her sister? But that would only make her panic, and she wasn't up for that type of call. Her brother? But Marco was overseas. And her parents, well, they would flip out that she'd been attacked in a domestic.

She sighed.

Maybe Jeff's sister, who looked after the café that she and Jeff had owned together. Tears pricked her eyes afresh as her mind drifted to Jeff's wish in his will. He had wanted her to run the café. But she didn't want to. His family knew everything about restaurants and cafes. Maybe after this event, she should have that long-overdue conversation and give it to them. Jeff had left her enough money to complete her midwifery studies without needing to work. Although Liz enjoyed working at the café, she didn't like the "ownership" part.

Liz had often found herself in the café to be with her husband while he worked. Now, she didn't desire to grace its doors. She also fought the internal tug-of-war of walking away totally from what her husband loved. Somehow, with God's ability, she had to find her way back to that café and see her family. Jeff's family.

A doctor approached her bedside. Her breath hitched. Her eyes pinned him as she held a lungful of air.

"Liz, I am Dr Cartwright. I performed the surgery on Steph. Surprisingly, there was only one nick to her stomach lining, and it was a clean cut in and out that needed suturing. She's a lucky woman. I don't see many knife attacks that are so simple."

Air whooshed out of her lungs and tears flooded her eyes again. At the rate she was going, she'd have no liquid left to cry.

She mentally thanked her Heavenly Father as the doctor stood studying her for a beat longer.

"Liz, we found a problem. She had bleeding on her brain from head trauma. We've stopped it, but she is in an induced coma until the swelling goes down. You may visit her when you're ready."

She sucked in a lungful of air and held it. Waiting for him to go on.

He didn't.

"Is she going to be alright?" The question gushed out as she exhaled the air.

"Yes, we will be keeping a close eye on her."

"Thank you, Doctor." What else could she say? Her brain had gone blank.

He shook Liz's good hand and, with a nod, walked off.

Liz pushed herself up on the bed quietly, praying for Steph's healing to come quickly. She opened her eyes to see her pastor and his wife walk through the emergency curtain.

"Liz, we won't stay long," her pastor said in greeting. "We've come to pray with you and to see if there is anything you need us to do."

"Thank you. There certainly is something I need," she answered squeezing his wife's offered hand. "My ute is in the car park with Steph's stuff piled high in it. A police officer drove me here. Could you drive it to my place? I don't trust that the gear will still be there by the time I get out of here." She half laughed as she said it, knowing it was the truth of the area the hospital was in.

"Yeah, and I will go one step further," the pastor said, gathering her hand in his. His warm hand comforted her while his wife's hand gripped the fingers of her injured arm. "I will ask another man to help me unload it. Where would you like us to put the gear?"

"Really?"

"Absolutely. Liz, look at you. You aren't lifting anything. Let me and another guy do it."

"Thanks." Her heart softened as she took in the sweet pastor who treated her like his own daughter. "Can you put it in both the spare bedrooms if it'll all fit. Here are the car keys and house keys. Thanks heaps."

"We will drop the keys back to you on our way home when we're finished."

"Okay, ta."

"Another thing, Liz," his wife said before turning. She laid a hand on her sheeted leg. "We have organised some women to bring meals around for you over the next two weeks and to help with cleaning."

Her eyes were leaking again. They had become taps that she couldn't turn off. They had a mind of their own. She swiped at them, nodded her head and, through her tears, gave a big smile. Although Liz didn't think she needed meals, she wasn't arguing. Having home-cooked dinners for two weeks would be amazing. Not to mention, delicious.

With that, the pastor and his wife turned and left the emergency room at the same time a police officer poked his head in, locking eyes with her.

Liz stopped a groan from escaping her lips. So much for getting some rest. Maybe she should tell him to come back later.

"Mrs Agius, the nurses said I could have a word with you. I know you have already given your statement, but I want to know whether you think the man responsible for this may try to follow you here."

"No, I don't think he would try to do that."

"Are you sure?"

"Yes."

"One more thing, Mrs Agius, do you want to press charges against him?"

"I'm not sure."

He nodded, handed her his card and asked her to call him if she had any further questions.

Wondering how much longer she had to wait for the results on her wrist, Liz closed her eyes to rest. Minutes later, a doctor entered and explained her injury.

A sprain and not a break. Good news.

"I thought it was a long shot," Alex replied as they sat around Jaymond's table a couple of days later, having lunch.

"It was worth a try," said Jeremy with a shrug. "At least we know the person who left the babies wasn't a criminal. Otherwise, their prints would be on file."

"You're gonna have to let it go, Alex," Solomon interjected. "No one's claiming them. There's not a whisper amongst our families about any twins."

"Not to mention the mum may have to go to court. A criminal conviction could be brought for abandoning children in the street." Jeremy tapped his fork against his plate.

"I've seen the girls," interrupted Jules, grabbing a piece of cake and sitting down to eat it. "They look beautiful and healthy," she said around bites of the carrot cake. "The carers look like a lovely couple. We have invited them over for dinner in a couple of weeks."

"That's good to hear," Alex murmured as he rubbed his hand down the side of his face. He wouldn't voice his irritation that the brothers had told him to let it go. He'd have to do his own research through his books because those baskets came from his farm, and you could only get one if you visited.

And that had only happened once.

It had been Kelly's idea to sell the concept of 'local farm produce to the plate' to advertise the marketplace. The local cafes and restaurants loved it, and it had generated enough community support that Alex hadn't needed to do another one.

"I'd better get going," Alex said as he rose from the table. "I've got a lot to do today."

Including finding out who visited my farm.

Kelly came through the door with two hot coffees. "Hi."

"Hey," Alex greeted with a lopsided grin from the kitchen table. "How's Philip's mum?" he asked as he took the coffee she offered.

"She's home and resting. How's the research going? Find anything useful?"

"Nah, I just started. I reckon we'll have at least twenty people to ring. I've been thinking how to go about it, and I can't just come out and say, 'Do you still have the basket we gave you or did you put a baby in it and leave it at The Coomera Marketplace?'"

Kelly laughed. "No, you can't. You need to ask them if they enjoyed the tour, as we are thinking of doing it again."

Alex turned to his sister, his eyes curious. "Go on. I'm listening."

"Financially, we don't need to do another because we're busy already. But maybe we can do a Christmas gift draw for our loyal customers and take the two lucky winners on a farm tour."

Alex's eyes narrowed at his sister. He could see her mind ticking, and he tapped his pen on the kitchen table as he asked her to continue.

"That way we're not lying when we ring up."

He chuckled. "You've really thought this through." He leaned sideways and hugged his sister. "The last couple of weeks, I've run myself to the ground trying to figure out who would've done this to me. And now you've come up with a plan that might work to extract that information."

Her eyes sparkled as he sang her praises.

"Okay, Miss Nancy Drew, how are you proposing the basket question?" His exhale was a little louder than he'd planned as he looked across the table at the two baskets sitting there.

Kelly placed her hand on his forearm as she spoke, grabbing his attention. "It'll work out. I'm not sure how, but it will."

Her voice calmed the anxiety building inside of him ever since the first baby had been discovered at his shop.

She waved her free hand in the air as she thought. "I don't know, I might be able to get them talking, and then I'll ask if they liked the basket idea that we did last time." She shrugged.

"That's a good idea."

Leaning over, Kelly picked up one of the baskets and spun it in her hand. "You never know, someone may offer information about what they used their basket for?" She raised one shoulder, tilting her head sideways at her brother as she thought.

He knew she was trying to sound casual, but this was his life, and now he had a set of abandoned twins attached to it. Frowning, he looked at his sister and said, "I feel like you're enjoying this somehow?"

"Well, just a little bit of an investigation has churned my Nancy Drew fantasy into real life."

He couldn't help but smile. "Okay, you find the numbers. I'll go look for the photo album of that day and bring it back."

Alex wasn't gone long rummaging through the hall cupboard for the year-old photo album when he heard Kelly call out, "Alex, I found the list of names and numbers."

He snatched up the album and scurried back to the kitchen table, where Kelly had the list spread out.

"If we can eliminate customers whom we know personally, then we are narrowing down our suspects," Kelly suggested.

"How will it work if they gave their baskets away to someone or to a charity?" Alex pondered out loud.

"Let's just begin with what we've got and go from there. You look at the photos and see if you recognise any as regulars. The person responsible knows you and trusts you," Kelly said confidently.

"Hmpf." He still didn't like the sound of it.

Kelly had marked, noted, jotted messages and circled names by lunchtime. She'd even spoken to over half of the people. "Who would have thought so many would still have the baskets?" Kelly mused, toying with the leftover lunch remnants on her plate.

"How many are you talking about?" Alex asked.

"Nine of the chefs or owners of the cafes and restaurants still have them, using them in some way or another. And one cafe owner had a phone number that was no longer connected, so I haven't spoken to them yet," Kelly summarised as she scraped her fork on her plate, making Alex zero in on it.

"What about the customer list?" Alex took a swig of cold water and the fork from Kelly at the same time.

She took it back and finished her salad before answering.

"I have only spoken to two ladies, and both of them are elderly and use the baskets to hold their knitting needles and wool," Kelly ended with a smile.

A slow smirk spread across Alex's lips. "At least they're being put to good use. So" – he tapped his knuckles on the table as he thought – "we haven't found either culprit yet. Hopefully, the remainder of the calls are answered, and we get some direction."

The rest of the Saturday afternoon passed by quietly until Kelly waltzed in from the hammock she'd been lying in with three names circled in red pen. "Of the two customers I have written down for further enquiries, one said she didn't know what she'd done with it while the other said she gave it to a lady in their church with groceries in it for families in need."

"And that sounds like a deep, dark pit with no answers."

"Don't be so deflated, my brother." Kelly stood, shoulders back, looking confident.

Alex felt his eyes narrow in on her mischievous grin.

"What we have are two names listed for follow-up because we need further answers. And one cafe owner who still must be contacted. That, my friend, sounds like a whole lot of success and achievement for one afternoon." Kelly looked entirely pleased with herself. Her face radiated her joy.

"Seriously, Kelly, I would have had a boring afternoon had I done this by myself. And an even slower one had I not taken the Nancy Drew approach."

Seeing the smile broaden on his little sister's face pricked tears in his eyes. Staring at her was like looking at his mother. He had to blink the tears back before they fell.

Their mum had carried herself with a zest for life, just like his sister.

Leaning in to hug him, she kissed him on the cheek. She seriously had no idea how her presence in his life had helped carry him through their heartache. Leaning back, she squeezed his shoulders. "Once I have contacted these last three names, you can pass the information on to Jeremy. I hope his weight in law enforcement can prompt more investigations."

CHAPTER 6

"Ouch," Liz muttered as she rolled over and hit the snooze button on her alarm.

Her body ached all over. She'd slept through when her pain medication was due and was now suffering for it.

Her phone beeped with an incoming text message. Pulling it from her bedside, she read that her meal was on its way, and, as if on cue, her stomach growled. She hadn't eaten since last night at the hospital, and it was now five o'clock, Sunday.

After a slow and painful shower, Liz sat on the couch, thinking about going back to the hospital. Steph had still not woken up from the coma, but she wanted to visit her.

A knock at the door startled Liz.

Dinner. Yes.

While she ate, she scrolled through the missed calls from Saturday and saw a number she didn't recognise. Her finger hovered over the button and thought better of it.

She already had enough on her plate today. She had to get to Steph. No use listening to messages from people she didn't know.

It was surreal to see Steph in a coma. It had only been twenty-four hours since they'd sat and walked together yesterday. Now, here she sat staring at a lifeless form. Tears fell again.

What was with her face being a waterfall?

Liz prayed, read her Bible and crooned away on some melodic songs by Steph's bedside. She did everything to keep her company. She even pictured Steph humming along in her head. An hour passed, and Liz began to yawn. She headed home to a house shrouded in darkness.

Muttering at her lack of thought to leave the lights on, she paused and looked around her front garden. Her car lights lit the garage roller door, but everything else was in darkness. She shooed away the negative thoughts, climbed out and ran to the roller door.

Her neighbourhood was safe.

A shudder ran through Liz as her key slid into the roller door lock.

What would happen if Rick found out where she lived? No chance, surely. He didn't know she had stayed there when Steph was pregnant, and he wouldn't find out now. Hopefully.

"Alex, it's only been two days since we left a message. Relax and go outside and do some work," moaned Kelly mid-morning, Monday, over the phone. She was at the marketplace doing the books, and Alex was in a sour mood at home.

Instead of working, he was annoying his sister. He should know better, but he didn't care.

"I'll ring as soon as she contacts me. Their café is still on the books to receive deliveries Monday, Wednesday and Friday."

"But don't you go to that café and buy coffee?" Alex wanted his sister to do more to get answers.

"Yes, but I don't make friends with all the owners. I don't even do the deliveries to know the owners."

"That's it."

"That's what?" Kelly's voice came across the phone, confused.

"I'll make the deliveries this week to their café, get to know them, and feel out the situation."

Kelly sighed loudly into Alex's ear as he let out a whoop. If his sister thought she was Miss Nancy Drew, then she was in for some competition.

He was not giving up until he figured out who had used his baskets to put two little bubbas in them and leave them on the doorstep of his Coomera Marketplace.

The next two days flew by as Alex absorbed himself in his farm work. Even the goats had co-operated with him and hadn't tried to escape. Wednesday morning had rolled around quickly, and Alex was pumped. Was he about to meet the lady who left the babies at his store?

An hour later, disappointed but not defeated, Alex sat in The Coomera Marketplace office chair opposite his sister, squishing a stress ball in his right hand.

"So, let me get this right, the café owner was killed in a car accident, and his wife hasn't set foot in the place since about eight months ago?"

"Yep." Alex nodded. "Now that you say it like that, it sounds tragic."

"And the lady you spoke with was his sister and is running the café in the interim," Kelly stated matter-of-factly, as if her brother hadn't interrupted her at all.

Alex stared at his sister as she pulled a section of auburn hair over her shoulder and began twirling it, mesmerising him with the in-and-out motion between her fingers. Wondering where she was going with the information, he stayed silent.

"So, she could have been a few weeks pregnant and didn't know it, have the babies prematurely and not be able to handle it if depressed, forcing her to give them up?" Kelly fiddled with a pen in her hand, looking satisfied with her summary.

"Good in theory, but flawed for one main reason. The abandoned babies are Samoan. This couple are Maltese."

"Ohh." She exhaled in exaggeration. "But what came of her basket?"

"I couldn't bring myself to ask. Not the place nor the time to ask." Alex rose from his chair and paced the small distance to the door. "I'll see you through the week when you come out." With a nod of his head, he said goodbye and walked out the door.

By the end of the week the swelling had finally gone down on Steph's face and around her brain. She was coming out of the induced coma, and Liz wanted to be the first one she saw.

"Hey, fighter," Liz remarked as she saw her friend's eyes try to focus on her.

Steph only mumbled a reply, but that was good enough for Liz. They sat and talked. Well, Liz dribbled on about anything that came to mind while Steph drifted in and out of sleep, her body fighting to wake up. She wanted Steph to know she was not alone.

She told her how she had finally worked up the courage to go back to the café, that it wasn't as bad as she'd first thought, and that her in-laws were very understanding and loving. She told Steph how she'd realised fear was the worst disease. It crippled a person and destroyed a healthy life.

Generally speaking.

Okay, with exceptions. Fear could be a good motivator at times to overcome challenges, but most of the time, it locks people behind unseen bars. The fear of how she'd cope walking into the café after Jeff was killed had been real but not warranted. She was glad she'd overcome it.

"Mrs Agius?"

Startled from her recollections, Liz looked up to find a young police officer standing inside the hospital door.

"Excuse me," he said, "the doctor said Steph was awake and we would like a report of her account of the attack and want to know if she would like to press charges."

Frustrated at the ill-timing but glad they were prompt and, on the ball, Liz shook her head. "Sorry, officer, she's not fully awake."

Gazing at Steph's face and injuries as he took a step closer, the officer stated the obvious. "You need to encourage your friend to press charges and get a DVO on the person who did this. Next time, she may not survive."

Swallowing bile rising in her throat, Liz stood and crossed the short distance to stand in front of him. She looked up at him after reading his name badge, and, with a boldness she did not feel, she spoke. "Constable Kirk, with all due respect, I'm trying to be comforting in my voice and words as Steph wakes up." Lowering her voice, not wanting Steph to hear her next sentence, Liz focused on Officer Kirk in front of her. "I am well aware of the danger she is in and how close she came to death, and even how my life was put at risk. I assure you, I will do everything possible to convince her to take the necessary action." She turned and went back to Steph's bed, hoping he got the hint to leave.

Constable Kirk didn't.

The officer coughed to get her attention.

Annoyed, Liz looked at him again, and he waved her over with a flick of the hand.

Resisting a growl, she wished she could fob him off with her own wave of the hand, but she didn't. Instead, she rose and, for the second time, closed the gap between them.

"Mrs Agius, I need you to know a man who identified as her boyfriend has visited the hospital twice since the weekend and asked to see her. The second time, he became angry and demanded that the front desk tell him what ward and room number she was in."

"Sounds like him. Thank you, sir, for coming by." She looked down at the floor, wanting the conversation to hurry up and end. She was concerned her fear would show.

She'd love a hug right now, but not from Constable Kirk.

She missed her husband. Missed the feeling of being safe and loved in his arms.

A cough brought her attention back to the man in front of her.

He was not her husband. Not the man she wanted. She firmed her jaw and sensed her eyes harden.

The officer bid her good evening with a nod of his head, spun on his heels and strode away.

Liz looked down at her wristwatch and flinched at the lateness of the hour, so she strolled back to the bed and bent down to lay a kiss on Steph's cheek. She was out like a light. Liz whispered a promise to be back the next day.

The car park was wrapped in darkness by the time Liz descended to it. The few working lights were dim and nowhere near her car. She made a mental note to park under the lights the next time she visited.

Flicking on her phone torch, she rummaged in her bag for her car keys.

Footsteps sounded behind her. A hand grabbed her shoulder and spun her around.

She shrieked and tried to pull away, but his grip held fast, and his hold was warm on her skin, seeping through her clothing. She forced a step back and shone her phone torch in the man's face, temporarily blinding him.

It wasn't Rick. So what did this man want?

He grabbed her phone in one quick movement and shoved it in his back pocket, securely removing her ability to dial 000. "You sure are prettier than the photo Rick gave me." His voice was a deep baritone.

Oh no, he was connected to this mess and not some random person. Fear pricked its ugly head in a flash.

He had been waiting for her.

He knew her car.

Did he know where she lived?

Trying to contain her shaking body and control her nerves, she hid her fear. "What does Rick want from me?"

"To tell you, no one takes his girl from him."

He took a step closer and his breath tickled her skin as he dropped his voice to a whisper. "I'm warning you, stay out of this or you'll get hurt."

Shocked, Liz mocked him, holding up her left arm. "And this isn't called getting hurt?"

No reply. He just backed up, pulled her phone from his back pocket, dropped it back in her handbag, and walked off into the night.

Liz fumbled with her keys, jumped into her car without looking around and locked her doors. With trembling hands, she took longer than necessary to put the key into the ignition before cranking the engine over and taking off.

Panicked and afraid, Liz prayed, and the words, 'go to the police station' came to her mind. She listened. That threat was enough. Now she needed protection for herself and Steph.

Going through the front door of the police department, she aimed straight for the front reception. Liz studied the posters on the wall after ringing a bell. There were posters about crime watch and when to call 000.

"Can I help you?" a lady asked coming from behind a wall.

"Yes, I need to speak to an officer on duty." Moments later, she sat in an interview room. How much should she say? How much longer would Steph keep her silence?

Interrupting her thoughts, there was a knock at the door, and the police officer who had been at the hospital only thirty minutes before entered. Surprise flickered through his eyes, but he regained composure. "What can I help you with, Mrs Agius?"

"I know I just saw you, Constable Kirk, but something happened as I left the hospital," Liz said with unease.

Getting a pen and notebook out, he sat at the table across from her. "Go on."

"I left not long after you. When I was getting my car keys from my bag, I heard footsteps behind me, and then a hand on my shoulder spun me around. A man I have never met before stepped inches from my face and gave me a message from Rick."

"Which was?"

Leaving out the bit of her being pretty, she continued, "He said, 'No one takes Rick's girl from him'. Then he whispered, 'I'm warning you, stay out of this or you'll get hurt.'"

Constable Kirk scribbled notes in his notebook and then looked up. "Can you give me a description of the man?"

"It was dimly lit. I couldn't see him very well."

"Anything about him will help."

Liz told him what she could remember and then added, "I'm afraid if I go back, they'll be waiting again."

"Then I suggest you don't go late at night. Stick to daytime hours and change the times you go. Don't set a pattern for them to follow."

Liz thanked the officer for his time and drove home. Just as she was pulling up to her house, another car pulled up behind her. She was already on edge, so she froze. Her eyes were glued to the rearview mirror. If a man hopped out, she'd take off and go straight back from where she'd come from.

Breathing a sigh of relief, she watched as a woman stepped from the driver's side, followed by another younger version of the driver exiting the front passenger side. They were carrying a dish, then Liz realised that it was time for her meal to be dropped off. Quickly, she exited her car and walked to meet them on the path leading to her door.

"Hi, you must be Liz," the older woman began. "I'm Christina Niko, and this is my daughter, Cheriece."

"Hi, thank you. I'd take the meal off you to save you coming inside if I could," she said, holding up her bandaged arm, "but it still hurts."

"That's okay, sweetheart," the older lady said. "We have a few minutes."

Liz unlocked her front door and invited them in, showing them the way to the kitchen.

"This is a lovely place you have here." Cheriece gestured to the open view of a backyard surrounded by the valley view.

"Thanks. I never get tired of it. My husband, Jeff, and I had this place built with this view as the focus," Liz replied as she walked to join her.

Turning to her, Cheriece answered, "Well, I guess we'll get out of your way so you can begin your weekend together."

Sadness filled Liz's heart, but surprisingly, no tears threatened, which was a welcome surprise. "He won't be coming home. He was killed in a car accident a little over eight months ago."

Christina walked over, put a hand on Liz's uninjured forearm and smiled at her. The look was one of compassion.

Stepping back, tears rimmed her eyes as her hand covered her open mouth. "Thank you for um…dinner." Liz stood at the door and waved as they drove off, wondering how strangers could be so kind in such a brief encounter.

It had been three weeks since her attack, and she'd finally left the hospital. Steph was surprised Rick hadn't turned up, but then again, maybe he had and somehow her room had been kept a secret.

And like the calm before a storm, she knew something was brewing. She could feel it.

She hadn't talked about him and hadn't wanted to. Liz had probed, but what was there to say?

The man who did this to her and Liz could do it again, and that felt wrong on all fronts.

The emotion.

The fear.

The grief.

The trauma.

It all simmered underneath.

It felt better not to talk about it. Other than the statement she'd rattled off to the police, Steph had said nothing else.

She'd been on a liquid diet for her stomach, which was still healing. Solid foods were too much. And Liz's concoctions weren't too bad to drink.

She and Liz sat on a couch together, watching a TV show of a woman being chased through the streets of Brooklyn by some psychopath. It didn't thrill her as a choice of afternoon activity, but she wanted to spend time with Liz, and this was how they did it.

'Suck it up, princess' came to mind.

When it was finished, Liz hit the off button. Turning to face her, Liz pinned her with a question. "Steph, why haven't you brought Rick up at all?"

She'd avoided this question for three weeks. She groaned and didn't hide it.

Liz waited for her. Silence and the waning afternoon sun peeking through the window were their only friends.

It had become awkward between the two ever since the knife attack. The elephant in the room was not an elephant. It was a T-Rex threatening to destroy their relationship, devouring the two of them if it had the chance. Steph knew their lives were in danger. Rick was out there somewhere, plotting something. He would not disappear that easily. He had stated as much and more.

Steph studied the grey loops of the carpet as they gently curled in underneath each other. They represented a far cry from what her jagged life looked like. "I haven't known what to say other than the initial apology for Rick inflicting injuries upon you. I couldn't bring myself to talk about him. More to the point, I don't want to talk about him."

She could see Liz studying her, taking her in, trying to read her downcast eyes.

She would only see sadness. Steph's once bright, mischievous look had been replaced by despondency and hopelessness years ago. Picking up to flick through the pages of a book from the coffee table, Steph continued. "Short of us having other males in our lives to protect us, I don't know how to stop Rick."

Steph had been tough once, when she was younger. To everyone around her, she was the one who started fights if necessary, standing up for the underdog, but there was another side to Steph that few people saw.

The side that longed for protection.

Liz gathered her hands in her lap. "You don't deserve your injuries, Steph. He attacked you because he doesn't want you to leave him. Remember, he told me through his messenger that you won't be able to leave him, so that makes this scarier for both of us." Liz paused. "I think it is time we went forward and told the police that you gave your babies up and why."

"No. No. We can't." She jumped up and threw her arms in the air, saying the same thing that she'd been saying the entire pregnancy.

Why couldn't Liz listen to her?

Liz joined her, pulling her into a bear hug, speaking into her soft black hair that hung loosely around her shoulders. "Steph, his family will understand why you cannot have them because of Rick. Heck, they might even be secretly glad you gave them up. But they will question why you left them the way you did."

Steph slumped into Liz's arms, releasing a sound of resignation. "You know, Liz, they'd be a couple of months old by now. I think of them every day. I have an immense open wound inside of me, and it won't heal because of what I was forced to do."

Liz kept her hold secure but relaxed her arms enough to go around her friend's waist as she pulled away to see her face.

Steph drew in a steady breath. "You know I've been clean of all drugs since before I was pregnant. I don't want any of that life, but I can't seem to be clean of Rick. And I don't want to put you in danger. I need to leave here. I can't have him find me."

Desperation clung to her voice.

"Okay, tomorrow we will go to the police station and tell them what we know and what we have done. We will get an early night and go first thing in the morning." Liz released her and leaned down to collect the cups and take them to the kitchen sink.

A smash of glass and a scream pierced the quiet night as a brick landed near her in the lounge.

CHAPTER 7

Running to where Steph stood, Liz's bare feet crunched on glass. Steph's eyes were wide with terror staring at the brick that lay a metre from her feet.

Liz grabbed Steph and dragged her to the bathroom, the closest room with a lock. Cut feet and blood didn't register in Liz's brain. Safety did. Calling 000 was a reflex memory, and thankfully, her phone was in her back pocket. Pulling it out, she hit the little round digit three times.

"Police, yes… I've had a brick thrown through my window, and my friend and I are locked in the bathroom… Intruders? I don't know. I ran with my friend before anyone entered. Come quickly… Yes… I can hear someone now banging on doors in my house."

Liz gave the address.

"Stay on the line," came the voice over the phone. "We have dispatched the police now. There is one on patrol not far from your house. You should hear sirens shortly."

"How will we know when to come out?" Liz asked, her voice reaching pitches she never thought possible.

Calm down. Calm down.

She zeroed in on Steph's wide eyes and shaking body, and it turned her fear to anger. "How dare Rick and…"

"Steph, I know you're in here. I told you, you can't leave me."

Sirens. Sweet sirens filled the air, again for the second time in a month for Liz.

"Come on, Rick. Leave 'em. Police are coming," said another male voice, drowned out by the sirens.

A few long minutes later, there was more banging on the bathroom door. "Police. Open up."

"How do we know it's the police and not Rick pretending?" whispered Steph.

Valid question.

"Dispatch, are police inside the house yet?" Liz whispered into her phone.

Relief flooded Liz as dispatch confirmed the affirmative and she stood to open the door, yelping in pain as glass cut deep into her bare feet.

A tall police officer and a plain-clothed man who flashed a police badge were standing on the other side of the bathroom door. Compassion flashed through the plain-clothed officer's eyes as he pulled out his phone from his pants pocket.

Another police officer joined them and nodded to his partner. "All clear. No one in the yard or the house."

Looking at the women, the first police officer spoke. "Your feet are cut. Can we carry you somewhere more comfortable?"

Feeling vulnerable and embarrassed, the thought to decline filtered through Liz's brain, but it didn't rest anywhere. To be lifted into the arms of these men would bring sure relief. "Okay," she mumbled.

Sitting at the kitchen table with bandages now on their feet, Liz thought they looked ridiculous. Thanks to the tireless work of the ambulance officers who had been called, shards of glass had slowly and painfully been removed from both girls' feet.

Turning to her friend, who still sported a bandage to her head, another peeking through her ruffled shirt, and now, with both feet wrapped, Liz chuckled.

Satisfied that the girls were medically sound, the ambulance officers motioned to the plain-clothes officer. "We're done here, Detective. Other than the cuts to their feet and some superficial bruising, they're fine. We will finish writing up our report and be off."

The detective nodded to the ambulance officer then turned to the women at the table. "Hi, I am Jeremy Niko, a detective from the Surfers Paradise Police Department. I need to talk with you both."

Liz's head swung up at the mention of his name, meeting his glance. She had met so many people these past weeks, but something rang a bell in the recesses of her mind. She couldn't figure it out, her mind was jumbled, but she would.

His gaze was swift, taking in their injuries.

"We look a sorry sight, I imagine," she snickered, relieving the tension that had been building inside her.

Steph chuckled, too, and Jeremy observed both women silently.

"Excuse me, Detective," Steph said. "Sorry to sound blunt, but ah, why are you here when we could have given our statements to the police officers?"

Showing no emotion, Detective Jeremy answered, "I'm here to find out who did this and why."

“That’s easy. My boyfriend… Ex-boyfriend,” Steph corrected. “His name is Rick Limo. He called out to me when we were hiding in the bathroom.”

Liz watched as Steph’s eyes turned to steel as she faced the detective and folded her arms across her chest. “He won’t let me leave him. He says I’m his, always will be, apparently.”

Steph was clearly uncomfortable and wanted him gone. Her short answer and body language told him that much.

Detective Niko studied her face. Her recent injury and the wounds she still carried from the last attempt of Rick’s ‘not letting her leave’ were evidence of his power of control.

He had read the notes about her in his office and read up about her attack simply because she was Samoan and had been put in the hospital due to a domestic violence attack. He was looking for any leads that could lead to the abandonment of the twin baby girls left a few months back. There was a slim chance these two fit that description, but since he was on call tonight, here he was.

Pulling a chair out, Jeremy sat down to reduce his intimidating frame. “Let’s back up a bit if we may. Tell me what Rick said to you at your house the day he caught you moving out.”

The pain on Steph’s face made him sorry he’d asked, but he needed the answer from her lips.

“I already gave my report when I was in the hospital.”

She’d shielded herself by angling her body away from him. Protective move.

Studying her fleeting, terrified eyes, Jeremy tried once more. “Sometimes you remember things that you’d forgotten previously.”

Breathing in and letting out an exhausted sigh, Steph told him what she could remember of that day.

"Has Rick ever mentioned an address where you could find him?" Jeremy questioned.

"I already told you I don't know where he lives." She paused. This time, her chocolate brooding eyes studied his. "Another thing, you don't find Rick. He finds you." A visible shudder passed through Steph.

Acknowledging the statement with a nod, Jeremy asked another question. "So why did you move out in the first place?"

A glance between the women and the look of panic that passed over Steph's face was so subtle, almost non-existent, that Jeremy would have missed it if he hadn't been watching.

Fidgeting with her jumper zipper, the Samoan woman remained silent.

Jeremy accepted the silence for now. Some undercurrent was behind the silence; he would get to the bottom of it later. Changing tactics but endeavouring to get the answer eventually, he turned to Liz. "Mrs Agius?"

"Call me Liz, please."

"Okay, Liz, how long have you known Rick?"

Again, the glance between them was slight as they each tucked hair behind their ears, but Jeremy hadn't missed it. What were they nervous about? What were these women hiding?

Liz murmured, and he had to lean forward to hear her. "Several months ago, when I turned up at Steph's house, he was there."

"So, you two have known each other since when?" Jeremy asked, looking from one woman to the other.

"Since we were children," answered Steph. Her voice was clear. "We were in the same grade at primary school." She pinned him with defiant eyes. He saw the challenge.

He knew that look. He'd seen it so many times before. She would give him what he wanted, but only enough of what she wanted to give. She would withhold the rest.

She'd control the conversation.

"Have you always been close?"

Jeremy watched Liz's body language, and it was evident she was uncomfortable.

Good. Maybe she might be the one who would buckle.

"Only in the last year," Liz offered.

"Go on," Jeremy prompted.

Pushing herself back into the chair, Liz continued. "My husband and I used to help at a domestic violence program at our church, and Steph and I ran into each other again. We have helped each other through hard times." This time, Liz looked pointedly at the floor as she continued. "And that's it. Her ex-boyfriend is jealous and controlling because I've taken Steph away from him."

"Until we find Rick, you women aren't safe here. They obviously followed you here, and they could track you down." His phone rang. "Let me get this, but while you wait for me, pack some bags because you are leaving tonight and going someplace else, and it may be for a while."

As Detective Jeremy stepped out of the kitchen and into the hallway to take the call, Steph whispered to Liz, "Have you got any family we can stay with?"

"Yeah. I will ring them and then pack a bag. Why don't you go pack a bag, too?"

Steph watched Liz hobble out of the kitchen. "I am so sorry, Liz," she whispered to herself as she rose to walk the hall to her own room. "The wounds that I have caused you, the emotional stress, the mental stress and now, because of me, you're forced to leave your own home. I need to leave and get away from you before something worse happens."

Steph had finished her private discourse when Liz waltzed into her room, announcing, "My sister and Jeff's family have both offered their homes to us, but I turned them down. While talking to them, I realised we can't risk going to either of their homes and possibly having the threat follow us there."

"Talking about risk, I don't want your life at risk anymore, either. I think I'll leave and go where Rick isn't." Tears filled her eyes. Steph stepped forward, closing the short distance between them. "Look out for my babies. Find them and keep track of them. I never wanted to let them go, but you've witnessed Rick's violence firsthand. I had to protect them from him." Sobbing, she embraced Liz.

Hugging Steph fiercely, Liz murmured, "You can't leave. We're in this together. We'll get your babies back somehow."

Detective Jeremy Niko had walked to the outside of Steph's room when he heard Liz's last words.

Darn it. He'd missed an important conversation, and it irked him. Not that he agreed with eavesdropping, but, if overhearing important pieces of information was necessary, then so be it.

They were hiding something because he had not read anywhere that Steph had babies.

Plural.

It would be interesting to know when that had occurred, but how would he get that info from them? Obviously, he was a detective. Obviously, it was his job to ask questions, but both women had withheld that major piece of information for a reason, and he would respect that for now.

He cleared his throat to alert them of his presence and watched them turn to face him. Liz was slower at hiding her emotions than her friend. "So, do you have anywhere to stay?"

Rubbing her head, Liz shifted gears. "We don't want to put any more people at risk, so we will stay in a motel for a couple of days to figure things out."

The detective signalled to one of the police officers, calling him over. "Drive these ladies to the motel of their choice. Make sure you aren't being tailed."

The officer nodded and carried their bags to their police car.

Handing Liz his card, Jeremy urged, "Ring me immediately or call 000 if something else happens. Don't wait."

He was serious.

Dead serious.

Too many women had died at the hands of their assailants.

Jeremy studied the two from the doorway. They certainly needed protecting, and a personal nurse, too. If it weren't such a sad situation, he would have laughed at the pair of them.

They had done that themselves earlier, but domestic violence was no laughing matter.

Victims suffered and sometimes fatally.

Indicating with a hand gesture for them to follow him, Jeremy turned and headed towards the front of the house. He prayed he would find their attacker before their attacker found them.

He watched their vulnerability as the women hobbled to the car with the help of two police officers.

"Dad, all we're doing is watching out for someone to discuss a mother, father or the twin girls," Jeremy said, defending himself to his retired cop and father a week later.

"Just don't go causing a scene. That's all I ask. We're having a large family gathering, and we don't need you three boys stirring a beehive." He patted him on the shoulder and marched out the door.

If Jeremy knew his dad well, he'd be doing the same, just on the sly.

Once a cop, always a cop.

Rick Limo's family was well known in the island community for all the good they did. The fact that Rick had turned sour was a surprise, especially when he'd had a good upbringing and bright future. Tonight could prove useful for Jeremy if he could have some questions answered.

The night was loud, with lots of laughter, music and dancing, with too many aunties asking why he wasn't married, embarrassing him with introductions to single women.

Jeremy had wanted to leave within the first half hour.

And by ten o'clock, he and Solomon offered to carry their nephews to the car for Jaymond and Jules. As Jaymond drove off with his family, the two brothers remained in the shadows talking, when suddenly Jeremy heard Rick's name being mentioned a few metres away.

Remaining obscure in the shadows, Jeremy and Solomon moved towards the voices. Two men were leaning against a car speaking together.

"Rick's gone too far, man. You need to talk to him. He's flipped or something."

"Why?" another man asked.

"Well, the other day his brother told me Rick hit Steph so badly that she ended up in the hospital. Then he had OJ threaten the other woman he hurt."

Both Niko brothers stood still, barely breathing.

"You're kidding me. You wait until I see him," started the second man. "Steph may have introduced him to that life, but when she fell pregnant, she stopped everything and made her life clean."

Jeremy was surprised. The man sounded like he was defending her. Interesting. His heart rushed at the mention of the pregnancy. It fitted with what he'd overheard the girls reveal. He hung on every word they said.

"But Rick wouldn't hit a pregnant woman. Not any woman. He isn't like that," the second man continued.

"You mean, he wasn't like that," said the other voice.

Jeremy figured they were as confused about Rick Limo's change as their Samoan community was.

The first guy continued talking. "Apparently, when Steph came back, she had no baby. That's what made Rick turn violent. Steph must have lost it or aborted it."

Jeremy signalled to Solomon, and they rounded the corner of the vehicle.

Immediately, the two men fell silent.

Jeremy recognised one of them. "How are you doing, boys?" Jeremy asked.

"All good, bro," the one who recognised him said.

"We couldn't help but overhear as we walked to our car." Solomon joined in on the conversation. "You know about Rick beating up Steph. Can you tell us anymore?"

"I know you're cops."

"I am. He's not," corrected Jeremy. "We'd appreciate it, bro, if you could tell us anything. We could find Rick and get him help before he hurts the women again." Jeremy appealed to the man's moral conscience.

"I don't know where to find Rick. He's transient. But if you find him, help him. Don't lock him up."

Jeremy studied the men in front of him in the dim light. A cigarette hung from one man's lips. The smell made him feel sick.

"Is there anything else you can give us?" Jeremy asked.

"Yeah, I'm his cousin, and he won't listen to me. Steph used to be important to him until he started using ice. He changed, and that's all I know. And I don't want to be brought into his mess."

"Fair enough." Jeremy thanked him and gave him his card before stepping away with Solomon.

"Let's get out of here and away from that smell," Jeremy said as they headed towards his vehicle. Jeremy was driving Solomon home when his phone rang. It was the police dispatch. "Niko speaking."

"Detective, sorry to disrupt your evening, but the women you visited a week ago just called because of a disturbance outside their motel. I've sent two police officers, but thought you may want to visit them as well."

"I'm on my way."

Turning to his brother, he stated the obvious. "Solomon, I've got to drop you home and then get to this case ASAP."

Hoping they hadn't been hurt again, Jeremy sped through the city towards the motel where the women were staying.

He didn't take long to arrive on the scene, cutting his engine as he pulled his vehicle to the curb. The dimly lit streetlight cast an unpleasant ambience on the night, matching a mangy dog slinking up the street towards the group gathered near the police vehicles.

Jeremy headed towards the six youths gathered around his police force team and was brought up to speed on the source of the disturbance.

It had come from these young men. They hadn't broken any laws. In their minds, they had been out on the town having a good time.

Jeremy excused himself and turned for the stairs of the motel, taking them two at a time. The smell of stale cigarettes hung in the darkness as he knocked on the door, making his head swim again.

Apparently, tonight he couldn't get away from the smell of nicotine.

A front porch light flicked on and off, irritating him further as he stopped outside the room number he'd been given. He wished he could get these women somewhere safer to stay, but they couldn't afford to be picky in such an emergency.

Steph jumped when she heard a knock on the door and stood grasping her chest to try to calm her heart's raging pace. She stepped over to look through the door's peephole and saw the detective on the other side.

Bracing the door frame with one hand and placing her other on the handle, she willed her heart to relax. She'd had enough of frights and fear. She was living on the edge every day, but as she opened the door, she greeted the detective, forcing a smile to her lips, and invited him in, ignoring the fear still exploding inside.

"Steph, Liz," he said with a nod. "I came to tell you the voices you heard outside your window were young boys having too much of a good time."

Another emotional shift detonated inside her, and Steph felt stupid. She didn't know how to deal with the rollercoaster of moods. "I'm sorry to disturb your night for something that was not serious."

"That's okay." Detective Jeremy's tone was kind and soft.

Another emotion rolled through her. He was showing kindness, and she didn't know how to deal with that. She stepped backwards. "After everything we've been through, I wasn't sure if it was Rick."

"It's our job to respond to disturbances." His eyes were soft, his attempt at lightening the mood, she guessed. "It's good to see your bandages are off. You must feel slightly normal now that you can get around more easily?"

"Yeah," she replied, looking up at him. "I do feel better. The stab wound has healed well, too." She coughed out the last word as she caught Liz's eyes roaming up and down the detective's handsome body. Elbowing her friend as she made her way to the door to open it, she added, "I see we interrupted your evening."

Jeremy nodded, and a slight curl hinted at his lips. "I'd better get going since there's nothing else I need to do." Before turning to leave, he added, "Remember, Rick may find you. He has people on the street willing to help him find you."

"What are you doing checking out the detective like that?" Steph hissed as soon as the door closed behind him.

Jeremy stepped out onto the verandah, waited to hear the lock turn, then smirked as he heard the hushed comment from Steph. He didn't need his aunties setting him up. He just needed to work less hours and get out more. But Steph's comment had him whistling all the way to his car with a spring in his step. Pondering his next move, he looked at his watch. "Let's see if anyone is willing to offer some information about Rick," he mumbled as he slid his car into gear and drove forward.

An hour and a half later, with no huge success and frustrated, he called it quits and headed home. He had been in the police force long enough to witness multiple times how family members stayed silent to protect relatives.

He pulled into his driveway and killed the engine. The front porch light was on, and so was Solomon's bedroom light. His brother was up, probably waiting for him.

Exiting his vehicle slowly, his mind drifted to the conversation he and Solomon had overheard at the family celebration.

'She must have lost it or aborted it.'

"What have you done, Steph?" Jeremy questioned as he turned the lock to his front door.

Pondering her plight, Jeremy knew she needed more help.

He needed to ask her more questions. She looked like she'd turned her life around, but at what cost? Liz appeared to be a good friend, but he knew they were hiding something. Someone. Babies, it appeared. But how exactly?

Interrupting his thoughts, Solomon called out from the lounge, "You've been gone a while. I was just about to head off to bed."

"Yeah. I've been driving around mostly." He plonked himself down opposite his brother.

"Based on what we overheard, I'm gathering Steph has experienced the dark, suffocating tunnel of domestic family violence and had the strength to leave," Solomon determined.

"True, bro." Taking his jacket off, Jeremy settled more comfortably into the recliner and stared out the window at the bush surrounding their home. "And as you and I know, most women don't leave," he continued, almost absentmindedly. "And of those who do leave, they are either seriously injured or killed in the process."

A silence hung thick in the room, as if it, too, was contributing to the heaviness of the conversation. Jeremy knew it wasn't just women who faced domestic family violence. The numbers were increasing for men, too.

CHAPTER 8

"Kelly, guess what? I just saw Liz walk into her shop," Alex announced over the phone.

It was a Monday morning, and he was seated in his Hilux across the road from the café, where he hadn't taken his eyes off its front door.

"What? You did?"

"Yep."

"When did this happen?"

Alex could hear the excitement in her voice building. "Just now. I pulled up outside the café to go in and saw her walk in. I had to ring you. My heart is racing. I don't know what to do."

"But how do you know it is her?"

Satisfied with his own Nancy Drew-style work, he smiled into the phone. "I remembered her face from the photo we took on the day. The one in my album. It's her. I'm positive."

"Wow, look at you go, big brother. So, what now?"

Alex heard her grin even though he couldn't see it. He imagined her standing with her hand on her hip as she gave him the compliment. Alex went quiet for a moment. "Maybe it's time to ring Jeremy with our idea of the baskets being used by the mother." He'd wrestled with the idea in his head. Staring through the café windows, he saw Liz laughing with a customer at the register. He couldn't imagine her, the owner of a café, doing something like that, but maybe she had. Maybe she'd given up a child, make that two and put them both in a basket?

"How will you ask her that without offending her?"

His sister stirred him from the incomprehensible thoughts.

"I'm not. That is Jeremy's job. I want him to take up our idea and interview everyone on our list. Maybe he will see something crack open."

"Great idea. Let me know how it goes."

"I'll ring Jeremy now. See ya, little sis." Alex disconnected the call and rang Jeremy.

On the third ring, his detective buddy answered. "Detective Niko speaking."

"Hey, Jeremy. Alex, here. I've got information you may be interested in. I haven't rung you before now because I didn't think it would lead anywhere." Pausing, suddenly unsure of himself, Alex sought his mind for the right words. "Kelly and I looked into some things."

"Okay, I'm listening."

Bolstering some courage, Alex forged ahead. "A few weeks ago, I got a call from the hospital to come and collect the two baskets the baby girls were found in—"

"Wait a minute. Wait a minute. Why did they ring you? And not the police?"

"I don't know. They found my logo and contact details on the inside of the basket," Alex answered.

"And they confirmed the babies were brought to the hospital in them?"

"Yes."

"But we do not have any record of them coming from you."

"Well..." Alex paused and shifted in his seat, unsure of himself. "That's what Kelly and I have been working out, and it's the reason for my call. We think we have some answers."

"Go on."

"You see, I held a farm tour for twenty people when I first opened The Coomera Marketplace. It was a form of advertising for the local farmers. We held a raffle, and ten café or restaurant owners were selected, and ten customers were selected."

"Okay, but what is the connection between the baskets and the hospital?" asked Jeremy. "Alex, I want quick answers, not a walk around the park and show me all the pretty flowers kind of talk."

Alex coughed at the rebuff. "Sorry. I don't know how to tell you without saying everything." He leaned against his car door and focused on the café windows with a steely gaze to fortify himself. "On the tour day, we handed out baskets to the twenty people. They were given free products to place in the baskets as they went from farm to farm. We took a photo of the group and kept all their contact details on file."

Alex paused.

"Go on."

"Well, Kelly and I thought we would investigate and ring up all the twenty winners. The thing is, that was the only day I've ever handed out baskets with my name on them. And somehow, those baby girls ended up in my baskets."

"So, the hospital rang you to come and collect them." It was a statement more than a question.

Excitedly, Alex moved in his car's cab and accidentally hit the horn.

"Alex, are you driving?"

"Nope, officer. I'm parked out the front of one of the cafés whose owner had visited us on the tour."

"Are you doing your own investigation without telling them? And somehow gleaning information?"

Fidgeting for the first time, Alex hesitated. "Have Kelly and I broke some law?"

"No, you haven't," Jeremy answered. "But how did you get the information without some resistance?"

"First, we didn't think we'd be able to locate all the winners to ask any questions. But we did, bar one who I'm yet to speak with."

"Okay, I got a couple of questions. Can I have all your notes, numbers and photos? Secondly, who is the one you haven't spoken to?"

"First answer, yes, you can have all our contacts and photos of the day. Another thing you might find interesting is three out of the twenty baskets are unaccounted for unless everyone lied. But why would they lie unless they have something to hide? Right?"

"Correct."

Alex's voice rose in volume as he revealed everything he had learnt. "Of the people we have spoken to, seventeen of them still have the baskets in their possession." Alex shifted the phone from his ear. "Hold on a minute while I connect you to the Bluetooth in my car. I need to get going back to the farm."

"Yep."

Pulling out of the park, Alex took one more look in the café for Liz. There she was, laughing with the same customer as before. He resisted the urge to brake, driving away slowly with a smile forming on his lips.

"Alex, I'm waiting. Who is the one you haven't spoken to?"

"Yep, right. Of the three baskets unaccounted for, one lady gave it to an op shop, so it can't be tracked. The second one, which we haven't followed up on yet, was given to a church group that gives food to single mothers or families in need."

"That would be a good lead to follow. But Alex, you're taking me for a walk around a park and showing me the pretty flowers. Get to the point and tell me who you haven't spoken to?"

"I just saw her and was going to go in and talk to her, but chose to ring you instead."

"Alex."

"Her name is Liz Agius."

Jeremy sucked in an audible breath.

"You right, mate?" Alex was greeted with a ruffle of papers on the other end. "Jeremy, are you still there, mate?"

"Yeah. Anything else about Liz?"

"No, other than I went to the café to meet with her since she hasn't returned my calls."

"Have you spoken to her personally, though?" Jeremy pushed.

"No. I spoke with her in-laws. They told me she hasn't been in since her husband was killed in a car accident, probably nine or ten months ago now. I also learnt she was studying midwifery." Alex heard a bang on the other end. "Jeremy, what's going on over where you are?"

"Everything is okay. I'm taking notes, and that was me grabbing my pen that had slipped from my hand."

Unaware of any undercurrent on the phone, Alex kept talking. "Apparently, Liz deferred her degree, and they spoke of her with fondness. She's a kind woman who believes in God and goes to church."

"Thanks for ringing, Alex. I need to get going. And I will come by tonight and pick up the information you have. That is a lot of investigating on your end. Thank Kelly for me, and be sure to tell her, if she ever gets bored crunching numbers for you, she could work for me."

Alex chuckled. "I will be sure to tell her. She'll think she's maybe too good to work her current job." Alex ended the conversation and kept listening to the music that rolled into his ears from his Spotify playlist. After all this time, it felt like they were a step closer to finding the mother who desperately wanted to stay hidden.

Leaning back in his chair, Jeremy rubbed a hand through his hair. "*Dear God, I need your help.*"

Finishing his short prayer, he looked Liz up online to learn more about her. Surely, the woman he'd been called to for the domestic on the weekend wouldn't have anything to do with a desperate mum and two abandoned babies. All without going to the police?

But if he'd learnt one thing in his field of work, it was that anything was possible.

He jotted down his thoughts as well as anything that stood out online. That was, if what Alex said was true, it explained why her social media presence had been tiny over the past year in comparison to what had been posted in the previous years.

Ten minutes had gone by, and Jeremy had browsed Liz's Facebook page, Instagram posts and café website. What he could learn about a person online without too much effort was scary.

What had begun as a niggling curiosity was growing into a fully-fledged conviction that a possible professional investigation may need to be opened.

Why did the information about her being a midwife stand out among the rest of her posts?

"We can't keep living like this," Liz pleaded with her friend. "I'm afraid to go out and shop in case Rick sees me, and you can't go out. We need help, and I think we can trust Jeremy enough to tell him the truth."

Steph gasped. How many times must they go over the same topic? Her blood no longer went slowly to a boil when Liz brought that up. It went straight to one hundred degrees Celsius. Exasperated, Steph threw her hands in the air and raced down the concrete stairway. "I wish I'd never brought you into my mess," she bit back over her shoulder as she flew down the stairs two at a time, fleeing to get to who knew where.

"Too late. I'm already in it!"

Shocked that Liz had kept up the pace, Steph swung her body around when she landed on the bottom pavement, and the girls went eyeball to eyeball. She didn't want to fist fight her friend in the car park of some backward motel, but she had just about had it with the 'we need to go forward, I can't keep living like this' type of statement. "Liz," Steph ground through clenched teeth, holding tightened fists by her side. "Don't you think for one minute I haven't had enough of living like this, too?" She held her hand up, uncurling her fist to silence her friend, who had opened her mouth to answer. "Rhetorical. You don't get to answer."

Steph was more than fuming. She was wild. She was furious at the world. At Rick and at herself. She blinked. She would deal with herself later. She couldn't dwell on that now. She was focused on the person who stood toe-to-toe with her.

She cut her friend a look that was more foe than friend. "I agree we can't keep living like this, but I don't trust Jeremy. He's a cop, and he will throw us in jail for what we did." She could feel the pulse in her neck beating almost out of her throat. How could her desire to keep her babies safe end up in such a mess? She was running from the law, running from Rick and ruining her friend's life all at the same time.

Her friend's face was desperate, shattered.

"Do you think it's safe to go back to your place?" she blurted out to Liz. It had to be better than where they were.

"You have got to be kiddin' me." The look Liz threw her confirmed the feeling Steph felt about herself.

She'd lost her marbles. She watched her friend twirl her long, thick ponytail between her fingers, considering her with her hazel eyes.

"Maybe Rick has lost interest in watching your place. It's been a few days, and we haven't heard anything from him," Steph tried again.

Liz blinked at her and said nothing.

Smart move, chickee. I wouldn't trust me either right now. Steph turned and pounded the pavement outside the motel. She needed to think. "Surely, we can go get the window fixed… I'm paying for that. And you can collect your car to drive to the caf—"

"Steph, stop."

Exasperated, Liz expelled air loud enough for Steph to hear, but she ignored her and paced the same route until a taxi pulled up to the curb.

Steph followed her friend outside and watched her turn on the hose to water the plants. Guilt overtook her. Maybe she should take off so Liz could develop some type of life again without the darkness she'd dragged her into following her around. She couldn't bear the thought of Liz getting hurt again.

"What do you reckon, Steph?" Liz asked.

Steph squinted at her in the sunlight. "Sorry, my thoughts were elsewhere. What were you saying?"

"I was just asking if you wanted to come into the café with me the next time I go?"

"Yeah, I guess," Steph mumbled. If she was still in the city, but she left that part unsaid.

The women finished up at Liz's house, locked up and drove back to the motel in her car, stopping to gather a few food items at the local IGA.

A plan began to unfold in Steph's mind.

Liz's phone rang, and Steph answered it for her. "Hi, Detective. Yes… Liz is driving." A pause. "We just went by her house to do a few things." Another pause. "Yes, we can meet with you tomorrow. Ten o'clock at the motel." Steph looked at Liz, touched her arm and raised a palm upside to gesture if that was cool with her.

Liz nodded.

"Okay, that's fine. See you tomorrow." She hung up the phone. "The detective wasn't happy we'd gone to the house. He said if we must go back, we aren't to stay long in case Rick is staking the house out."

Liz replied with a nod, and Steph stared out the side window for the remainder of the drive. By tomorrow, ten o'clock, she would have to convince Liz to keep her mouth shut.

Jeremy was not to know their story, her story.

Ten o'clock came around, and Jeremy arrived at the motel with his partner, Brendan, and a wad of papers under his arm. He studied the women seated before him at the little round table. Both looked nervous with their eyes averted from him.

He wasn't there about Rick so he needed to get straight to the point. Turning to Liz, he eyed her. The police force had taught him how to detect discomfort even when appearing uninterested. "Something has come to light that I hope you can help me with. Not long ago, twin baby girls were left at The Coomera Marketplace." Jeremy paused, watching as Liz's face paled.

She looked away, and the swallow in her throat was obvious, as was Steph's immediate inhalation, which she tried to cover with a cough.

They were obviously involved. However, the law required a verbal confession.

He resumed his speech. "It appears that the marketplace was selected deliberately." Jeremy gave them time to process what he'd said. Suddenly, the carpet became more appealing to the pair of them. "Just wondering if you girls have ever shopped there?" Jeremy's gaze flittered between the two.

Liz had turned her face back to him, trying her best, he guessed, to appear unperturbed.

Attempting to put them at ease, he added, "We're not here to accuse either of you. We have come to ask you both some questions."

Liz leaned forward on her chair, mouth moving, but no words came out.

Giving pause for the women to gather themselves, he waited only a beat before continuing. "The reason I'm here today is that attention has been thrown on twenty people who were clients or customers of Alex's store a year ago."

Liz's eyes widened. She opened her mouth to say something, then must have thought better of it and closed it again. Jeremy took that moment to look at Steph. She had her head down and was picking at an invisible speck on her pants.

"Liz, you're one of those twenty people who are of interest."

"What?" She had found her voice.

Steph found the comment interesting also, as she swung her head up to meet his gaze.

Jeremy's silence lingered a little longer before continuing, allowing the news to sink in. "Alex handed out the baskets so the people on the farm tour could place produce in them to take home." Jeremy turned directly to Liz. "I know you were there because your name and photo are in these records." He pushed the papers towards her, showing her photos and her name."

Her hands trembled as she moved them to her mouth. She turned to face Steph, who had resumed picking invisible lint from her pants.

Jeremy could see in Liz's eyes that she was thinking about what to say. Jeremy chose a simple question. "Liz, can you tell me whether you still have the basket?"

He watched her struggle to swallow, and, barely above a whisper, she answered. "No."

"Can you tell me where it is?"

"No."

She hadn't lied directly. Jeremy guessed that much. If she had been involved, she wouldn't have a clue that it was back in Alex's hands.

Steph pushed her chair back and stood abruptly. "Does anyone want a drink?"

Jeremy watched Brendan's eyes follow her to the small bar fridge near where they sat. She was trying to escape them. Jeremy knew that. But why was she nervous? Her fidgeting. Her lack of eye contact all spoke that she knew something, but what?

"A cool drink would be great," replied Liz when Steph turned.

Jeremy noticed she hadn't looked at either him or Brendan. Her eyes had landed solely on the only other person in the room.

Jeremy could take a hint. The conversation was over. He wouldn't push anymore. He stood, gathered the papers and strode the short distance to the door, speaking as he turned the door handle. "One last thing, Alex only goes twice a week to The Coomera Marketplace, and those were the two days the babies were left outside."

Steph awoke with a massive headache. She'd spent until lunchtime in her room, writing a letter, scrunching it up, only to write it again. Saying sorry was not enough. Asking for forgiveness wouldn't fix it. Nothing would. So instead of making Liz's life any worse, after today's commitment to having her window fixed, Steph would leave town.

For good.

As Steph stared out the window of the tiny motel bedroom, a sad smile formed on her full lips as she watched a dry leaf scoot across the car park below and down the drain.

A fitting picture of her life. "My life scattered as I know it, down a dark pit into the unknown," she spoke into the air. "By this afternoon, I'll be out of the city, making it impossible to be talked out of leaving. And impossible to find."

A bird chirped outside her window. It was the only other soul who'd heard her misery.

Looking down at the note she'd written, a tear dropped onto the ink, making a letter run. Liz would be sad, but she would bounce back. Steph was sure.

The window was measured up and paid for in advance. Steph did not want Liz to be charged for it after the installation in a few weeks. All her Centrelink money went to a window and a bus ticket.

The glazier man had packed up and gone, leaving Steph outside Liz's quiet house all alone. She looked up and down. No cars in sight.

Steph phoned for a taxi. It said they were five minutes away. She had her bags by the curb, where she paced, hoping the taxi would turn up quickly so she could get out of there. She didn't trust her heart. It could betray her at any moment.

When it turned the corner, she gathered her bags. As soon as the taxi stopped, she loaded them in, sat in the back and requested the bus stop.

As the taxi turned the corner, Steph slid down into the back seat. Feeling guilty, she peeked out the back window and watched Liz's house go out of sight.

CHAPTER 9

Where was she? Liz had walked through her house calling Steph's name. She had mentioned she was getting her window fixed. Walking back through the house to the front door, she got her phone out of her pocket to dial Steph's number and opened the front door with her head down.

"Well, well. Who have we here?" came a familiar voice.

Her heart froze, but she looked up, ignoring the panic flooding her system. Fear, no doubt, emanated from her face as she stared Rick in the eye. He loved the power play, but she would not give in to it.

"I was driving past your house, watching for your return." His words dripped with venom. "I missed you, Liz." He stroked a finger down her cheek, and she fought to recoil from his touch.

Liz put the phone behind her back after punching in 000 and hitting speaker phone, hoping the people on the other end would hear whatever went down.

How many times had she called those three little digits?

"What do you want, Rick? Steph's not here," she said as calmly as possible, stepping through her front door and pulling it shut.

"If she's not here, then I'm taking you with me."

"No, I'm not going anywhere with you." Liz side-stepped Rick, which he allowed. Fighting fear, she hurried to her car.

Another man, the one from the hospital, stepped out from behind the tree on her front lawn. She eyed him cautiously as he headed towards her.

"Remember, Liz, I warned you Rick wouldn't let Steph be taken from him. If we have you, we'll get her," the other man said.

It hit her what their plan was.

She wouldn't go down without a fight.

At the top of her lungs, Liz screamed for help and took off running. She zig-zagged as she had been taught by her self-defence coach months ago. She'd hoped she would never need it when she'd signed up, but the time had come for it to be used. Keeping her voice clear, she yelled her address out loud as she zig-zagged down her street, hoping the 000-response person would hear her. Thinking quickly, she hit the location button on her phone while she ran and then slipped it back into her pants pocket.

The footsteps behind her grew louder.

Suddenly, she was being tackled, footy style, around the ankles, and her feet were taken out from under her. She hit the ground hard with a thump and groaned. The man was on top of her, and then, before she could blink, she was lifted off the ground and thrown into a waiting car.

She kicked and screamed, making it hard for the man to shut the door. She heard him grunt as her foot connected with his chest. "*God, help me. Don't let them hurt me. And protect Steph,*" she yelled out loud. She was frantic. She raked her hands towards Rick, who sat behind the steering wheel.

Spinning in his seat, he yelled, "Get her hands tied, OJ. She'll rip my eyes out before I get driving."

"Perfect," Liz spat as she lunged forward again, just as the other man, OJ, wrestled her in the back seat, pushing his whole body on top of her to tie her hands. She was panting when he finished. At least he had the decency to tie her hands at the front and not at the back. His breath was ragged. She had given him a workout.

Good.

OJ studied her with eyes that almost looked apologetic as they roamed over her body, taking her in.

She felt like spitting in his face. But of course, her manners got the better of her. Or maybe it was her logic. He'd probably slap her face if she did that.

So she didn't.

"Liz, where is she?" demanded Rick.

Dragging her eyes away from the man who could do her the most harm, she focused on the one who had used a few extra choice words. She couldn't concentrate. The stress was too much in the small space of the car.

Rick's eyes raged. She felt a fear she'd never known. His words were lost to her growing angst as he threw the car in gear and screeched off down the road. He was saying something about ringing Steph, but before Liz could realise what was happening, OJ ran his hands over her body.

"Hey!" She bashed his hands away with her tied-up ones. "What do you think you're doing?"

"I'm searching for your phone."

OJ grabbed her flying hands and moved his face within inches of hers, his voice calm and gentle. His minty breath warm on her face.

His soft response threw her off kilter. "Hang on a minute," she stuttered. "I'll get it." Her eyes never left his face.

"No," Rick ordered from the driver's seat. "OJ, get her phone. I don't trust her. She could ring the police."

Oops, too late.

Holding her two bound hands firmly in his one, he reached around her body and felt her phone in her back jeans pocket.

His cologne threw her senses for a spin. His voice hadn't threatened her. His eyes hadn't scared her, his hold was gentle, and his smell was not that of some animal who wanted to hunt her. Yet here she was in the back seat of a car, tied up like an animal ready for slaughter all because of him.

From the corner of her eye, she watched OJ turn her phone over in his hand, staring at the bling on its case. "What's Steph's number?" he asked, his voice almost inaudible.

Turning her head to study him, she didn't reply. Instead, she waited until he looked up at her with the question still in his eyes. She was not going to be a pushover.

"Liz, give him Steph's phone number, or you'll be one sorry girl!" Rick roared from the driver's seat.

Neither of the passengers turned their heads to Rick. They were too busy studying each other's faces. The pulse on his neck had ticked faster when Rick's voice rose, then slower when Rick stopped.

He was a mystery man. One she didn't trust, but still a mystery.

Liz watched as OJ pressed her phone's homepage screen, revealing a close-up of her and Jeff laughing in each other's arms. A pain pricked her heart. Her privacy felt invaded. If only he were alive. She knew he would have saved her.

"Password, Liz."

She turned her head and said the password to the window.

"Again," OJ said. This time, he spun her to face him, holding her chin in his fingers and watching her lips move as she repeated the numbers.

The man had patience. She would give him that.

She shuddered as a scene from a movie flashed before her eyes. A woman had been struck across the head for not cooperating with her kidnappers. Realising she was no match for the man beside her, she decided right then to at least not cop unwarranted beatings.

He sucked in air.

She swung her head as he turned the phone to face her.

The screen lit up with the call to 000 still ticking over. He hit end. His eyes flew to hers then up to Rick's in the rearview mirror and back down to the phone, all in a matter of seconds.

She held her breath, waiting to be hit across the face. Waiting for the consequences of being found out. She trembled. Her body had a mind of its own. As much as she tried to bring it into submission, it wouldn't listen.

Fear of the unknown nearly undid her.

But OJ's finger went to his lips, and he shook his head.

What had he just communicated to her in silence? That he was not going to say anything to Rick.

Her heart skipped a beat as she watched him scroll through her contacts to find Steph's number and hit dial.

Her phone went to voicemail.

Liz watched as OJ saved Steph's number to his phone and pocketed her phone in the back of his jeans. He shifted in his seat to face her and stayed watching her for a beat longer than she liked before turning to glance at the passing scenery.

Her heart had slowed somewhat, but her mind hadn't. She prayed under her breath as she watched him fold his arms across his broad chest and take a deep breath.

Steph looked at her phone screen as the bus sped north out of the city. It was Liz's number. She had ignored it. She was not being talked out of leaving. Turning her phone to silent, she lay her head back against the seat and closed her eyes. No one knew where she was headed. She didn't even know. She had bought a one-way ticket to the town farthest north. She would get off sooner if she chose.

"Jeremy, you need to get to Liz Agius' house immediately," came the dispatcher's voice over the car's radio. "We just got a 000 call, heard muffled voices, a scream for help and then the sound of running feet. It ended with a thump of some sort, talking in a car, Rick's name being said, and the call disconnected."

Turning his car around with a screech of wheels, Jeremy flicked on his sirens and flashing lights and sped along the suburban streets in the direction of Liz's house.

He growled and banged the steering wheel. "Brendan, until now, the girls have been kept hidden, so the error occurred because they went back to Liz's house. Not good," he ground through clenched teeth.

"The men must have been watching for them."

Jeremy swung his eyes at his partner; daggers not intended for him hit him all the same. "Why would they not listen?" Now one or both are in trouble. "You know, Brendan, Solomon sees plenty of this in his field of work, and Jaymond attends many house calls as a paramedic for DV. I wonder what we're about to find?" Jeremy hated this aspect of his job. Domestic and family violence callouts had increased dramatically.

"I hear you. These women have just gone through one attack. Now, they have experienced something else. It's never-ending."

Jeremy raced along the back streets, thinking about his sisters. If they were ever attracted to a man like Rick, he would not be able to control himself, cop or not. He would manhandle him. He hit the steering wheel just thinking about it.

Brendan glanced at him, raising an eyebrow.

Jeremy ignored the look he saw from his peripheral vision.

After driving for about twenty minutes, the detectives arrived at Liz's house. A police vehicle with two officers was already there.

"This is what we found down the street where the skid marks were," said one of them as Jeremy walked towards them.

In the afternoon sun, his partner reached out to receive a clear bag holding a set of keys. "I bet they belong to Liz and were dropped when the scuffle occurred."

"Only one way to find out," Jeremy suggested. With one press, the car unlocked. "Let's get the crime squad out, and they can check out the area and look for prints. You boys stay put until the crime scene guys get here," Jeremy told the officers as he jumped back into his vehicle. Jeremy's gut rolled. His mind spun. He had two women, who were possible suspects for abandoning the twin girls, who were now likely victims of a kidnapping.

It was inconceivable. He rubbed a hand down his short, trim-bearded face.

He stared over his steering wheel to gather his thoughts as Brendan plonked into the seat beside him, the car shifting with his weight. "Brendan, try both the girls' phones. With any luck, one of them will answer." He spoke without looking at him. He had to think where they could be. Slamming his door in frustration, Jeremy spun the car around and skidded his wheels as he sped off back towards the Gold Coast city.

"Both phone numbers have gone through to the message bank."

Jeremy stared at Brendan for a second. "Well, hopefully, they're at the motel." Jeremy hit the lights and swung the car left at the next set of lights to go where he had last seen them.

Pounding up the staircase two steps at a time, Jeremy suddenly stopped outside the girls' door, Brendan on his heels. He had to act calm, not panicked. They could be inside. He didn't need to freak them out.

Knocking on the door didn't prove successful.

"Brendan, go to the office on-site and get key access to the girls' room."

Brendan bounded down the stairs the same way and returned moments later with a key in his hand.

Jeremy stood back as Brendan unlocked the door. "From the look of the room, it doesn't appear that there has been a forced entry or a struggle inside." Jeremy dragged a hand over the back of his neck as he took in every detail of the small space.

"I agree. The room is tidy and nothing looks amiss except…" Brendan's words fell away as he stepped towards the kitchen table where two pieces of paper lay folded neatly in half. Intrigued, he unfolded the top one and glanced at the bottom of the page. It was from Steph. Brendan read it.

Handing the letters to Jeremy, Brendan scanned the bedrooms and came back out. "One is cleared of everything and the other is not. Based on the notes, the cleared-out room is Steph's, and I can almost guarantee Liz had no idea she was leaving town from the second note on the table."

Pulling out his phone, Jeremy rang the station. "Can you get a location on two numbers for me?" Jeremy read the numbers out. "Let me know as soon as you get them." He hit the off button.

"Where to now?" his partner inquired as he locked the motel room door.

"Before we leave here, we need this room cordoned off for investigation. Nothing leaves this room without our saying so. We need to inform the office staff that no one enters the room."

"All right. I'm onto it." Brendan was on the phone immediately.

Jeremy listened to his partner organise a couple of police officers to come and stand guard. Studying his partner, Jeremy appreciated how much alike they were. They were in sync, and he wouldn't want it any other way. They entrusted their lives to each other.

Brendan hung up the phone and turned to face Jeremy. "Niko, they won't be long. There's a squad car five minutes away attending a break and enter. Apparently, they are finishing up and will be over shortly."

"Right. Good." Jeremy looked across the car park. "It's only mid-afternoon. If the dispatch call to 000 was indeed Liz, then how could a possible kidnapping take place in broad daylight?"

Brendan hadn't had time to answer when Jeremy's phone reverberated.

"What have you found?" There was a pause as Jeremy listened to the operator on the other end.

"Okay, that's about half an hour from here. Get some units over there straight away but do it quietly. No sirens. We don't want to spook them if they're there."

Both men sat in the car, itching for the squad car to arrive. They had a place they both wanted to be.

Rick removed his foot from the accelerator and pulled his car to the side of the road. Jumping out, he stood by the back window and pinned OJ with a dark look. "Give me Liz's phone."

OJ was bigger and stronger than Rick, so it almost seemed funny that he would take orders from him. Liz had observed the two men as they interacted during the drive. Rick gave the impression of having a lack of control, while OJ appeared to be in complete control of his emotions and responses. Where Rick demanded authority by yelling and screaming, OJ obtained his authority just by his presence. Funny how she could see their differences so quickly.

"Come on, bro, give it over. I don't have time to waste," Rick urged.

OJ handed the phone over without comment, but a slight pause in his movement caused Liz to turn to look at him. He was eyeing Rick, suspicious.

"Wait here in the car with Liz. I'll be back." He strode off.

They were left in the car alone.

Hoping OJ wouldn't try anything, Liz pulled her thighs away from touching his. They hadn't trusted her to sit near the door, guessing she might unlock it and jump out, so she had felt his body against hers the whole ride and was itching to move away.

"Did I hurt you, landing on you?" His voice was soft in the silence of the car.

What type of question was that? Liz turned her head to glare at her foe. She should have been afraid, but the question shocked her. "Why would you ask me that?" She raised an eyebrow skyward. "What do you care? You just kidnapped me." Her long ponytail whipped him in the face as she turned her head to look back out the other window.

How dare he?

She was stuck in a car with a man who had kidnapped her, and he had asked if he had hurt her in the process. If she could hit him in anger and revolt, she would, but she couldn't.

Her hands were tied.

She was still trying to figure out how to get out of the car without being knocked out or killed when she felt fingers on her chin. She froze. Her heart in her throat. She dared not move. What was his intention?

His hand cupped her chin, and she fought against him to turn her head. Her whole body shook as she yanked herself away. He overpowered her and forced her to look at him. Sitting with her hips against her captors on the back seat of the car, it wasn't like she could escape. He forced her to stare into his deep chocolate irises.

Their brown depths somehow appeared calm.

They weren't angry.

His lips parted. "Listen, Liz, I do care, and I can't tell you how or why I'm messed up in this, but I need you to trust me and to stick close to me."

Now that scared her.

"Trust you?" she spat out. "Why would I trust you?" Her eyes blazed with anger. "Stick close to you? What are you? Some kind of psycho?"

Pain flickered across his eyes, and he dropped his hand, turning his face away from her.

Liz looked past him, following his gaze out through his window, and saw Rick a distance away, strolling back with a smile on his face.

OJ pivoted, and Liz focused on his eyes and saw an urgency in them. Alarm struck her. He clasped her tied hands, and his next words were clipped and frightening. "When we leave from here, Liz, we're going to a place where a beautiful woman like you should not be. Don't try to escape, but promise me, do what I say. Trust me and stick close to me."

His eyes radiated sincerity, but how could she trust him? She fought her internal dialogue. Her body trembled, looking into her kidnapper's eyes. She couldn't hide her shakes even if she tried. Her words fumbled from her mouth. "Why should I trust you? You tackled me to the ground and threw me into a car."

His eyes darted between her and Rick. His breath was short. "Yes, I remember. I was there." He sounded irritated. "But I'm also your only hope of getting out of here unharmed."

He smelled nice. She got a whiff of his woody cologne as he shuffled his body in the back seat. Why her brain went there when she needed to focus was outright wrong. She tamed her thoughts and berated herself for dropping her guard. She had no idea what all his bravado meant, but deep inside she sensed she could trust him. She didn't know how, but she did.

Was it his eyes or voice that oozed trust?

She shouldn't trust him, but her sixth sense, if that was what you called it, said she could.

Maybe it was God telling her, but she didn't want to put God's name to it in case it went pear-shaped and then she had nowhere to go with that kind of statement.

Rick whistled a tune as he approached the car, opened the driver's side door and plonked himself down, throwing a bag onto the front seat beside him. Turning the engine over, he looked in the rear-view mirror at her. "Did you get acquainted with OJ?"

His smirk disgusted her.

She rolled her eyes and looked over at OJ in time to see his jaw clench and his eyes harden. He pivoted his head and look out the window, clucking his tongue behind his teeth at the same time.

Liz shuddered and closed her eyes.

Maybe she could trust OJ. His response showed her that maybe, and that was a *big* maybe, that he thought Rick was as uncouth as she did.

Perhaps he didn't want to hurt her because he had passed up a perfect opportunity to get acquainted with her. Instead of hurting her or intimidating her, he had tried to convince her he would protect her.

Speeding away, Rick yelled over his shoulder, "I got a few hundred bucks for your phone. I bought myself some nice treats with the money." He laughed as he held up the bag in the front. "The police will arrest some innocent kid after they track your phone to this 7-Eleven." Rick continued to laugh. His joke only pleased himself.

He repulsed her.

CHAPTER 10

OJ had scouted the house out earlier. Windows were barred, the back door bolted and locked, and there were no exits except past Rick's men posted at the front. There was no way to escape.

It was dark when the car slowed to a crawl down the deserted street, no streetlights lighting the way. They had left suburbia a while back. The car pulled to a stop outside a lone house with only one light on at the front.

"Welcome home," Rick joked as he opened his door. Turning to face Liz with dark, brooding eyes, he smirked. "This is where we'll be staying. You do as I say, Liz, and you won't get hurt. OJ will take good care of you, won't you, OJ?"

OJ looked from Liz to Rick and nodded. His clenched fist remained unseen in the dark. He wanted to strike his cousin as he watched Rick glide his dirty hand down Liz's face.

"In this world, women are property. We're not equal. Right now, I've given you to OJ, but you're also fair game. OJ knows the rules, and you're about to find them out."

In the back seat, OJ felt Liz's warm, soft body stiffen beside him. He hadn't even got her inside, and she was already freaking out. She was in trouble. He prayed God would hide her inside this evil dwelling.

"One other thing," Rick added. "You're the bait to get Steph. If she cares for you, she'll give her life for yours. But then again, by then, we may not want to hand you over." Laughing, he exited the car. After grabbing his bag off the front seat, he sauntered to the front door.

OJ motioned Liz out of the car and followed closely behind her towards the house, which was gloomy in more ways than one.

OJ studied the men at the front door as he approached. Both wore black, were roughly his height but more muscular and no doubt had concealed weapons. Brute force wouldn't take these boys down. He would have to plan Liz's escape well.

She took a glance at them as she tripped her way through the front door. Had Liz just moved herself closer to him on purpose? Or was she that afraid she had stumbled over her own feet?

He had no idea but caught her before she tumbled down. Securing her in his grip, he held her close as they entered the stark building. He didn't trust a soul.

Once inside, OJ removed the tie binding Liz's hands together. The place reeked of so many foul odours that OJ's gut churned. Guiding his charge down a dark, short hallway to a bedroom on the left, OJ felt a weight of responsibility settle heavily upon his shoulders.

How could he keep his promise to Liz in the darkness of such a place?

Shutting the door behind them, OJ moved away. He heard her gasp and knew her pulse would skyrocket. With the room pitch black, he could only imagine what was going through her mind. Rick hadn't bothered to replace the broken light switch by the door, so OJ felt his way towards the bedside lamp and pressed the switch.

Liz hadn't moved from the spot he had left her in. He watched her eyes adjust and take in that she was alone in a room with a strange man. He wanted to step towards her, to tell her he could be trusted, but how could he do that?

He had done nothing but endanger her.

Choosing instead to study her from where he stood, OJ could see glimpses of fear and resolve. He looked away. He hated being the reason a woman was afraid. No way could he tell her why he was messed up with Rick, but he'd do his best to protect her in the horror she'd just entered.

Liz pivoted on the spot, taking in the room. "I'm not sharing a bed with you," she whispered.

Her voice was almost inaudible. OJ was thankful he had this moment to be alone with her. He knew virtually nothing about her, but he had to gain her trust quickly and without tipping his hand.

Drawing her attention, OJ stepped towards her.

She instinctively stepped backwards.

Good. Defences are up.

"As you can see, the room is very basic. You can have the double bed. I will sleep on the floor." He held up his hand when he saw her mouth open to most likely protest sharing the same room, but he had to be clear. It was going to be this way and no other. He took another step towards her as her focus was on the bookshelf.

Her head turned in his direction. "Why are there no clothes drawers but only a bookshelf housing these clothes?"

Strange question.

In the dim light, it was too hard to read what he saw in her eyes, but her slight step backwards indicated he had come too close again. A shrug of his shoulders was all he could offer. He could guess why there were no clothes cupboards, but the less he said about the activities in this house, the better. Hoping she wouldn't turn and bolt, he took a few short paces to stand in front of her.

She stepped backwards again, placing her back against the door whilst her hand landed on the door handle. Her eyes widened with fear, her pupils dilated. Her neck vein increased its speed.

In the short time it took, OJ witnessed her body being pumped with adrenaline, preparing her for the fight or flight response. Even if she fought him and ran from the room, Rick would grab her and inflict some form of punishment.

Raising a hand above her body, he placed it against the door and leaned into her, invading her personal space. OJ spoke firmly in a whisper. "Liz, I know you have no reason to trust me, but I'm not going to hurt you. I can't promise others won't, but I'll do my best to protect you." His chin was just above her left ear, so he could feel her warm breath on his neck and right bicep outstretched over her.

"Why do you care?"

Her attempt at composure was to be admired. From where OJ stood, she came out sounding more like a squeaking, terrified mouse. "Believe it or not, I'm not like Rick or these men. I respect women."

"Huh. You have a funny way of showing it. Did you forget, you just footy tackled me and threw me into a car?"

Bold and feisty. "That attitude might get you into trouble here."

"Well, what are you doing here, caught up in this, if you respect women?" Her voice was breathy, struggling to speak, but she wasn't letting up, as she waved her hand around to the side of his face.

"It's business."

"So that's it?" The fighter had appeared. She pinned him with her eyes as they narrowed in the reduced light. "That's what this is about. Money? Women are discarded for money." She spat the words out with disgust. Her nose almost touched his. She squished herself farther against the door but failed.

OJ hadn't moved from his position, and he hadn't let her escape from hers either. Covering his free hand over her mouth, he leaned closer until their bodies were touching. "Shh. That is what will get you into danger here." OJ felt her breathing increase as she exhaled through her nostrils, and he could feel the quick rise and fall of her chest pressing against him. Inches from her wild eyes, he looked at the vein pulsing in her neck. She was afraid and should be. "That feisty attitude must stop. When you want to speak, don't, unless it is to me."

She flung both her arms at him, but he blocked them, spun her around and trapped her arms behind her. She was too easy to restrain; it almost crushed him. He felt her legs tense, and he pre-empted the backward leg action that was coming and side-stepped it.

But she did a swift head jerk backwards, catching him in the nose, causing him to let go, and she ran to the door and threw it open. She got as far as the threshold before Rick bellowed her name, and she came to a screeching halt.

OJ's heart shuddered. Three quick steps, and he grabbed her backwards, forcing her back into the room before Rick got to her. OJ's hand pressed across her mouth for the second time, and this time, he led her to the bed and forced her to sit. She momentarily sat between his legs with her back crushed against his chest. He had her restrained, arms behind her back and mouth still covered.

He needed to get his bearings. His head spun as blood dripped onto his lip.

She had made him bleed. She had done a good job. Her shoulders heaved in front of him as she breathed heavily in and out. He guessed from adrenaline. But one thing was good: She was not fighting him.

Rick threw open the door, anger in his eyes, but when he saw the position of OJ with her on the bed, he let out a laugh. "Good, you're going to teach her a lesson, OJ."

OJ felt her flinch under his hold.

Rick slammed the door shut, laughing.

OJ let his hand go from around her mouth and spun her body to face his. He needed to get some things straight. She had to know the rules of the house if she wanted to survive it. "Liz, I'm not going to hurt you. You must trust me. And you cannot go outside this room without me."

Her hazel-coloured eyes expanded but remained steady on him. Unblinking. Her long black lashes were poised. "You're bleeding from your nose."

"Yeah." He wiped a forearm across the bottom of his nose. "You whacked me good." His voice came out harsher than he intended, and she shied away from him. He gave her a smirk. "Where did you learn a move like that?"

"Self-defence."

That surprised him. "Good."

He could smell her wonderful perfume, and that was dangerous. He moved away. "Come, I'll show you the bathroom." He gently grabbed her hand and led her out of the room, snagging an old shirt from the bookshelf to hold to his nose.

Liz stood glued to the floor, refusing to enter the bathroom. Her eyes darted around at the mould and dirt. Her hand flew to cover her nostrils. "It smells of rotten fish. There are more stains on these tiles than there is grease in a mechanic's shop," she whispered through gritted teeth. "And what is that? It looks like blood," she murmured as she turned to face her kidnapper.

"Yep, it probably is, but try not to think about it," OJ replied, trying to sound casual.

"Try not to think about it. Are you serious? How can I not think about it?"

"Liz, shush. You cannot let fear rule you here. Weakness is like a bullseye on your back in this world. I need to get going soon, and I want you safely back in my room before I go, so if you need to use the bathroom, do it now while I wait out here."

OJ urged her into action by stepping out and shutting the door behind him.

He could still see the shock on her face even as he stood behind the closed door. The bathroom was bad. He wondered if she would use the toilet paper. Even to him as a bloke, the tissue paper looked dirty, like it had fallen on the floor and rolled across its grime. But what could he do about it? What could she do about it? She had to use it.

OJ heard the tap turn on. Gingerly, she exited the bathroom. Leaning into OJ's space, Liz remarked, "There is no soap, the toilet paper is filthy, and the door doesn't even lock."

"Now you know why I stayed outside the door." He saw her visibly shake the heebie-jeebies from her body. Forbidding the chuckle that wanted to rise to the surface, his lips twitched. "I'm going to take you to the bathroom every time you need to use it. And don't exit my room without me. Remember, you are prey here." OJ held her elbow and guided her back to the safety of his room, even as she dragged her feet beside him, fighting him the short distance back. He inwardly groaned, hoping she wouldn't try to run away from him. She wouldn't get far if she did.

He shuddered at the thought of what would happen to her if she tried.

At the 7-Eleven where Liz's phone was traced stood one terrified teenage boy. Jeremy bet his bottom dollar this kid thought he had got a good deal with a phone, until a policeman screamed at him to put his hands in the air.

Jeremy and Brendan had just finished talking with him. It was Rick, all right. The boy had identified him from a group of photos. But where Rick went after that was anyone's guess. The kid didn't see a car outside the shop.

The girl at the front who gave him his purchases said he was alone.

Jeremy sat in his car, considering Rick's next move. Either he was within walking distance from this place, or he had driven off in a car that had been parked down at the corner.

Lord, you know where they are. I trust you to lead me to Liz and help me not to be too late.

The sad thing for Liz, based on what Jeremy had learnt, was that her life had been quiet, peaceful and enjoyable, apart from the heartache of losing her husband. Now, after meeting Steph and because of helping her, this caring woman's life had spiralled into the unthinkable.

He had to get her back, and when he did, he would hide her in the one safe place he could think of, Alex's farm. Of course, he would have to convince Alex and Kelly. But only they and a few others would know where she was until Rick was behind bars and Steph had been found. That was, if she wanted to be found.

The room was dark as Liz struggled to remember where she was. Waking up in an unusual place disoriented her. She rolled over and hit something or, moreover, someone, as a soft groan came from the body.

She screamed, scrambling to get off the bed. She hit the person a second time as her arms frantically swung around in protection mode. Before she could get herself off the bed, a hand grabbed her wrist, and another one struggled to find her face as it clamped around her mouth yet again.

"Shh, Liz. It's me, OJ."

As if that was meant to calm her. It didn't.

She flung her legs around and connected with his torso, effectively tying herself up in a sheet in the process.

His legs commando twisted around her, and now he was on top of her.

What the heck? How had he managed to do that? In the dark. In seconds.

She was wedged underneath him. His hands held her wrists while his legs straddled her body. She lay panting in the dark, trying to catch her breath. At least she had wrangled free of his hand over her mouth.

She could feel his breath warm against her face. She had no clue what he was thinking. Fair enough, she had startled him awake. He had gone from sleeping to being attacked and then commando rolled himself into self-defence in seconds.

What was he? Some ninja?

Her brain was warped, she knew, but she was impressed with him. What did this guy do for a living to be able to respond like that within seconds?

How could she have fallen asleep in a bed beside a guy she didn't know?

Hang on a minute. He was meant to be on the floor.

"Why are you in the bed?" She'd found her voice. Although it was weak, she'd still said it.

He didn't reply.

She felt movement on the bed as his hands left her wrists. His body shifted off her.

Her ribs expanded as she sucked in air.

The small lamp beside the bed went on. Liz looked around the room. Her gaze fell hard on the rugged face looking sleepily back at her then roamed over his body. He was clothed. She looked at herself and breathed out the breath she hadn't known she was holding in.

He hadn't moved far. It was a double bed after all. He had his head propped up on his hand, looking mighty relaxed, lying on his side, watching her.

Waving a hand between the two of them, she growled in a whisper, "Why are you in my bed? Nothing happened, did it? You didn't drug me and do anything, did you?" Looking into OJ's eyes, she watched closely for anything that would indicate a lie. Instead, she saw a sparkle that caused her to automatically look at his mouth.

It twitched into a smile. "No, Liz, nothing happened between us," he replied, waving his hand back and forth to copy her movement.

Chiding herself for liking the sound of his sleepy voice, she whispered, "But you think it's funny?"

"Well, yes, that you are so flustered. But no, that you thought I would take advantage of you."

"It's not like I have a habit of waking up to a strange man in my bed."

"Well, first, it's my bed," OJ corrected, "for now anyway. And second, I don't have the habit of waking up to a strange woman in my bed either."

She eyed him suspiciously. He looked relieved that he could correct her. He confused her. "So why are we sharing a bed? I thought you said you would sleep on the floor?"

"To protect you."

"By sharing my bed?"

"The door would not lock, so the safest place was beside you. I don't trust the men here. Like I said, they'll hurt you."

"What if I don't trust you?"

"True," he said, shrugging one shoulder.

"So why be here?" Propping herself up on her elbow beside him, she eyeballed him. "Do you protect all the women who come here then?"

"Nope, most women who frequent this house want the same thing as the men, the same life. I'll step in if I see a bloke beating on a woman or vice versa, but I normally stay out of it, you know, the other stuff. Also, you're different. You didn't ask to be here. Rick wanted you, and I had to help get you. He was determined to keep you in the picture to get Steph."

Liz shuddered and said nothing.

"Because Steph left him to live with you." He shrugged one shoulder. "I guess he's kinda angry with you."

"Kinda? What type of statement is that?"

He held his hands up in defence, and Liz could almost kiss his palms he was that close.

Her eyes roamed from his face to his hands before she swatted them down.

"Well, he has taken you as bait to get her back," OJ reasoned.

"But I'm sure Rick can have any woman he chooses," she bit back. Her eyes narrowed in on his. "Why do all this for her when she clearly doesn't want him?"

"Shush, keep your voice down." He placed a finger over her lips and continued. "Rick is unpredictable," he whispered back. "I don't think he would have turned violent if it weren't for the drugs. I've known him a long time." He removed his finger from her lips and rolled onto his back, folding his hands under his head. "You know, Liz, in the past, if Rick didn't get his way, he'd get wild and swear, but he'd never hit a woman or attack someone. Now, it's like he doesn't care."

Liz pushed herself up to a sitting position. She didn't like feeling this vulnerable in a bed with a man. Plus, she was feeling mighty confused about the casual undercurrent to the conversation. It was like they were mates discussing a friend. "But that doesn't answer why he has done this if it's clear Steph doesn't want him."

OJ propped himself up on his elbow and dragged a pillow under his head.

Again, the position made him closer to her, making it almost intimate. She wriggled backwards as far as the bed allowed.

Keeping his voice low, OJ surprised her by continuing the conversation. This kidnapping was far from what she'd seen in movies or heard on TV. She expected to be gagged, shoved in a room, blindfolded and beaten. Yet here she was having a respectable conversation with her assailant.

Weird.

"Liz, in Rick's mind, Steph loves him, and he loves her back. He'll do whatever he can to get her back. He doesn't like to be beaten. It's as simple as that."

"That's absurd. It's not a competition."

"For you and me, we understand that. But to someone who must be in control, when they're not, they do what they must to get the control back."

"Even if that means hurting people and kidnapping them," Liz mumbled as she shuffled her back against the bedhead, eyeing him cautiously.

For a long moment, neither of them spoke. They just studied each other. The silence was not awkward, but the intense gaze he gave her had her heart beating faster.

She was too afraid to fall asleep. How had she fallen asleep earlier?

Now she would pull an all-nighter if she had to.

CHAPTER 11

Her slender build lay less than a foot from his body. The sliver of moonlight peeking through the broken blind revealed her ribs moving in and out as she breathed. He had turned the light off only after she had dropped off to sleep.

She had fought the drooping of her eyelids for as long as she could, then her head had lolled forward, and he had lifted her athletic frame down to the mattress. Her broad shoulders could probably pack a good punch had she awakened from the movement.

She had put up a decent fight earlier, but still, she was either too tired to think straight or too naive to consider the danger.

She had told him she had learnt self-defence. That was one good thing, but to fall asleep on a bed beside him for the second time. He shook his head as he looked at her.

He ran a tired hand down his face and flinched when he hit the sore spot on his nose. He'd probably have a black eye in the morning. She should have at least fought him again and kicked at him or something. But there she was, within arm's reach, lying beside him with her back to him, a stranger.

Baffled, he rolled onto his back and stared up at the ceiling. Maybe she sensed some peace and safety from him, but honestly, not inflicting more pain was not a good sign. And not getting up off the bed and moving against the wall was not a good sign either.

Father, help me keep her safe. And don't let me get attached to her. There may be no ring on her finger, but the faint suntan line shows that there had been one there recently. Help me get her back to her husband or partner, if she has one. Thanks.

OJ tilted his head sideways to glance at Liz as she moved to face him. Her eyes remained closed. Surely she hadn't fallen asleep that quickly? Keeping his distance to one side of the bed, the broken blind gave him plenty of moonlight to watch her snuggle into the pillow to get comfortable.

He wrestled with his conscience. He should lie on the floor, but a man could step over him and be on her. Maybe he should sleep against the door? It would be safer for them both.

Quietly, he crept off the bed and lay down against the door. It might not be comfortable, but it would be safer. Eventually, sleep took over, and OJ slept for the remaining hours of the night on the hard wooden floor.

Jeremy's phone chimed, and he rolled over and snagged it from his bedside.

"Jeremy, I saw the news while I was having breakfast. The café owner, Liz, was kidnapped?" Alex's voice sounded concerned.

Scrunching his face at the early morning wake-up call, he pulled the phone away to check the time. Oh, it was a decent hour. "Yeah, Alex, she was. The case kept me up late last night, but I can't talk about it." He shut down any questions Alex might have had. "I have a question for you, though. When Liz is found, can she stay at your farm? I know you don't know her, and this is a big ask."

"What? Why here?"

Contemplating how much to say, Jeremy paused. "She was safe at the motel, but couldn't afford to stay at one long term. She can't stay at her home because that was where she was kidnapped. Your place is hidden away, and my boss okayed it."

"Can I think about it?"

"By all means. I would expect that. I will keep you updated with any news."

"Thanks, Jeremy."

Jeremy had to get to work. He had to find out if the baskets that hadn't been accounted for were linked to Liz and Steph. The conversation a couple of days earlier indicated they were. Now Jeremy couldn't get information from either woman, so he had to go to the only lead he had, the church that gave out meals to single parents and struggling families.

Brendan walked through the police station door just as Jeremy trudged up the steps. "You look as tired as I feel, partner." Brendan smirked.

"Yup, but I have coffee for both of us to keep us going. Let's go get some clues on Liz and these baskets."

"Baskets?" Looking confused, Brendan took the coffee Jeremy offered.

"Yeah, I've been looking into something in my downtime that I now suspect is linked to these two women."

"Okay." Brendan followed him to the office.

Shutting the door, Jeremy sat at his desk and breathed in the rich dark aroma coming from the cup. He sighed. "You ever like the smell of coffee more than the taste?"

"That's a bit of a left-field question, don't you think?"

"A question with a question. I like it. Well?"

"Yes, to answer your question. I do like the smell of coffee better than its taste most of the time."

Jeremy raised an eyebrow and raised his cup to him. "Same." He tipped forward on his chair and put his cup down after a long drink.

Brendan put his own cup on the table, crossed his ankles and his arms and focused on him.

"I will give you the shortened version of everything I know."

Jeremy didn't have to wait long before Brendan was already on the phone ringing the church in question. Smiling at his partner's efficiency, Jeremy rang the op shop for an unrealistic but hopeful outcome that someone would remember who bought the basket all those months ago. Not liking his odds, Jeremy dialled anyway.

He was already off the phone with a "No, can't help you…that was too long ago," answer when he heard his partner ask, "Do you mind if I come over and ask you a few questions?"

Hanging up his phone, Brendan turned to his partner. "You want to come for a ride? I have the address of a lady who delivers meals to single mums and struggling women. She is happy to give us any information if it helps an investigation."

"Let's go."

The detectives drove through the peaceful suburb until they arrived at the front of a lovely single-storey white rendered brick home. The front lawn showed off a garden with an array of colourful flowers skirted by a neatly trimmed Lilly Pilly hedge.

A short woman with greying hair pulled up into a bun met them at the front door. She reminded Jeremy of a friend's nonna. If this lady cooked like his friend's grandma, then anyone who received a meal from her was in for a treat. They showed their badges, and she led them to a comfortable lounge off the kitchen.

"Mrs Borg, thank you for meeting with us at such short notice. I spoke with you on the phone. I'm Detective Brendan Miller, and this is Detective Jeremy Niko."

"Ah, Niko. I know that name," the grey-haired woman commented as she sat looking at Jeremy. "You remind me of Mr Niko from the church a few suburbs over. He works with victims of domestic violence and their perpetrators. Our church joined with his on this mission to help change our community."

"That's a great thing you are all doing." Avoiding giving out information about his father, he skirted to the next topic. "In fact, we're here to ask you a few questions about who you deliver meals to."

"Gentlemen, I hope I can help you."

Without going into the details as to why they needed the identity of some of the women, Brendan and Jeremy took turns asking questions, hoping to eventually get some sort of answers. Finally, they came across some information that could lead somewhere.

"Yes, I remember several months back, I was called to deliver a meal to a woman who had contacted the church, saying her boyfriend spends the money they get on drugs, and if she could receive some noodles or tinned food. I went a step further and cooked her a meal as well. I bought her some groceries and put them in a basket that I usually kept in the garage for when I went shopping."

Pausing and staring beyond the window to the outside, Jeremy watched as Mrs Borg's eyes took on a distant look. He didn't rush her but gave her the time to think until she focused back on them in the lounge.

"Now, I don't know why I used my basket, but I filled it with food and gave it to her."

Interrupting, Brendan asked, "Mrs Borg, do you remember the name of the lady?"

"No, but I can give you a few addresses I visited that day. Will that help?" Rising, she looked from one man to the next. "Am I getting into trouble for delivering meals?"

Answering quickly, Jeremy replied, "Not at all, Mrs Borg. You are helping us find someone who needs our help."

Satisfied with that, the kind-hearted woman left the room and came back holding her diary. "Detectives, you need to know I never went to her house. If the women are not known by the church or have had previous visits from anyone within the church, we don't go to their homes purely for safety reasons."

"That's wise," Jeremy countered.

"It is domestic violence we deal with mainly, and the drug scene, so a car park in a shopping centre is where we met. If these people are serious about needing help, then they turn up."

"So, you don't have her home address or name?" Jeremy turned to Brendan, hoping he had an idea. He did. Jeremy could see it in his eyes.

"Mrs Borg, what was the shopping centre you went to, to deliver the basket of food?"

The information was given, and both men rose, shaking her hand.

"CCTV footage will show them meeting together. I know the place. We've got the date and a rough time," Brendan stated as they got in the car.

An hour later, the men were peering at a TV screen. "Bingo!" exclaimed Jeremy as he watched Mrs Borg approach a woman who looked very much like Steph.

Rewinding the footage to play it again and zooming in on the screen, Jeremy and Brendan watched the exchange take place. She didn't have a pregnant belly. Either she wasn't showing yet, or she was not pregnant.

Either way, Jeremy and Brendan now had two baskets linked to the two women who were hiding something. Couple that with the conversation Jeremy had overheard the girls discussing getting the babies back, then on the weekend when Rick's cousin said he knew Steph was pregnant but she went away and came back not pregnant.

Suspicious circumstances all pointing in their direction.

Unless one or both women were found, the mystery of why the baskets were in their hands and used to possibly cocoon twin girls would remain a mystery. Was it even possible that either of them was connected to the twin girls?

"Alex, did Jeremy say why he wanted to keep Liz at your place?" questioned Solomon as he threw tackle boxes and lines in the boat. "And why not Steph? She needs somewhere safe, too." Solomon undid the boat from its trailer with a little bit more force than necessary.

Alex eyed his friend, remaining silent.

"All clear!" yelled Solomon to Jaymond, who had driven the boat and trailer down the ramp.

Pulling away from the water slowly, Jaymond drove to park up for the day.

The ocean wind was gentle as it blew across the crystal-clear water. All going well, the three fishermen would come back with enough fish for a big family feed.

"Okay, Alex, for a second time, what's this about, Jeremy asking you to hide Liz at your place?" Jaymond asked, breaking the otherwise silent fishing trip.

"This morning, I rang him because of the news of Liz's disappearance and apparent kidnapping. Jeremy didn't say much, but he asked me to think about lodging her at my farmhouse because no one would know she was there."

"Um, doesn't telling us make this suggestion null and void?" Solomon remarked, smirking at his friend.

"Well, I suppose it does. But other than Kelly and her husband knowing, I have only spoken to you two. And I am speaking to you two to ask your opinion. I need help to decide what is best."

"Well, let's keep it that way. No one else needs to know. We need to tell Jeremy we now know, maybe a few more than he intended. Maybe we might need to protect the girls should they come forward."

"You're sounding a little hopeful there, bro," remarked his brother.

Alex eyed Solomon as he went still from the comment.

Solomon looked at his line, which had just yanked downwards.

"Perfect timing for a fish to bite, don't you think?" said Alex.

Concentrating on the task at hand, Solomon worked the fish to eventually bring it aboard the boat.

"Way to go, bro." Jaymond slapped his brother on the back. "Now we just need a few more to feed the family tonight."

Silence reigned again for a good ten minutes before Alex spoke again. "Ok, Solo, spill. We aren't going to let you ignore the question. Talk to us, mate."

Keeping to the facts, Solomon told them what he and Jeremy overheard during the weekend of the family get-together.

"But why is your concern with Steph and not Liz?" probed Alex. He wasn't going to let it go. He could tell the younger Niko brother liked the girl, or at least showed an interest in her.

"I don't know. There's just something about her. She's probably related, anyway."

"Whoa, bro," Jay burst out. "You like her, but you can't. She's a client." He elbowed Solomon in the ribs as Alex did the same on the other side, causing the fishing boat to rock.

Realising he had revealed too much, Solomon looked away, annoyed that he caught the other two smiling at him. "She's not a client," he ground back at Jaymond, eyes defensive.

Jay assumed a surrendered stance, arms raised for a split second before he folded over laughing, clapping his brother on the shoulder.

"Whatever, bro." Solomon shook him off and went back to fishing. His black curls were blowing in the wind, escaping from his cap.

Saving his hide and giving him respect, Alex changed the topic. "Kelly and I talked, thinking it would be okay to house Liz and, obviously, Steph if she needs it. But I'm not sure how it would work.

I'm single. They're both single, and that would make it awkward for me."

"What, you aren't good around women?" Solomon asked.

"And you are?" Jaymond laughed.

"Back on me, fullas." Alex waved an arm in his direction.

Jaymond quit laughing. "Sorry, bro, I couldn't help myself. Go on."

"I need help to decide. I can't be there all the time to make sure the girls are safe. Any ideas?"

"I don't think Jeremy intends for you to babysit Liz or Steph. I think he just wants them tucked away as soon as they're found," Solomon answered.

"I agree," Jaymond said as he reeled a fish in on his line.

Exasperated that Steph still hadn't returned her call, Liz resorted to sending a text. It had been two days now, and hoping her friend was alive and safe, she sent a cryptic message that only Steph would understand.

OJ had trusted her and given her his phone to text Steph. He really did want them safe, or so it seemed.

Rick was getting madder by the minute. If it wasn't for the respect for his older cousin, Liz was sure he would have abused her somehow by now.

OJ had kept his word, much to Liz's surprise. He hadn't touched her, and he'd slept on the floor at the door since her panicked awakening on the first night.

Liz kept mostly to herself in the room. She played numerous games of Patience with a pack of cards OJ had bought for her. She'd read a car magazine that held no interest to her and spent many hours staring out the window at the dead grass and ugly weed-filled lawn that was scattered with paper and bottles.

Liz tossed the phone on the bed and resumed her position of staring out the back window. Her mind wandered to an event that had happened on the first day, when Rick had wanted to speak with her but OJ had told her not to leave the bedroom.

OJ was nowhere in sight, and she didn't want to disobey Rick, so off she traipsed to a common area, the loungeroom. It had stunk of rotten potatoes, so she'd covered her nose with her shirt sleeve. She stared at the dirty carpet stained with blood and shuddered at the thought of what else.

She did not want to be in that room. She did not want to be in that house, period.

Liz stood against a wall watching a lady opposite her jerk side to side on a chair. As she eyed her with caution, Liz hugged herself closer against the wall when, as if in a slow-motion video, the woman's face contorted into an anguished look as her body jerked forward and was thrust onto the floor, writhing like a snake into the corner.

In horror, Liz couldn't tear her eyes away from the scene playing out before her. The woman was yelling at something unseen, telling it to leave her alone, thrashing her arms and legs at the invisible assailant.

Liz watched on in terror, not knowing what to do.

"What are you doing in here?" came OJ's voice behind her. He didn't try to stop the woman. He'd simply come in and hustled Liz away.

Shortly later, Rick had stormed into OJ's room. "Stop protecting the woman. She's in our world now and will live like us."

Liz could see the fury in Rick's eyes and tone. He had his fist clenched at his side.

Glaring down at his cousin, OJ had remained calm with a protective hold on Liz, shielding her behind him. "She's not one of your women," he had said. "She does not belong to this world. Now get out of my room."

Anger had pooled in Rick's eyes. He swung a fist, but OJ was too quick. Releasing Liz and pushing her to the bed, he'd blocked his cousin's punch and hit back, connecting with Rick's jaw and hurling him backwards against the wall.

Powerless to stop them, Liz had climbed farther against the bedhead and prayed silently that they would stop and that OJ would not get hurt. Without him, she knew she wouldn't survive in that house.

At one moment during the fight, Rick had landed on the bed beside her and grabbed her arm, reefing her onto the floor with a thump. And somehow, OJ had edged his way between the two of them, picked his cousin up and shoved him out the door.

"You wait, Liz," Rick had roared over his shoulder. "I'll make you one of ours, and OJ won't be able to stop it."

Liz had wobbled in OJ's arms as he lifted her and drew her to himself. Her legs hadn't worked after that. She hadn't been able to hold herself up. She had wept against his chest, spilling tears down the front of his shirt.

She had soaked it.

It was the only time she'd allowed him to hold her like that.

The strength and security she'd felt within his arms in that dark world was the weirdest thing imaginable.

OJ didn't fit that world, yet there he was in it.

The difference between Rick and OJ was like looking at night and day. The venom that spewed from Rick was fierce, whereas OJ oozed calmness and a peace that went beyond Liz's comprehension.

Liz realised that she never did find out what Rick had called her for that first day, and she hoped she never would find out either.

Now Liz sat looking out the window, frustrated that she was not allowed outdoors. But outside those bars lay an unknown. What would happen to her if she tried to escape?

Yet she remained a captive inside that dark house.

The only thing that would lighten it was when she talked to her Heavenly Father.

As a believer in Jesus, she knew she wasn't alone, but some days throughout the last year of grief, her faith had been tested to the point of breaking.

Some days she had felt completely alone.

Between the loss of her babies and the possibility of not having more children, then her husband's death and now this, some people would wonder why she had faith in God at all, particularly in One who would allow such heartache.

But what she had come to realise was that God had created mankind with free will. The free will to choose between right and wrong.

Liz took comfort in believing the words Jesus said in the Bible. That Christians would have trials, but He would give them His peace. That was something she could attest to. His peace had cloaked her when she would awake at night after Jeff had been killed.

She watched as a car slowed to a stop outside the house. Liz knew God had even given Rick the free will to choose what he was doing. He chose this life, and right now, he wanted to harm her. That was a man choosing to do evil.

That wasn't God's doing.

There was a battle going on between darkness and light. She could feel it inside the house.

It was tangible.

Evil had made war against good. Although OJ hadn't admitted it, she believed he was on her side, the good side.

The day dragged by. Yelling and abuse echoed throughout the house and tormented her. The occupants believed they were having pleasure, but it sounded more like torture.

The people terrified her. Their actions frightened her. She knew it was the drugs, as they were uncontrollable, and that was the scariest part.

She couldn't predict what they were going to do.

A knock on the door froze her in place. She didn't move.

"Liz, it's me, OJ. Open the door." His voice sounded strained.

Immediately, Liz's insides quivered. Something wasn't right, and she could tell it before she even saw him. Opening the bedroom door, he hustled in and shut it, leaning against it as if to keep the evil out.

She peered into his deep, dark, almost black-coloured eyes. A look of concern radiated from him as his gaze settled on her.

He had come to the door with sickening news. She could feel it.

"Liz, the men have chosen you tonight, and I can't stop them."

CHAPTER 12

OJ wasn't one to beat around the bush. He clenched his fist by his side. His vein on his forehead strained.

"OJ, you're scaring me. What does that mean?" Her words fumbled from her lips, almost not making sense.

His hand uncurled and cupped her face as his words came out jagged. "This isn't one man stumbling into your room, Liz. This is a planned gang rape where they drug you," he rasped.

"But you always protect me. You said you would." Her own voice sounded strained in her ears. She pushed away from him and punched his chest. Her vision became blurred. This couldn't be happening to her. "No, no, no." She flung her arms around and hit him in the chest, pummelling him, punching him harder and harder until she had no energy left.

He didn't try to stop her.

Her body shook as she collapsed into his arms.

Was this the life of some women who were caught up in ice? They were bodies to be used. She couldn't fathom it.

Gathering some resolve, she pushed back from his chest and asked a question. "What do you mean you cannot stop them?" Her eyes were glued to his as he looked away. She was afraid that he was going to admit to being a part of it, so she pushed against him, trying to free herself from his grasp.

OJ fought to hang on to her, not letting her go. His eyes penetrated hers.

She could tell in that one moment he was not hiding anything just by his look. "It means, even if you have a partner, not even they can stop this from happening. It is warned, accept it or die trying to stop it." His husky voice drew her in. OJ paused, swallowed and took a deep breath. "Liz, I'm sorry." He hung his head.

She shuddered and broke away from him.

This time, he didn't resist. Stepping back, she looked up into his eyes and watched him turn his head and look out the window. He didn't move away from her, and somehow that comforted her. His eyes held faint crease lines near their corners. He was worried, but as she stared at him, she could see a steely resolve start to emerge.

"What is it?"

"Liz..." He looked down at the floor, as if he couldn't bring himself to look into her eyes. Kicking the bedpost, he blurted out, "Do you believe in God?"

Shock reigned for a moment, then a peace flowed over her. "Yes."

His eyes found hers once again. "Good, because if you believe in Him, you need a miracle tonight. Somehow, He needs to hide you, protect you—"

Cutting him off, she spoke with confidence, her eyes glistening. "Hasn't He been doing that already?"

"Yes, I suppose He has."

"So why do I need to believe more now than before?"

"Tonight, the men, not me," he quickly added, "have planned to drug you and abuse you... A group of them."

"And you can't stop them. I know."

"The rule is, if I step in the way, they attack me, beat me or worse. But I want you to know, I will fight for you, Liz. I won't willingly let you go to those men."

She could hear the determination in his voice. See it in his eyes. Her breath hitched. "You would willingly die for me," she whispered as tears rolled down her cheeks. The blood drained from her face as she uttered the words. The reality of it hit her. She shook her head. "Why? Why, OJ? You kidnapped me, and now you could die because of me. It's not worth it."

"Shh, you're worth it." He embraced her once more.

She didn't feel afraid of him, yet she couldn't figure out why. He was confusing her.

"Then we pray that something happens to change their wicked plan so that I can get you out of here," he said into her hair.

She felt him release his grip, and she stepped back and looked up at him through her tears.

His deep, dark eyes locked onto hers as he reached out to one of her hands.

She didn't resist as he reached for the second. His eyes remained fixed on hers as he began to pray. *"Father, we need You to intervene and show me how to get Liz away from here before tonight. Amen."*

"Amen," she whispered.

He remained rooted to the floor, taking in her body, face and countenance.

She didn't feel exposed under his scrutiny. Instead, she wanted to hug him and thank him for being…she didn't know what. Kind? Caring? Sincere? She wasn't fully convinced of him yet. He had kidnapped her and put her in that place of hell after all.

She took in his body definition. His shoulders were muscular. She couldn't make out the tattoo hidden partially under his T-shirt, but it was wrapped around his right bicep. Her eyes travelled down to his toned forearms. She realised she was now giving him the once-over and didn't care what he thought. She wanted to take in who stood before her.

He was her guardian, and she had no idea why.

He let go of her hands.

She had made him feel uncomfortable. Her cheeks flushed pink. She forced her eyes upwards to his. They weren't angry, but they revealed discomfort. A battle was taking place inside him.

"Forgive me," she uttered.

His quietness forced her to look back at him and watch as a smile spread across his lips and into his eyes. She held her breath, waiting for his next move.

He simply nodded and scooped up his phone from the bed and strolled towards the door and left. She figured he had to put distance between them.

He was right.

She stared at the closed door long after he left. His prayer encouraged her. God would keep her from these wicked men, and OJ would witness it.

An hour later, OJ's phone chimed. He looked at the message. It was from Steph. He hurried through the long text, keen to see what it said. She was in Brisbane, ready to meet Rick. It stated they were to meet at a designated place.

She was offering her life for Liz's. No emotion. Just a factual account.

OJ had been sitting outside the house on an old drum, talking to a man quietly, when the phone had beeped. Squashing the soft drink can in his hand, OJ excused himself and went in search of Liz.

He didn't need to look far. She was in her normal safe space, his room, seated on his bed. Upon hearing someone approach, she looked up, slight fear running through her eyes, but it was quickly replaced with a smile when she registered it was him. It brought a smile to his own lips.

She was a rainbow after a storm, a breath of fresh air in a world of rubbish. How she did that baffled him.

A few moments later, he sat beside her on the bed. "Maybe this is the answer to our prayer," he said, handing Liz the phone.

He watched her soft, pink lips move slightly as she read the message. He could smell his deodorant on her body. That brought a sense of sadness to his heart. She had been whisked away from her home without even her handbag. She had nothing that was hers. Yet she hadn't complained. She hadn't said one word about not having personal belongings.

She radiated a beauty he couldn't fathom. She was experiencing something terrible, yet she exuded peace and beauty amidst it. He was still studying her lips and the curve of her cheek when he noticed a subtle change in her eyes. The sparkle had disappeared.

"Maybe this will stop the planned event tonight if we go and get Steph." Sadness broke through her voice as tears welled in her eyes.

"But..."

"But we can't bring her back here."

"My thoughts exactly. We can't have Steph take your place." He looked into her hazel eyes. They had a slight streak of blue running through them near the ring of her pupil.

She was breathtaking.

And she wasn't his.

He had to get her out of that pit hole of a place. She didn't belong there.

She was still turned towards him, looking at him but saying nothing. Her hair curled around her shoulders, and it reached out to meet him, but the soft tickle of her loose hair against his bare bicep caused him to pull away. He couldn't concentrate, and he knew that could be dangerous for them both.

Liz obviously hadn't noticed him distance himself as she leaned her head even closer, touching her forehead with his. Lowering her voice to just above a whisper, she spoke near his ear. "Can't I tell her to ring the police or Detective Jeremy?"

OJ froze.

He had to keep the police out of it. He was wondering what to say when Liz whispered again. "Of course, I would tell them you have done nothing but protect me, but then you did kidnap me, so that wouldn't work." She shrugged her shoulders and half laughed at the comment.

He raised an eyebrow in her direction.

"Sorry, I know it's not funny for you, but it is kinda weird, don't you think?" She raised her hands in the air, as if to make a point of air quotation marks, and said, "Kidnapper turns protector."

"Haha." He seriously needed some space away from Liz. He needed to think. "Give me a moment." He looked at his watch and stood up. The men would be here soon. He needed to find Rick and get her out of there, pronto. OJ left the room and told her to put the chair behind the door.

Moments later, the door handle rattled and Liz froze, not making a sound. Again, the door handle rattled, and this time, the chair was forced backwards a fraction, allowing the door to open marginally before it jammed.

There was only enough space for a man's head and shoulder to squeeze through, and to Liz's horror, a man whom she'd never seen was trying to force his way in. The door scraped some more on the floor as it shifted under his weight.

He gave her a once-over. "So, you're the darlin' we get to meet tonight."

Shuddering and praying his head and body would get stuck in the door, Liz took a step closer to finalising her plan.

A roar from his foul mouth erupted as Liz slammed the door against his body. "You wait, missy, there will be no mercy tonight!"

Trembling, Liz pushed on the door until he had no choice but to retreat. She leaned against the door as another bang was heard on the other side of the door, followed by a grunt.

"Liz, quick, let me in."

It was OJ's voice.

She opened the door just enough to let him squeeze through before she slammed it shut.

He held her to look at her. "Did he touch you?"

She pressed into his body, ignoring his question. She needed his closeness. A man had nearly reached her. She was not letting OJ go.

Leaning back, he asked again, "Liz, did he touch you?"

She couldn't speak. Her voice box failed her, so she shook her head. Noticing the blood on his lip, she reached up and allowed herself a moment to caress his bleeding lip. Tears filled her eyes as her fingers trembled, hovering over his jawline.

Covering her hand with one of his, he held it and drew it to his chest.

She knew he was trying to calm her down.

"Liz, this is all the more reason we need to get you out of here." The anger in OJ's eyes was lit like fire. "Rick agreed. We're leaving now. He's telling them you will be back, but you won't be coming back if I can help it, and neither will Steph."

OJ was still holding her against his body when Rick roared from the other side of the door for them to move.

In a protective gesture, OJ shielded Liz with his body towards the waiting vehicle. Only once inside the car, with OJ beside her, did she slightly relax. She couldn't speak.

She gripped OJ's hand as he slammed the door shut. Her hand was trembling inside his. She didn't care what he thought. She held on to her human lifeline. Only once they had turned a couple of corners did Liz turn to face OJ, who was already observing her. "Thank you, thank you, God, for saving me," was all she could utter before the tears fell from her eyes. She didn't try to stop them as they streamed down her face in silence.

As they sped along, OJ gave Liz his phone and whispered for her to text Steph with the update.

With trembling fingers, she sent a quick message updating Steph with the latest news. She felt a hand close over her free hand and give a reassuring squeeze.

What was with OJ?

Liz handed the phone back to him just as Rick threw his phone over the rear seat. "Ring Steph. Tell her, no police. If I see another person, we are gone, and you will go back to tonight's party."

Leaning in close to Liz's ear, OJ whispered, "When you can, run like the wind."

Looking into his eyes, she saw kindness. 'Thank you,' she mouthed. Still shaking, Liz dialled her friend's number. "Steph, it's Liz. I'm on the way to meet you with Rick and OJ. Rick wants me to tell you, no police. If there is, he takes me back to tonight's party."

Liz was now shaking more than before, and again, OJ grabbed hold of her free hand, giving her the strength to trust they would get out of this.

"Put it on speaker!" demanded Rick. "I don't need you two girls scheming anything."

Liz pressed the speaker button.

"Hi, Rick. Let Liz go. It's me you want." Steph sounded bold.

"Baby, you're coming back to me. I knew you would." His charm made Liz feel sick inside but as quickly as the charm appeared, it disappeared like a switch had been flicked. "Steph, what took you over two days to answer? You know your little friend was about to be initiated into our little group tonight, but your phone call saved her." Rick laughed.

On the other end of the phone, Steph breathed calmly. "The deal is Liz is released, and she will walk over to me freely. I will walk to you and will leave with you."

"When did you start telling me what to do?" Rick's voice rose. "Remember, you do as I say. No woman tells me what to do." Rick cussed into the phone. "One other thing, if I see one person, Steph, or one car, the deal is off, and we try this again another time after your friend has made friends with my mates."

Liz stared straight ahead as she held the phone in her hand, her body shaking. Could she run? Would her legs be able to move? At least darkness would be her friend tonight. She could hide and not be seen.

Again, Rick's voice sliced through the silence in the car. "Steph, you will walk to me and get in our car. Then Liz will get out."

"No way. Liz gets out, and then I walk."

"You don't tell me what to do. I will end up with both of you if you try anything stupid."

Steph disconnected.

Rick cussed and slammed his fist against the steering wheel.

Liz turned and looked at OJ. Even in the darkness, she could see the outline of his jaw set firmly. His lips were tight and his eyes were straight ahead.

This time, Liz grabbed his hand and squeezed it. He looked at her and gave a brief nod. She had no idea what that meant. Did it mean he'd let her get away?

She released his hand.

Soon they pulled into a deserted car park lit by only a single lamp. Liz scanned her surroundings, wondering if lurking in the shadows were police ready for action. Liz saw no one as they pulled into the edge of the park, farthest from the lights. Apparently, Rick wasn't trusting Steph either.

He faced the car towards the exit for a quick escape. Rick kept the car idling. Getting fidgety, he rolled the window down slightly, but not enough to reveal his identity through the dark-tinted windows.

OJ shifted in his seat. Liz prayed God would once again reveal His power.

A moment or two later, a lone figure stepped out of the shadows under the streetlamp. It was Steph. She didn't move.

OJ grabbed Liz's arm as he opened the back passenger door and got out but left a trembling Liz inside beside him. He stood by her side, leaning against the door. His leg blocked her exit.

Steph started walking but stopped several metres from the car. "Rick, I move no further until Liz gets out of the car," Steph yelled across the car park.

Rick's hand slammed against the steering wheel. Turning around to face them, Liz saw the fury in his eyes. "Walk Liz over, OJ, but first tie her hands and feet."

OJ cocked his head sideways to see through the gap in the door to his cousin. "Come on, bro, let Liz go. That was the plan from the start. Use Liz to get Steph."

"Plans change. Plus, don't you like her company?" sneered Rick. "Tie her up."

OJ didn't move. He stood there glaring at his cousin. Liz watched the verbal fight, hoping OJ would think of a way to get her away.

"You think I won't hurt you?" Rick stared his cousin down.

"This has gone on far too long. This is not who you are." OJ took one more chance. "Give this life up, man. Get help. Let the girls go."

"You're forgetting something, bro. If the girls walk, your face and mine will be all over the news. We, no doubt, are wanted for kidnapping and drug charges. If the police catch us, that's jail time for you and me. I'm not going to jail, bro. Now tie her up!"

❁

Steph stood watching the heated exchange, but in the shadows, she couldn't see who was beside Liz. Her heart raced as she saw the man tying Liz's hands and feet. How could she run?

This was no exchange. Rick was going to take them both. Where were the police? She'd rung Jeremy and left a message, but he hadn't returned her call. She could only hope he'd gotten the message and understood to stay hidden.

Finally, Liz and her guard stepped away from the car.

Steph was not going willingly unless either man produced a weapon. She wouldn't get in unless she was physically carried. Rick would have to get out of the car and risk being seen.

That was the only way she was going.

Steph scanned the car park, hoping to see the police. She also hoped no one would drive into the car park by mistake. Rick would see it as a set-up and bundle Liz up, throw her back in the car, and take her back to the place of hell she'd just escaped.

Rick yelled at her to move, then, at the exact moment she had decided to placate him and take a step, her nightmare happened. The crunching of gravel under tyres sounded as a car slowed. Voices shouted. Cars revved.

Liz's guard had only moved her about two metres when she saw her being yanked back towards it.

"No!" Steph yelled above the noise. "I didn't set this up. I don't know who they are." She screamed for help, running towards Liz. She had to save her. She had to at least fight. Her arms flew at the man holding Liz. She connected to him. Punching his arms and torso.

Rick shouted orders. "You wait, Steph. I'm coming for you. I'll find you." To his mate, he yelled, "Pick her up! Get them both in the car!"

"I can't."

Liz screamed then slumped over, hitting the pavement hard.

Steph turned just as an elbow side-swiped her cheek. Grunting in pain, she swung her arms at the bulky man. She was being picked up and carried. Kicking and screaming, she cried for help. Her foot connected with flesh, and a groan resounded out into the night.

Everything was happening so fast. The car was still driving towards them.

Rick hollered, "Get her in the car."

With one last effort, Steph kicked again, and the man let her go and dove into the open door. Steph hit the ground hard with a thud, jolting her body. She hit her head and, just as she saw darkness in her vision and the streetlamp fade from view, she heard men's voices coming closer.

She was too weak to fight them off. She couldn't.

She succumbed to the darkness.

She succumbed to them.

CHAPTER 13

Brendan and Jeremy stood under the dim light of the car park, surveying the scene before them. Thinking through the night's event, Jeremy rubbed the back of his head as he stretched and yawned.

He had received Steph's call late and had not made it to the car park in time to hide out.

Looking over at the squad car with its flashing lights, Jeremy focused on its back seat. There sat one of the men who had placed the call. The other one stood in front of him.

"I'm telling you, I don't know the two girls."

"Uh, huh. And you just happened to be going along this stretch of the road with your buddy for a drive and saw it take place?" Jeremy towered over the man.

He watched him shift from foot to foot under his scrutinised glare, but he looked innocent enough, perhaps a little intimidated.

"What exactly did you see?" Brendan asked.

"I already told the other officer." The man jerked a hand to the police officer over at the patrol car.

"Yes, and you can tell us again," Brendan said.

Jeremy smiled at his partner. The man had the patience of a saint.

"We were out driving, and from the road, a woman looked bound around the ankles with her hands behind her back. Straight away, we knew it wasn't good, so we drove in as a man knocked the bound woman out, then fought off the second woman."

"And when did you ring 000?" Brendan asked.

"Straight away. To me, it looked like a kidnapping."

This time, Jeremy interrupted the conversation. "What was the make and model of the vehicle?"

The young man searched his phone and pulled up a photo on the screen. "Here, I took a photo."

Jeremy was impressed. If that were him, he would have thought about it after the fact, and he was a cop. Jeremy zoomed in on the screen. The car was easy to make out and the registration was clear enough. "So, then what happened?" He shifted his stance and directed his line of sight to the police officer over at the patrol car, to keep tabs on what his team were doing.

"The man outside the car jumped inside the waiting vehicle as it sped off."

"Did you see the driver of the vehicle?" Brendan jumped in with the question.

The man shook his head. "Nah, it was too dark a tint. Couldn't see in. Plus, it's nighttime, and this light is the only one in the car park." He made a point of looking up at it and spinning around.

"Speaking about that." Jeremy shifted tactics. "How did you see what you did in the dimness of light?"

The man paused and scratched his head before going on. "I guess the unbound woman walked from this direction where we are standing, and the others were within reach of their car lights."

He ended with a shrug of his shoulders. "I'm just telling you what I saw, Officer."

The conversation went back and forth for a while longer until Jeremy felt satisfied that they had enough to go on. Leaving Brendan with the man, Jeremy stepped away to make a call to his brother, who had been the first paramedic on the scene. "Jay, it's Jeremy. Are you still at the hospital? I need to come and get a statement from you."

Thirty minutes later the sterile smell of the hospital assaulted Jeremy's nostrils as soon as the automatic doors opened.

"Excuse me, detectives." A doctor greeted them down the corridor from the girls' rooms. "I've spoken to the families, and I've updated them on their conditions."

Jeremy didn't bother to correct him that Solomon and his mother were unrelated to Steph. He didn't need to know. Jeremy had organised for them to be there for Steph. That was all that mattered. She had no family listed to ring, so he figured his family were the best option.

The doctor continued. "Firstly, both women are awake. They're a little groggy, but that's understandable, considering they both had a good knock to their heads. Neither has any brain injuries or internal injuries. You can go ahead and see them, but I do suggest delaying any questions until tomorrow."

"Thank you, doctor." Jeremy turned to Brendan as the doctor walked away. "So, we post a guard overnight outside their doors. We cannot afford for these women to disappear overnight."

"Good idea, and I suggest we bring Alex in to meet them asap, since they'll be staying at his house."

They walked the short distance to Liz's room. From the door, she looked weaker since he'd last seen her. The past few days had taken their toll. He wanted to know what she had been through and if Rick was behind it. Not wanting to interrupt the time with her sister, he'd obey the doctor's orders and come back to Liz.

He and Brendan left to visit Steph.

"I'll wait outside while you go in," Brendan said.

She was talking quietly to his mum when he strolled in. Both women stopped to look up to greet him. Jeremy nodded at his brother, who was standing by the window.

"Have you learnt anything?" he asked, dropping his voice as he wandered over.

Solomon shook his head. "Not much. She drifts in and out of sleep. At the start, she asked if Liz was safe or if they'd taken her back." Solomon turned to look at Steph as he spoke. "Jeremy, she said it with such dread in her eyes that I wondered what pain Liz might have endured."

"The fact that we have both women is amazing. Now, our job is to keep them. They've had multiple attacks, and who knows what else Steph has experienced while she's been with Rick. Did she mention who the "they" were?" Jeremy turned and took in Steph's injuries while he waited for his brother to answer. His heart had to stay neutral to remain unbiased, but he sure hated violent attacks on women.

Another bandage to her head and bruising to her face joined the scrapes down the side of her face where she had landed on the bitumen.

"Nah, bro. She didn't say who they were."

With a gentle slap to his brother's back, he bid him goodnight. He and Brendan had to get going. He may be dog-gone tired, but reporting waited for no one.

Pulling his phone from his pocket, he dialled his brother. "Jay, I'm at the hospital now. Can we do your statement… Yep… Where are you? Okay, Brendan and I are headed your way. In a minute."

"Alex, what do you want me to buy to decorate the two spare rooms? I'm standing at the bedding section inside Target. Are they single beds or double?"

"The décor hasn't changed since you and I left home after year twelve. Anything fresh and new has got to be better than what's in there now."

"Single or double?" His sister sighed into the phone.

"Neither. Mum replaced our old beds with queen-size ones. They're the only things different in the two rooms. Wall colour and furnishings are all the same."

"What? You haven't spent any time or money renovating the house since moving back home?"

"Nope. Haven't you spent any time walking around the house you grew up in to notice? Plus, why would I?"

"Because…maybe it's your house now, and maybe I don't snoop around. Plus, you're not just visiting Mum and Dad anymore. You can turn it into your style. Make it your home," suggested Kelly.

"I did. I changed the main bedroom after Mum and Dad left. Why bother with the other two since I don't have visitors except for the odd occasion when our parents visit?"

Kelly sighed into the phone. "Right. Fine. I'll buy what I like, and I don't want to hear any complaints from you. Okay."

Alex groaned into the phone and looked at Jeremy, who shared the lift with him. He didn't try to hide his smile.

"Alex?"

"Yes, okay." He thought of the expenses he would incur. "Also, Kelly, I won't be home when you get home. Decorate how you wish. Jeremy asked me to meet him at the hospital so I could be introduced to Steph and Liz."

"All right. I'll see you when you get back."

The lift jolted to a stop, and the men exited. Alex's heart rate rose as he turned the corner and heard loud voices echoing down the quiet hall.

Jeremy quickened his pace, with Alex hot on his heels.

They found a man right outside Liz's door arguing with the police officer. "Officer Kent, what seems to be the problem?"

"This man claims to be Liz's cousin and demands to see her."

Jeremy showed the stranger his badge and asked him his name. "Once I have confirmation from Liz that she knows you, I'll let you in."

Alex felt invisible following Jeremy into the room, leaving the other man outside.

Liz's sister was seated on the bed with her back to them. "Knock, knock," Jeremy murmured as he strolled closer to them.

"Hi, I'm Mikela. I was expecting you," Mikela whispered, looking between Jeremy and Alex.

"Hi, I'm Detective Jeremy Niko, and this is Alex. How is Liz?"

"She's been sleeping on and off for most of the morning. What was the commotion outside the door?"

"A man claiming to be your cousin." He rattled off the man's name.

"Oh… Yes, he is. He is also a reporter for the Courier Mail."

"Okay, so your sister doesn't need to be visited by him just yet, even if he is your cousin. I will tell him to give us a minute."

Still feeling invisible, Alex remained silent while the exchange took place. Awkwardly, Alex turned and looked out the window. He was not good around women, especially a woman who studied him as frankly as Liz's sister now did. He could just about hear her cogs churning. Who are you? What are you doing here? Does Liz know you?

He took a quick look in her direction. She still faced him. He turned back to staring out the window. Jeremy could deal with the questions.

"So, tell me how you know my sister."

Drats. So much for that. Turning to look into her hazel eyes, he became nervous.

Get a grip, man.

She's only looking out for her sister. Same thing he'd do. Reminding himself he was not a teenager but a man, he answered her with his heart beating in his throat. "Liz and her husband visited my farm once as clients. She owns a café and buys produce from me."

"Okay, so why be here beside her hospital bed if you've only met her once?" She was suspicious as she eyed him. Both eyebrows raised skyward.

Alex didn't blame her. Her chocolate-coloured hair fell against her olive skin.

Jeremy approached from behind them. "Mikela, I will answer that with Liz at the end of our visit, but first, I need to talk to her about the kidnapping once she wakes."

Movement on the bed caused all three of them to turn. "Hi, Detective."

The sister peppered Liz with more questions than what Owen would have drilled her with.

Looking into her sister's eyes, she smiled. "I know you mean well, but I need to do this. I may as well get it out of the way. I'm up to it."

"You don't look up to it," her sister drawled back.

"Well, I am." Liz ended the argument with a turn of her head and focused her eyes on the one man in the room she didn't know.

Alex shifted under her gaze. Heck, he sweated under it. Was the aircon even on? He stopped himself from slipping his fingers between his neck and shirt collar just in time. That would have been a slip-up for sure, bringing the party who were staring at him to doubt his capabilities of looking after Liz on his property. He was a farmer. A hardworking one who had worked the land, broke horses or the more modern term, started horses. Surely, he could handle being in a room with a pretty woman, make that two, staring at him.

"Liz, this is Alex. I will explain why he's here in a minute. Alex, this is Liz. First, Liz, I need to know whether you want your cousin, Owen Jackson, in to see you. He's camped outside your door and won't leave until he gets word from you that you're fine," Jeremy stated.

The sisters shared a glance and nodded.

"We were close with Owen growing up. He's like a brother to us. There are two girls and our older brother," answered Mikela.

"Before I allow him in, I would like to ask you a few questions first, if I may. Where are your parents? And your brother? You were kidnapped and now have escaped."

"My parents are holidaying in Malta. They went back to visit family." Although her voice was shaky, Liz answered the detective's questions with a quiet confidence that spoke through her eyes.

"And your brother?"

"First, you need to know we haven't been able to speak to Mum and Dad about the news Liz has been found," Mikela answered. "By the time I reached them with Liz's kidnapping, they were adamant our brother, Marco, had to fly back with them. He was in Cyprus for work, so they'll all arrive late this afternoon. If they don't check their voice messages, they'll think Liz is still missing." She paused to swallow and glance at Liz with a sheen of moisture in her eyes. "Hopefully, when they land, they will switch their phones straight on and hear my latest message that Liz is safe and we are at the hospital."

Liz's gaze shifted from Jeremy to settle on Alex. He moved his stance awkwardly under the scrutiny.

Why focus on him, a stranger, he had no idea, but he couldn't tear his eyes away. It was then he saw a hint of blue hidden near the hazel rims of her irises.

She was mesmerising him. He needed to snap out of it. What was wrong with him?

She broke the grip on him by turning her head to look at her sister. "Owen is the closest family we have in Brisbane right now. I would like to talk with him. You know, when my husband was killed just under a year ago, Owen researched it and is still convinced it wasn't an accident."

The shift in conversation confused Alex, but he figured Liz had a purpose for that.

Alex's heart ramped up about her being married and then shattered by her husband's death, to this kidnapping, all in a space of a year. He lost track of what was being said. His world on the farm certainly kept him out of all the chaos.

"What did he learn that made him think that?" Jeremy asked.

"It was a single-vehicle accident on a wet night. He had stopped to get dinner on the way home. As he walked out of the Chinese takeaway shop, he saw one of the men we had helped get off drugs. They shared a few words, and he kept going. He rang me before he drove off, and that was the last conversation I had with him." Liz's eyes took on a distant stare.

Alex watched on in obscurity as he stood back against the window.

"And?" Jeremy prompted.

"Well, the man he spoke to was found dead not long after." Liz turned back to look at Jeremy. "I don't believe in coincidences, and nor does Owen. You need to talk to my cousin about it."

A sad smile touched the edge of Mikela's lips. "Sis, if you're ready for Owen's questions, I'll go get him."

"Hang on a sec, Mikela," Jeremy interrupted. "You can get him only after Liz gives me the details of the day of the kidnapping." Shifting his stance to concentrate on Liz, Jeremy stood with his legs shoulder-width apart. "Are you happy to have your sister hear it all? And Alex?"

Pausing, Liz pivoted her head to flick a look in Alex's direction. Slowly, she nodded whilst not removing her intense gaze from him.

"Tell me the events as you remember them. It may be hard, but I need to know everything."

Alex could hear the detective speaking, but he had taken on a muted sound. He was locked in the stare of the woman lying before him. It scared the living daylights out of him. He wanted to bolt, but his feet were like lead on the floor.

Over the next hour, Liz detailed her traumatic experience and highlighted a man named OJ, who was her beacon of hope in that dark world. Alex was amazed at Liz's ability to distance herself from the event. Maybe it was a trauma-informed approach she had adopted to survive the terrifying ordeal? He didn't know. But he was fascinated and captivated by her capacity to survive.

After waking a sleeping Owen and allowing him in, Alex watched the family converse with each other. Owen clearly cared about Liz and her well-being, but could he be trusted to keep the information from the papers until the police were ready to release it?

Only time would tell.

After a long hour of discussions, Mikela and Owen left together. Now alone, Jeremy had the privacy to tell Liz the logic of Alex visiting. "The reason I asked Alex to join us today is because he needs to know what you have gone through, who captured you, and what the men look like, because once you are released from the hospital" – he paused and looked directly at her – "you and Steph will be hiding out at Alex's farm."

Shock registered on her face.

"For how long?" she managed to utter.

"We're unsure. If we can locate Rick, then hopefully it won't be too long. We need all the information about where he kept you and what he is after, so we can find those responsible and charge them. Once they're in custody, all going well, you should be safe to go home. But until then, you and Steph will stay at Alex's and won't leave unless we okay it."

She sighed and crossed her arms across her chest, clearly not impressed. She looked from Jeremy to Alex and back to Jeremy. "Do I have a choice?"

"I'm afraid not."

"Okay. Fine," she huffed.

"And you cannot tell anyone where you are. We already have my two brothers, Alex, his sister and her husband and a limited number in my team who know. We won't tell your family anything. All they will know is that you are in an undisclosed location." Jeremy paused with intention before continuing. "Rick will come after you if he finds out. Trust me, he will be angry with himself, with you, with Steph, and with everyone, and stewing on it will only make him worse."

A visible shudder went through Liz's body.

Alex hated seeing the fear in her eyes. If he could do his part well and keep her safe, then that's what mattered.

Walking into the police station, Jeremy headed straight to his boss's office. "Boss?"

"Yes, Niko. Come in."

Shutting the door behind him, Jeremy approached his boss. "Sir, is there an undercover cop on a drug sting at the moment that would be connected to our investigation with Liz Agius?"

Looking up from his computer screen, his superior glanced at him. "Why?"

"I've just come from an interview with Liz Agius, and there was a guy who didn't cause her harm at all. She had to share a room with him, and, given the circumstances, any male who spends a night in a room with an attractive…"

His boss raised an eyebrow.

"I am just stating the obvious, sir. Liz is attractive. She was there three nights, but this guy, OJ, didn't try anything, and if he was a criminal in a drug ring, do the math. Just saying." Jeremy turned and paced the small room back to the door and pivoted on his heels and faced his boss, who was watching him.

"I hear you. What else did Liz Agius say?"

"That OJ protected her on multiple occasions from men who could have harmed her. She even said the night she escaped, they were supposed to swap her over for Steph, but Rick told OJ he wanted Liz, too. She was the woman they 'chose' for that night. That men were waiting for her back at the house." Jeremy spat the words out. His eyes pierced his boss. "OJ told her he would somehow try to get her out. So, is there an undercover cop named OJ?"

His boss sat studying him for a beat, twirling a pen between his fingers. Jeremy had dropped a bombshell, and he had not reacted.

Jeremy's eyes narrowed. "You know something, and you didn't tell me." His voice rose a decibel.

"Niko, I don't know of anyone undercover. Besides, the drug arm squad do not share their information with us. Maybe I could get something from them if I tell them we are after this group for a kidnapping."

"Thank you, sir. I would rather know so that if it comes down to it, we don't open fire on one of our own."

"I understand we now have an open case involving an OJ of unknown origins, and if we find him, he will be taken into custody. And Niko." He paused. "Don't shoot him if we don't get word back."

"Yes, sir." Jeremy turned to leave and opened the door.

"Also, Niko, did Steph happen to know anything about this OJ?"

Jeremy spun back around and leaned against the door frame. "No, she hadn't met an OJ or heard Rick talk of him the whole time they were together."

"What was Steph's involvement in the kidnapping bust?"

"She had caught a bus out of town on Wednesday just before Liz sent the 000 call. Steph said she wanted Liz safe and, therefore, had to leave town. Ironically, that decision made Liz more vulnerable. Rick wanted Steph, and Liz was the pawn to get her back."

"Right. One last thing, is Alex's place ready for the women once they're released from the hospital?"

With a final nod, Jeremy walked out the door to his own office. He would search the system for anybody called OJ and see if Liz could identify the man.

CHAPTER 14

Jeremy arrived nice and early at the hospital the next morning with Brendan. The women were being released after the doctor's visit, but there was a problem.

The one media release they did yesterday with Owen's brief write-up caused a media frenzy, so reporters were already camped out at the hospital by the time the detectives got there.

Jeremy had to force his way through the front door. There was no way they were bringing the girls through that entrance. "Brendan, go to the head of staff and ask for a secure back way out of here. We can't bring them through there. We'll be tailed for sure."

Jeremy went to Liz's room to find a doctor with her. Stationing himself outside her door, waiting for the doctor to finish, he considered what he'd learnt about OJ.

Nothing.

He had no criminal record, or maybe it was that he hadn't been caught yet.

The doctor nodded to Jeremy as he walked out, informing him that Liz could leave when she was ready. Knocking on the door, he waited for Liz to answer. She didn't. He peeked around the door and heard a muffled sob.

Not good. He made a noise by clearing his throat. She still didn't look up.

Walking into the room, he risked a rebuke, but he didn't care. He wanted to know what had made her cry. "Knock, knock," he verbalised as he strolled closer. He didn't want to startle her. She'd been through enough of those already.

In slow motion, she turned to look at him, her eyes broken and vulnerable.

What he wanted to do and what he could do were opposites. He jammed his hands in his jacket pockets, waiting for her to speak.

"I'm scared," she whispered as she bit her bottom lip.

He pulled the chair nearer and sat to the side of her dangling legs. Trying to strengthen her with his presence, he leaned forward and grabbed both her hands, looking straight into her eyes.

Ignoring the slight tremor in her fingers and the fear in her hazel eyes was easier than ignoring the quiver in her bottom lip. As hard as she tried to bite it to get it to stop, it wouldn't.

He looked from her lips to her eyes, and, with a gentleness intertwined with strength, he held her gaze as he spoke. "Liz, it's normal for you to be scared. I have done what I can to secure Alex's place. Brendan has put up security cameras at each entrance point to the house and around the yard. We have protected your privacy by not putting any inside the house. As long as no one follows us today to his property and you don't venture into town, your location is secure."

Just then, Steph entered, with Solomon following, carrying her bag.

Solomon coughed, and Jeremy looked up to catch his brother's gaze on their hands. His brother's brief look was not shock but rather a subtle glint that Jeremy understood.

Dropping Liz's hands and returning a hidden bro nod, he rose from the chair. "Good timing. Steph, I need you and Liz to listen to me carefully." Jeremy waited until Steph's curious look had turned from Liz to him. "We're assuming Rick will have lookouts at the hospital again. Probably, even this OJ could be standing in the crowd." He made a point of directing his next comment to Liz. "You're the only one who could recognise OJ in a line-up, so keep an eye out for him." Flicking his gaze back and forth between the two, he laid out the rules for leaving the hospital.

"Do your vehicles have tinted windows so no one can see in?" Steph asked, fidgeting with her fingernails while her eyes stayed on him.

"Yes. No one can see in, but you will be able to see out. Bulletproof, too." Not that he needed to add the last part, but he did.

He noted Liz's face pale, but Steph's eyes steeled. He could see she was ready for battle. She had been through enough and was ready for war.

Hopefully, his men and his defensive plan were enough to stop her from needing to put herself on the line again.

He admired the two women before him. The number of women like them was growing, and it grated on him. He ground his teeth. He would work to stop Rick and whoever else was behind it and make sure they didn't get off lightly.

Men like him not only needed a sentence. They needed reform.

"Once we get you out of here," he continued, knowing he had to get them moving, "and on the road, we will make sure we're not being tailed before we head to Alex's property." He paused and targeted each one with a pointed glare. "I need to remind you, your location must remain top secret. Do not answer the door if someone knocks. Ignore it if Alex is not home. You cannot afford for someone to recognise either of you. Solomon, Jaymond, Kelly, and I will be the only ones who will visit the house. Any questions?"

Both women shook their heads.

Looking at Solomon, Jeremy nodded, glad to have his brother as backup. Besides Brendan, Jeremy knew his two brothers and Alex would do anything to protect the women.

Steph let out a deep sigh. They had achieved the first hurdle: getting to the car without being seen. She let her head loll back against the headrest as she took in a deep lungful of air and released it, counting to six. She began to remove her scarf and sunglasses when a car door banged, and a hand landed on hers. She jumped and clenched her fist to fight. Adrenaline pumped through her veins.

"I'm sorry, Steph. I didn't mean to frighten you. I said your name, but you didn't hear me."

She stared into the dark chocolate-brown eyes of the man she was getting to know. His black locks dangled beside his face as he shifted in the seat beside her. He removed his warm hand from hers, and she could breathe again.

"Jeremy said to leave the disguises on. Although the tints are dark, keep 'em on. Scan the crowds, look for anyone you know."

His eyes were warm. His voice calmed her racing heart.

Once outside the hospital grounds, it was Brendan who spoke. "Can you see anything or anybody you recognise?"

"No," came Liz's answer.

Steph gave a more indirect answer. "Yes and no. Yes, to a few buddies from my old life who probably want a glimpse of me. They aren't directly linked to Rick, so probably not a lookout person. And no to anything else odd or recognisable."

"Ok, we'll take that with some caution as we drive to your location."

Brendan glanced at her in the rearview mirror and flicked his gaze to catch Jeremy's brief look and nod as they sped through the streets towards Alex's farm.

Other than the one car with an elderly man driving too close for comfort, the trip was uneventful.

Upon approaching Alex's farm, Steph watched as Liz's countenance transformed. Her fidgeting in the car and cautious glances out the window changed to wide open eyes, leaning forward and a keenness to get the door open.

What was with that? She nudged her friend and did a slight shake of the head as if to say, "What's up?"

A huge smile and a sheen of tears were given in return. She would be getting the downlow from her bestie as soon as they were alone.

Was Liz her bestie? She'd never had one. Could she call her that?

She swallowed deep as the car rolled forward into the shadows and the garage door slid down. Adjusting her eyes to the limited light, Steph waited as the men climbed out first then opened the doors for the girls.

Liz bounced on the balls of her feet, chewing her bottom lip.

Steph eyed her friend. What the heck was wrong with her?

Jeremy's voice cut through the darkness as shuffling sounded behind them. A light came on, and two bags were pushed to the side of the vehicle.

"We had a female officer go to your motel and pack up everything you both left there. I brought it all here earlier." Jeremy pointed to a collection of bags. "If you need anything else, the same officer can go to your home, Liz, and collect it. She will leave it at the station for us to transport here. Or Kelly will go to town for you and purchase what you need."

Steph nodded as she looked around, followed the men inside, and took up the spot behind Liz.

Taking in the surroundings of the inside of the house, Steph felt the country charm immediately. The smell of the farm outside the windows and the tickle to her taste buds of a banana loaf fresh from the oven had her mouth watering and her heart easing to a steady sixty-beats-per-minute rhythm. She had normalised for the first time in weeks as she followed the men into the lounge.

After placing the bags down, Brendan and Jeremy turned and motioned for the girls to take a seat.

"Try to feel comfortable, which I understand will be awkward to start with," offered Jeremy. "But the quicker you work on relaxing, the better it will be. I don't need to warn you that Alex is quiet around women." He spoke, having no idea Alex stood right behind with his arms crossed in front of his chest, eyeballing him. "You've already witnessed that at the hospital," Jeremy continued with ease. "Give him time to warm to the idea of females other than his sister in his home."

"Hey, I'm pretty sure you can't talk much better yourself. What women have graced your home, pal?"

Jeremy spun around and laughed. "Cheriece and Shontelle—"

"Sisters don't count, I recall."

Steph's shoulders relaxed as the two men bantered between themselves. It was no doubt going to be interesting times ahead.

"Drinks?" Solomon entered with a tray sporting glasses, water and a couple of cans of soft drinks.

Alex faced Liz and Steph. "Grab a drink, and I'll show you the two bedrooms, and you can decide who gets which room. I'll give you a tour, so you know where everything is, and then I'll sit with the detectives to catch up on what else I need to know."

At some point towards the afternoon, Steph fell asleep. She'd been stretched out on the queen-sized bed, her chatting growing slower, and the yawns had increased when, overcome with sheer exhaustion, she rested her head on her arm and drifted off to sleep.

Liz watched her friend for a moment, taking in how her relaxed face made her look younger and free of fear.

Wanting to journal her thoughts, Liz eased herself from the bed, her movements gradual, her eyes glued to Steph's face to ensure she didn't wake her. At the edge of the bed, Liz swung her feet to the floor, mindful of her movements.

She crept across the room to the door and cracked it open to sneak into the hallway. Liz hesitated for a moment to get her bearings, then, following her nose, she made her way to the kitchen. Her dry mouth yearned for a cup of tea. As the kettle boiled, she heard the back door open.

Liz stiffened, her eyes flicking towards the knife block, making a quick decision to reach for one just as Alex strolled in, deep in thought.

He stopped mid-stride when his eyes locked onto hers, travelling from her face, down her arm, to where her hand rested against a knife handle.

Tension skimmed through his eyes and his jaw tightened. He said nothing. He remained pivoted on his heel and toe stance, rooted to the spot, as his eyes flew back to her and locked in place.

She couldn't read what they were saying. Wariness. Compassion. Don't do it.

She didn't know, but her heart skipped several beats, and, realising there was no threat, it slowed to a calm rhythm. Her hand dropped to her side, and she slumped forward, her head on her forearm as she rested on the bench.

Alex didn't move.

She didn't blame him.

She'd stay away from someone who'd grabbed for a knife, too. She had a bad memory of that with Rick, and she had ended up sliced.

She wouldn't cry. She'd already shed too many tears in front of Jeremy. She wouldn't do it again in front of a stranger.

Tears with Steph, yes. Anyone else, no.

She lifted her head at a slight angle to catch a glimpse of Alex's face. She was afraid to read what she saw, but she needed to apologise.

The poor man wouldn't feel safe walking around in his own home.

"Alex." Her lip quivered. "I'm…I'm so sorry. I guess after that we should leave."

He reached for her and stopped halfway, pulling his hand back to jam in his front jean pocket. "Liz, it's okay, really. You've been through a lot. It would be normal to be a bit jumpy." He looked around the kitchen, propped his hip against the bench and crossed his socked feet.

She could feel her heart softening for the kind farmer standing before her. His Akubra hat was off his head, and his hair was indented where it had been sitting.

He was trying hard to make her not feel so bad. He ran his hand through his hair, making it stick up in all different directions. "After all," he added with a slight shrug, "you're in a new place with a new bloke around."

His mouth curled at the corner, and with his hair everywhere, he looked so…adorable.

Slamming his beer can down, Rick cursed. "How could my plan have gone so wrong?" he roared. "If we hadn't been spooked by that car, we would have Steph and Liz."

OJ peered over his phone at his cousin's bruised face. Anger was an understatement.

The news playing in the background stated two brothers had been out for a drive when one of them saw something suspicious going on.

They weren't cops.

OJ was glad. He hadn't fancied a bullet flying his direction last night.

Rick had sped off as soon as the car arrived, leaving the women behind. They'd arrived back at the house without the women who had been promised, and an inferno of cursing and fist fights broke out.

OJ shook his head as he rubbed his hand down his weary face. His eye and lip sported a bruise. Heck, he probably needed stitches, but that would need explaining. He was glad no one pulled a gun on them. He would have had to pull his, and that would not have ended well for the other guy.

"OJ, you're going to help me figure out how to get them back. Steph belongs to me and no one else."

OJ kept his eyes averted and said nothing as Rick crushed the beer can in his hand, dropping it to the bench.

"And Liz, well, she's beautiful and an asset to my growing business. If only I could convince you to share her."

OJ's free hand clenched at his side. He hated the way his cousin spoke about women. He was there to learn about Rick's growing business, and that was it. Nothing else. And not to hook up with women.

OJ's scout had told him that Steph and Liz had left the hospital in an unmarked police car. He would bide his time. The ladies would resurface, and he would wait until they did.

OJ continued to listen silently as his cousin rambled on.

"Money buys people, OJ. There are plenty of people who will sit and keep watch for a few bucks." Rick smirked. "We need to get those women back, and you're going to help me."

OJ didn't say a word. Instead, he chewed on a toothpick as Rick stood and paced back and forth in the small kitchen. OJ had witnessed how anger had become Rick's tool to gain control. People were afraid of him, and that worked to his advantage. "Plus, let's get out of this dump. The boys can use this, but you and I," he said, turning to OJ, "can live in something better."

Again, OJ said nothing. He simply listened to his cousin continue about his plans to live a better life.

OJ knew of that better life, but he had committed to this lifestyle for now, and as ugly and degrading as it was, he was in it until he got what he needed. Hopefully, dragging Rick out of the deep, dark pit he'd found himself in would be part of it.

At least, that was what he told himself.

CHAPTER 15

Steph had found joy in the simplest of tasks over the two weeks she'd been at Alex's house. Cooking dinners and baking sweets were her forte. She was knocking out some great dishes, and her treats, well, they'd be a hit if Liz could get them into the café.

Whoever visited the house was the guinea pig to her creations. That meant Solomon, Jaymond, Jeremy and Alex were the ones who sampled everything. Liz, on the other hand, was strict on herself, saying she'd end up the size of a house since she wasn't allowed outside to exercise.

It was a Friday afternoon, and Steph was in the kitchen making choc-chip and macadamia nut biscuits when Jeremy and Solomon walked in. Although she wouldn't admit it to anyone, she'd started to relax around the men over the last few days.

She'd learnt the three were brothers who had answered all the mannerism questions that were piling up in her head to ask.

"Is Liz close by?" Jeremy asked as he walked over and picked up a spoon to sample some biscuit dough.

Swatting his outstretched hand, Steph's brows raised to her hairline in a challenge. "She's outside with Alex learning how to milk a goat that doesn't want to be milked." Eyeing Jeremy as he spooned the mixture into his mouth, she was ready to swat his hand again if that spoon went back for a second dip.

Jeremy must have noticed her eyeballing him. "What?"

"That won't work on me, mister," she said as she landed her hand on a hip.

His lazy boy grin tried to win him another spoonful. She clucked her teeth and stayed guarding her biscuit dough until he put the spoon down and raised his hands in surrender. He backed away, still smiling.

"As I was saying, Liz is outside if you need her."

Jeremy saluted as he walked out the back door.

Cheeky.

But it brought a smile to her lips. The men had been food to her soul. Refreshing like water to parched ground. She turned to Solomon, who had now replaced his elder brother's spot, and groaned. He had snuck his own spoonful of mixture into his mouth.

"What is it with you Niko brothers? Each time I'm making something sweet, you're without a doubt, guaranteed, to walk into the kitchen and sample it?"

"Homing device."

"A homing device?" she repeated as her thick eyebrow raised slightly on the corner.

"Instinct," Solomon said, folding his arms. "Our mother raised us to sample everything she cooked or baked. Jaymond still samples his wife's baking. She's given up asking him to stop."

All this family talk and kitchen duties was making Steph's heart ache.

She blinked back tears.

She looked up quickly and saw Solomon's eyes trained on her. She tried to hide her emotions, but her hands trembled and her heart raced. She hoped the increased pulse on her neck would remain hidden.

Reining in her thoughts, she gained control and quickly turned her body to hide the tears forming in her eyes. She went back to her biscuit making, hoping Solomon hadn't noticed. Could she ever trust a man again, have the relationship Jaymond and his wife had and get her babies back?

She didn't know the answer to that. Only time would tell.

Laughter echoed across the lawn, causing both her and Solomon to move to the kitchen window and peer out. There was Liz on the ground laughing with a baby goat jumping across her legs as Jeremy fell, trying to catch it.

It looked impossible that either of them would be able to grab such a bouncing ball of energy as its sibling pranced and flipped in mid-air beside it, egging it on.

Steph couldn't help but chuckle at the kid goats' antics. They were free and without fear. What a place to be. If only she could feel free and without fear. Was that even possible?

Her mind reeled with questions and possibilities. It hadn't stopped since she had found the haven of the farm.

Sure, Liz had been helping her, prodding her along the journey. And at times being her conscience. She'd talked with her about the power and the peace that Jesus gives during a storm.

Remembering back to a year ago, Steph recalled praying to Him and literally feeling a peace settle over her and inside her, just as the Bible described. But she hadn't gone any further down that path.

✻

Alex walked over and lifted Liz to her feet.

"Why are we bottle-feeding them? Where's their mother?" she asked as she swept a hand across her face to remove the hair that had escaped the once neat high ponytail. She wiped her eyes from the tears that had remained after her fits of laughter.

"She died from a snake bite not long after giving birth. They were maybe four or five weeks old when that happened."

"So you became their foster mum," she answered with a smirk, looking at the ball of energy in his arms.

He bent and placed the kid he was holding onto the ground and indicated with a curve of his arm towards the shed. They walked together back to where the food was stored.

Chewing on her bottom lip, Liz followed. Steph had chosen the right guy, but how did her friend know he was so soft and caring about abandoned things? "What makes you do this?" Catching his arm and turning him, she waved a hand at the thriving baby goats. "I know you said their mother died, but you're a busy man. You run a diverse farm, a marketplace that sells produce, and you still have time to take in poor, defenceless baby creatures, not to mention two unknown women."

Her eyes darted away as she referenced her last phrase. She couldn't hold his gaze. It was too intense, yet he was too gentle.

Liz hoped she hadn't tipped her hand, but the weight of their secret was weighing her down more each day, especially when living with the man they'd left the babies with.

Talk about God wanting to sort your life out.

"For me, it's simple." Alex lifted his hat and ran a hand through his hair to place it back down again with a snug squish. "I've always been this way. From a young boy, I often cared for sick or injured animals on the farm, much to my dad's disgust." He chuckled to himself. "I remember one time, my cousin and I were supposed to kill a chicken to prove we weren't little boys anymore." He bent and plucked a blade of grass, then twirled it between his fingers and thumb. His honey-coloured eyes stared at the rotation, glazing over for a time. "You see, it was Dad's job." He glanced at her, drawing her in to his storytelling. "To kill the many roosters we'd bred, for a meal. One day, it was my turn. Dad showed me what to do, how to make it a clean cut so as not to torture the bird. I'd tied the rooster's legs together, laid it on the chopping block, and raised the axe for the kill, when a mangy cat walked into my view."

"A what?"

"A mangy cat. You know…scrawny, mite infested, sick looking."

"Yep, yep, so what happened next?"

"I laid the axe down and handed the rooster to my dad and said, 'You do it. I'm going to take care of that cat.'"

"What did your dad say?" Liz tried to hide her amusement with a hand to her mouth.

"Don't worry, you can laugh." Alex held her captive with his eyes for a beat before continuing. Her heart skipped a beat. "Dad shook his head in disgust and said, 'What type of man are you going to be? Running off to save something or provide for your family?' I walked off without answering him."

"It's a surprise you're not a vet or a doctor, or something like that?" She turned it into a question more than a statement.

"Yeah, well, I was looking at being a vet, but being the only son, my dad had plans for me to take over the farm."

"Do you regret the direction you took?" she asked, engrossed in the man's narrative.

"Not one bit. Farming is hard work, but being on the land is freedom. Look around you." He pivoted on his feet as he half held his hands out from his side and looked around.

She followed his eyes, roaming the farmland.

"Sure, I have The Coomera Marketplace, but my sister manages that mostly, so I can enjoy being here and doing this life on the land." Alex's face softened as he spoke.

She could hear the passion in his voice. He truly was happy.

That was the feeling she'd felt the day she and Steph had rocked up to begin their hidden life on the farm. It was the same feeling she'd had the day she and Jeff had visited his farm with the others. She remembered he had spoken much the same way. He was content with his life and enjoyed what he did. Liz pondered how she desired that for herself.

"You know, Liz," Alex spoke, interrupting her thoughts. "I've been meaning to ask you something but don't know…" His voice trailed off as he busied himself with cleaning the bottles and putting items away that were on the bench.

It was obvious he was uncomfortable. She didn't know why, but she would give him his space. She collected the broom from the corner of the room and began sweeping up the spilt grain from the concrete floor.

From the corner of her eye, Liz saw Alex lean his hip against the bench and fold his legs at the ankles. He was readying himself for the question, but why was he fidgeting with his Akubra hat, spinning it in his hands?

He cleared his voice as if to dislodge the object blocking his ability to speak. "Liz, do you remember the day you and your husband came to this farm for a tour?"

Her broom stilled ever so slightly. How could he know she'd been thinking about that day?

"Remember, you visited several farms and took produce home in a basket…"

She kept sweeping, ignorant of the fact that she'd already swept that spot. Her face paled with each sweep of the broom.

Alex kept going. Did he notice her discomfort?

"Liz, I'm curious if you still have the basket."

She stopped and looked him straight in the eye. Her hands that were holding the broom began to take on a mind of their own. She opened her mouth and then closed it. She shook her head from side to side and then fled out of the shed. She had to get to the safety of her room before she broke down.

Alex watched her pace quicken toward the house. She was shaken. She knew something about the baskets. Now all he had to do was get her to trust him so she didn't have to carry whatever she knew alone anymore.

A sadness so deep had pooled in her eyes when she'd looked back at him. He had seen it before she took off. He hadn't wanted to push her, so he had stayed rooted to the ground to assess his next move.

Moments later, Jeremy waltzed out the back door towards him.

Obviously, Liz hadn't done a very good job at concealing her distress, or maybe that had something to do with Jeremy being a detective? Whatever the case may be, Alex braced himself for what was coming.

"Okay, bro, what did you do to make her cry? She was laughing not long ago. Now, she flies in the back door with her tail between her legs, trying to hide her tears. She and Steph took flight to a bedroom."

Sighing heavily, Alex figured he might as well get his friend's perspective on what had just gone down. He was a detective after all. Experienced in human profiling. "We were talking about how I came to be farming. I brought up her visit to the farm and then asked if she still had the basket."

"And?" Jeremy picked up the broom and swept where he could see animal feed on the floor, a small pile of dust swirled in the afternoon sun following him as he went. Jeremy began sneezing and set the broom aside. "Bruh." He shook his head. "I need to step outside." Jeremy reached for a handkerchief in his pocket. "How do you do that?" Jeremy asked around sneezes.

Alex shrugged. "Used to it, I guess."

Taking his Akubra off and twirling it between his hands, Alex stared out across the yard, waiting for his mate to finish his sneeze attack. "You know, when I mentioned the basket, she swept over the same spot as her face paled. Then, when I asked if she still had it, she looked into my eyes with such sadness and shook her head slowly and then took off." Placing his hat to the side and picking up the dirt pile Jeremy had created, he sank it in the bin.

Jeremy braved the insides of the farm shed and clapped Alex on his back. "Well, we will just give her time, and then I will ask her myself. We need answers. Hopefully, she will come to us herself. Either way, it's not going to be easy for her based on the reactions she has expressed. I noticed a while back, but hadn't pushed for answers. However, I think it's time for both Liz and Steph to tell their story."

"That's a good plan. How about our next plan is preparing dinner?"

"Great idea." Jeremy clapped his hands together.

"Okay, guys, it's been two weeks since Steph and Liz moved in here," Jeremy began. "I understand you ladies need to get out and probably desire to get back to some routine in your lives. We've heard nothing of Rick or OJ. They've gone quiet and most likely gone into hiding as well. There's no word around the community about their whereabouts. But we still need to be cautious."

Jeremy looked around at who was seated at the back table and wondered what they all thought. He couldn't help but notice Liz's crossed-legged position with her right foot doing a rhythmic, gentle kick under the table.

"Here are my ideas, and I want your feedback," continued Jeremy. "Steph, you're enjoying cooking and baking. How about we take some of your creations into Liz's café and see what people like? Liz, I have spoken to your sister-in-law, and she's happy to try a few new products."

Steph nodded and smiled, clearly pleased with the option.

"I've talked with my boss, and he's suggested we take both of you in on the same day for an hour or two, but you're not to leave the store at all. It's only been two weeks since your release from the hospital, and all it takes is one person to say something, and the media will be there. You know they want to know more about you, and to have them broadcasting where you are puts you in danger."

"So, what are the precautions we take?" Solomon asked his brother.

"Liz, your suggestions will help. You know the café's pace more than all of us. What about going in on a slower day?" Jeremy suggested.

"Yes, that's an option, but how about we go in before the shop opens and deliver the products? That way, I can catch up with my in-laws. I can see how the business is going without interruptions." Her response was quiet.

"Good idea," Jeremy replied. Turning to look at Steph, he wanted her thoughts, too. "What do you think?"

"Sounds great. Plus, it gives me a reason to keep baking other than to fatten Alex up." She smirked at her new friend, who had opened his home to her.

Jeremy observed her easy banter, pondering the contrast of her relaxed mood and peaceful countenance from two weeks ago.

"Hey, I resent that. I'm not getting fat, am I?" Alex tapped his gut.

"Maybe you've put on a few kilos, big brother." Kelly slapped his bicep in good fun, laughing.

"Just more of me to love, eh, sis?" he retorted with a smile that reached his eyes.

Jeremy brought the conversation back on track. "Hopefully, taking these steps will give you girls something to look forward to and stem your boredom, but it's only once a week for now. Any other ideas?"

Looking at Liz, Steph asked her friend. "What about continuing your studies, externally, of course?"

"I've thought about it. It's been nearly a year, but I'm not sure if that's an option." Her answer was just above a whisper.

Jeremy wasn't sure if anyone else had noticed, but Liz's eyes had darted back to Steph in a pleading motion. He narrowed his gaze on the girls, noticing Steph had either not picked up on the non-verbal cue or ignored it on purpose to ask her a follow-up question.

"Wouldn't Jeff want you to finish it?"

The question hung in the air. If Liz's first answer was quiet, her response to the next one was quieter. "Probably, but what I can do and what Jeff wants are two different things." Shutting down the conversation, Liz got up from the table and sat near the pot plant on the steps. Liz's shoulders dropped. Her hands held her head as she stared across the backyard at the last rays of pink and orange sunlight.

Jeremy couldn't help but notice the pained look of sadness.

Alex got up and joined her on the step, placing his hand gently on her arm. "Are you all right?" he asked.

She didn't answer.

Alex roamed Liz's olive-skinned forearm where his large hand sat. What was going through the man's mind? Alex removed his hand and leaned forward, placing his elbows on his knees.

Jeremy wanted to move closer to hear what the conversation was about. He wanted to know what had spooked Liz to flee the table. He could see it in her darting eyes and the fidgeting of her hands. It all pointed to an ongoing internal battle.

But what?

❋

Taking a deep breath and keeping her eyes down and voice low, Liz started. “First, I want to apologise for racing off like that earlier. I can’t explain the reason yet, but hopefully, I will soon.” She snuck a peek in Steph’s direction when she tucked a loose strand of hair behind her ear, but Alex caught her. “I need to talk to Steph first. Next, I want to thank you for opening your home to us. We were strangers when you took us in two weeks ago.” Her voice wobbled.

Not trusting himself, Alex turned his gaze away from the woman beside him. If he saw tears or fear, he was a goner. “I knew who you were. I just didn’t know you personally. And Steph, well, yeah, I can say she was a stranger.” He stared out across his lawn, tracking the bird’s flight west to roost for the night.

A comfortable silence fell between them. He didn’t need Liz to say anything else.

A warm hand landed on his forearm, causing him to turn to look into the blue-rimmed hazel eyes he had been trying to ignore. Darn it. His heart picked up its beat.

“Yeah, but Steph knew you.” Her eyes were glassy as her voice trailed the soft words as a caress on her lips. “She knew what you stood for, the type of man you were.” She cast her eyes downward as a tear dripped from them. “We may have only met each other at your farm tour, but like Steph, I’d heard of you in the community and in my church, too.”

That was news to him. He angled his body to look at her. “What things did you hear?”

A chair scraped back, followed by another.

Liz withdrew her hand from Alex’s arm.

"Excuse us, Alex and Liz, we need to get going." Philip and Kelly bent down to hug Alex goodbye over his shoulder before turning to everyone else and waving goodbye. Philip clamped a hand on his shoulder, and he and Kelly left.

"Alex, we'll help you clean up, and then we need to think of going, too." Jeremy elbowed Solomon to comply.

"Ouch, bro, you don't have to dig me in the ribs. I can see our brother here wants some time alone without ears around." Solomon's eyes danced with playfulness.

Alex's brows drew together as his vision travelled from Solomon to Liz.

Her cheeks had turned crimson as she stuttered, "Nah, I was just telling Alex I need to uh…talk to Steph. If you aren't in a rush, I want you all to stay." With that, in a split second, she rose, and, keeping her head down, she went to her friend, grabbed her arm and dragged her down the three porch steps and out across the grass to the bench chair that sat under the big lone Jacaranda tree.

All three men stood silently as they watched the girl's backs disappear in the dim light.

"What was all that about?" asked Solomon to no one in particular.

"I believe that is a conversation that will have them changing the current course of their lives," replied Alex.

CHAPTER 16

Liz shoved Steph down on the chair, then turned and stood in front of her. Steph could tell the short march had bolstered her friend's determination to say what was on her mind.

Before Steph had a chance to gather any further thoughts, Liz stood with fists on her hips and blurted the dreaded words. "I'm done with keeping secrets from these men. All they have shown is love, care, and compassion, and all we have given in return are lies and deceit."

"Hey, I care. I cook them food," interjected Steph.

"Yeah, and you cooked food for Rick," Liz countered. "Plus, it's not about cooking. It's about what's going on in here." Liz pointed to her own heart, where her inner self sat. "I'm getting depressed, Steph, keeping this from them." Her speech rose louder at each punctuated word.

Steph may not have been able to see the anger in her friend's eyes, but she could feel and hear it radiating. She tried to diffuse the tension by stepping away and looking across the lawn to where they had just come from. "You don't think I'm done with keeping it inside?" Steph swung around with the accusation, her arms flailing. "But I just can't reveal it. It will show how bad a person I really am." Steph absorbed the darkness of the night, she let it cloak her the same way her shame cloaked her. It gave her a place to hide. But it surrounded her to the point she couldn't see clearly.

She swung back to look at the house, frustrated, noticing the lamps on the back porch. The little bit of light they gave shooed the darkness from around them. "This is going to look bad on you, Liz. I mean, really bad. I've made it worse for you by asking you to keep quiet all these months now."

Her lips trembled.

She was coming undone.

The little lamps on the back porch were drawing her. Speaking to her heart. Maybe there was hope in the darkness she had been drowning in. A flicker of light that wasn't at the end of the tunnel but one that had been placed right beside her.

She slowly pivoted on her toes and sat dejected, pulling Liz down beside her. Her friend had been watching her outrageous meltdown, saying nothing.

Placing her head between her hands and letting her brown locks cover her face, Steph wanted to hide from the reality of what she'd done. "You know," she whispered, "my babies would be nearly five months old…and I am no closer to seeing them, possibly further away if a judge or child safety have their way." She didn't bother to try to stop the tremble in her voice. "I wonder what their names are."

The statement hung between them. Neither woman said a word.

Steph kept her head down as she spoke what had been on a replay loop since she'd given birth and left the babies unnamed at Alex's store. "You know, the Scripture in the Bible about Jacob wrestling with the Angel and him being changed forever after that encounter? Well, I'd read it the night before I gave birth to the girls, and something powerful happened inside of me."

"Really? You never told me."

Steph looked up and faced Liz. "I began to weep. I realised the man's name was changed from Jacob, 'a deceiver', to Israel, meaning, 'let God prevail', after that encounter. It was like that story was my life being played out before my very eyes, but that event took place about 1745 B.C. That man, Jacob, represented everything I did. I have lied, stolen and used people for my benefit."

Steph took a long pause, gathering herself, before continuing. She needed to tell Liz why she hadn't wanted to name her babies. It had plagued her since letting them go. She hadn't been fully honest with her friend because she'd been afraid of being abandoned. Much like Jacob had been afraid of his brother Esau, but the wrestle with the Angel had changed all of that.

He had come back a different man.

Steph had begun to realise her life was changing. She was emerging into a different person. Transforming. Maybe she hadn't wrestled with an Angel or had her hip dislocated to get her transformation, but she had given up her babies. That had led to her transformation. Even Liz, being in her life, had helped shift her thought processes.

Reading that passage had shown her that she had been on an internal journey.

Holding Liz's hand and swiping tears that had begun to stream down her face, she gathered the fortitude she needed to keep going. "I realised that night, I could not name my girls. Names are powerful. Just like I changed my name from something pretty to something plain, I didn't trust myself to name them. I didn't trust where I was in my life to choose names that would do my girls justice. I was broken, and I didn't want them tethered to me."

Her voice broke to a sob. She could no longer hold it in. She wailed a heartfelt cry into the quiet night. The birds above her head that had been roosting for the night took flight in fright.

Liz held her tight as she gathered her in her arms and let her cry, holding her hair back as the tears flowed.

Steph had no clue how long they had stayed outside for. She had lost all track of time. At some point, she pulled back and wiped her eyes on her sleeve.

"The thing is," Liz said, her voice a hoarse whisper, "I think we committed a crime leaving your babies. That's my fear. That we could go to jail."

"I'm scared, too. I want to bury this, but in the years to come, I know I would regret that if I did. Can we trust them? I mean, the three men inside that house?" Agonising over what lay ahead, Steph murmured, "Abandoning babies is criminal. It must be. So, can we trust a fair trial considering the circumstances? I bet Rick's parents will file something against us."

"Remaining silent is only going to make it worse for both of us in the long run. Are you agreeing to discuss it tonight?" Liz nagged.

Steph sucked in a long, shaky breath. "Yes, let's go in before I change my mind."

The girls stood and embraced, bolstering each other, fortifying themselves in each other's love.

Pulling back, Steph stared at her friend. "Hey, off the topic, what is the go between you and Alex?"

Feigning ignorance, Liz shook her head. "Nothing is going on between me and Alex."

"Hmm. I'm not convinced." She dragged out her words. Not falling for her friend's innocent, battered-eye look, Steph persisted further. "I suppose that conversation can wait for another day. I thought you looked eager to get out of the car when you arrived," she said gleefully.

Liz's head swung nearly off her neck to look at her, flicking her hair in Steph's face. "Whatever do you mean?" she floundered and blubbered her words out.

Steph laughed and keeled forward. "When we arrived, your eyes lit up, your face changed from fear of looking over your shoulder to one that was keen to be here. And it got me thinking." She gave her friend a little brow waggle and a broad smile.

"I would have you know…" Liz stopped up short, her brows knitted together. "I was thinking of me and Jeff, and of our wonderful time here. We had a good memory of this place." Her face broadened into a smile at the memory as she stood, planting a hand on her hip. "The day of the farm tour was enjoyable, as Jeff and I tasted food and learned how the produce went from the farm to their café."

"So, it had nothing to do with a good-looking farmer?" Steph cocked an eyebrow at her friend, drumming up an enquiry.

"Not one bit," Liz defended and linked her arm with her friend.

Together they walked back towards the house. Steph would let her get away with it for now. She had a more pressing matter to deal with. Her heart pounded at the thought of the impending conversation.

The lights in the kitchen were out when the girls walked in the back door, but one shined from the lounge room. Walking towards the light seemed symbolic to Liz as she turned to Steph. "Let's trust

Jesus to work this out. We may have done wrong, but let's trust Him to work through these men. God's put them here. Let's see what happens."

Liz allowed Steph to walk in first, following closely behind. Solomon sat on the three-seater, and Steph chose to join him.

Interesting.

Liz couldn't deny he was gentle, soft spoken, oozed calmness, something Steph gravitated to, and his words often reflected his convictions.

Liz chose to sit on the floor and face the small semi-circle of people. Alex and Jeremy rose to offer their recliners, but she shook her head. The coffee table offered a barrier and some distance that she needed. She was ashamed of not stopping Steph's plan five months ago. Now, here she was, sitting in front of two people who were sworn to protect children. Would they see the women's actions in the light of protecting children or harming them?

Time would tell.

The men sat waiting for someone to speak. They all held hot drinks. It was Alex who disrupted the silence. "Coffee or tea, ladies?"

"No," came a unified answer. They wanted to get this over and done with.

Considering her friend, who sat rigid on the lounge chair, and showed no hint of starting the conversation, Liz spoke first.

Looking into Jeremy's dark brown, almost black eyes, she took in the rest of his features to gauge his position. His jaw was relaxed. His eyes open, not narrowed or pensive. His arms rested on his thighs with his ankles crossed. He appeared casual and comfortable.

She was anything but.

Was he friend or foe?

Taking a deep breath in, she plunged into the unknown with trepidation. "We know that what Steph and I tell you tonight will put you in a position to act, but we want to ask if it can be kept out of the papers."

Jeremy's eyes zoned in on hers.

Her heart rate doubled its speed.

"Anything to do with you women, at this moment, will be kept out of the papers. But depending on what you tell us, it will depend on who else in my department needs to know."

When Jeremy didn't offer anything else, she turned to his brother. Looking into Solomon's eyes was like looking at his brother. His eyes were so dark she could get lost in them. Looking down quickly, she regathered her focus.

She had to do this.

Looking up into kindness personified, she asked. "Solomon, what about you? Can you keep what we tell you from the papers?"

He cleared his throat. "Our department is not allowed to leak information about people either. Like Jeremy, depending on the nature of what you say will affect who I tell. If I can limit who I tell, I will."

"Alex?" Turning to face him, she looked, and tears were fought to stay unshed.

He sat on the lounge chair, with one ankle keeping a rhythm to an unheard beat as it rested on his knee. His head lay back on the headrest. Was he willing to keep what he'd hear to himself? His light brown eyes against his olive skin emanated peace and compassion. Those very attributes were the reasons Steph said she had picked this man in the first place.

Who would have thought she'd be sitting in his living room, ready to admit her part in abandoning the twins?

Alex shifted in his chair and regarded Steph before turning back to her. "What either of you says tonight will not be shared with anyone. I'm not a man to speak of other people's business around town."

Pleased with those answers, Liz shared a look with Steph. How did either of them start?

Steph glanced down. She was shaking. Liz could see it from where she sat. Her fingers were trembling. Maybe if Liz started, Steph would take over.

Here goes.

She focused on the cushion in her lap and began. "A little under twelve months ago, my life was pretty good. I was married to Jeff. He owned the café, and I would often go in with him, helping where I could. I was studying midwifery."

Taking in a deep breath, she continued but snuck a peek at Steph. Her head was still downcast.

"When Jeff died, I stopped going to the café. I deferred my midwifery studies and became lost in a life of grief. I was twenty-five years old and now a widow. I stayed home mostly, only going out for necessities. I even stopped going to church and doing the volunteer work that Jeff and I had done together."

She stopped talking. She hadn't borne her heart like this to anyone. Sure, she'd cried and talked to her family and Steph, but to monologue it in succession made her see the process of events that had led to her keeping such a secret.

She was coming to the part that haunted her. And it was at this point Steph looked up, giving her the courage to carry on.

She kept her eyes glued to her friend.

"Jeff and I saw Steph at one of the domestic violence events our church had put on. And because we were friends from childhood, and had lost contact, that dinner connected us back together." Liz gave Steph a teary smile. "That night, we decided to see more of each other. When Jeff died, the next time I saw Steph, I was at her house, drunk." She hiccupped the last words as she choked on a sob.

The more she talked, somehow, the better she felt. Even though it felt like her heart was being ripped from its insides all over again, she was beginning to feel lighter. Her fingers trembled, and at times her body shook. It took every ounce of control to pull herself together, to not get up and flee the room.

She knew her body's response was partly from fear of what could happen to her and Steph and partly from the grief of it all.

Liz flicked her gaze from Steph to Alex. She didn't know why, but it was instant and impulsive to see if there was any judgment in his eyes.

She saw none.

Looking back at Steph, who gave her a very slight nod, stopped her from continuing her story.

This time, Steph took a deep breath, but it didn't stop her hands from shaking or her voice from quivering. "The Liz I knew never drank alcohol." Steph maintained Liz's gaze and smiled. "She only ever showed me love. She knew the life I lived, yet she still wanted to see me for coffee or brekky, to bring normality, I suppose, into my bruised and battered world. So, for her to rock up on my doorstep, drunk, I knew something bad had happened. Thankfully, Rick wasn't home that night, so Liz slept off her hangover at my house. The next day, Liz invited me to live with her, encouraging me to leave Rick." Steph stopped and jumped to her feet. She didn't wait to assess the reaction of the people in the room as she stumbled towards the exit, one hand clasped over her mouth as she sucked in air and released a dry hacking sob.

Liz dashed after her.

When Steph saw her in the kitchen doorway, she gulped and dragged a hand across her face, wiping her tears away. "I can't do this, I just can't." She leaned forward, pressing her hands to her knees. "When they hear what a failure I am, they'll handcuff us both. I wanted to be a mum so much, but why couldn't I be a mum? Why am I such a failure?"

Liz didn't think her heart could break any more, but the emotions rolling through her body at the sound of Steph's rawness tore open any healing she thought she'd had. The strength of the broken woman astounded her. She'd given up her babies to save them, and now she stood before the men who could take her down with the harshest punishment.

Imprisonment.

But Steph's conscience would be clean. That was what destroyed her now. That was the torment Liz could see.

Jeremy watched the doorway, wondering if he should follow.

"Liz has got her. She'll bring her back." His brother knew him well.

Hoping his brother was right, Jeremy remained seated. He prayed for the strength the women needed to confess whatever weighed them down.

It was Steph who entered first. She looked scared. Her face showed fear, and she didn't sit down again. She stood near the doorway, ready to bolt.

Liz stayed beside her.

Steph's eyes swept the room. The men had not moved from their initial spots.

Tears sprang to her eyes, and she tried to blink them back. She didn't win. They pooled and dripped down her face. She swiped at them, annoyed.

She was wrestling with an inner battle.

After a moment more and regaining her resolve, Steph's mouth opened and closed. She tried a second time. "The night Liz turned up, I was nursing bruises from Rick. That morning, I had told Rick I was..." Pausing for the longest time, Steph looked between him and Solomon. "I told him...I was..." She stopped again.

Her eyes darted back and forth around the room. She looked like she was ready to bolt again.

Liz stepped closer to her, wrapping an arm around her shoulders. They stood side by side, linked in friendship and tragedy.

"I have never grown up with men as supporters, only as abusers."

The phrase made his heart sink.

Steph's eyes flooded with fresh tears that ran down her face in torrents. She didn't attempt to wipe them away. She sniffed and wiped her nose with her sleeve, her only effort at composure. He watched her forge ahead into no doubt scary territory.

She had chosen to reveal her story in front of them. Not in a clinical police interview room, but in Alex's lounge room. He knew the evidence she was about to admit could very well incriminate her, and he had to separate his heart from his mind.

He was a detective, but he was also a human.

He swore to uphold the law, but he swore to protect the innocent.

CHAPTER 17

"I told him I was pregnant, and Rick beat me."

She said it.

Relief flooded her soul as Liz squeezed her fingers with her other hand.

Steph kept going. She had to, the momentum of telling the truth pushed her forward.

"I was about twelve weeks and not showing. I thought he'd be happy. Instead, he erupted into a rage, ranting about how he wouldn't have me to himself and that I wouldn't be a good mother. He yelled about the cost of a baby and then told me to get rid of it." Steph looked at Alex, and she couldn't hold her tone steady. Her heart hammered in her chest. She thought her rib cage would burst. "I'd heard about you, Alex, amongst Liz's church group."

"What? How?" For the first time, Alex spoke, interrupting the girls. He clearly sounded baffled. "What did you hear?"

"I'd heard of how you cared for your farm animals. That you're a kind caring man. I knew right then, when Rick said that to me, that I would..." Her sobs shook her body as she collapsed to the floor. Her heart pounded. She thought she was about to have a heart attack.

The room went silent as they waited for her cries to subside. Sometime during that timeframe, Liz must have let go of her hand, for she was now shoving clean tissues into it. Blowing her nose and wiping her eyes so she could see through the blur, Steph carried on with her story that seemed more like a nightmare.

"I knew I could give my baby to someone who would care for them the same way you care for your animals." Remembering what Rick did to her next caused her to begin shaking all over again.

An arm came around her shoulders as she breathed in Liz's flowery scent.

Thankful she was not walking this journey alone, she thought of all the women like her who had no one. For them, she would carry on. "When I told him 'No, I wouldn't abort the baby', Rick picked up the closest object, a chair, and swung it hard against my body. I guess he thought he would beat the baby out of me."

A furious huff escaped from the direction of the three-seater recliner across the room.

Unperturbed, she ignored it. She knew it wasn't aimed at her. It was in her defence.

Grateful, she'd come to understand Solomon wasn't like Rick.

She couldn't look at him, though. She couldn't look at any of the men. She had not known men like that in her life. She knew she didn't want to run to them for their comfort. She'd only been hurt by men in the past when she did that.

Remaining beside Liz and in the security of her friend's embrace, she unravelled the rest of her story. "The chair broke in half, but that didn't stop Rick from slamming it a second time against my torso. I nearly crumpled to the floor in pain, but I knew if I wanted this baby to survive, I had to run. So, I ran out the door and kept running to the park not far from my house—"

Solomon shifted in his chair. "If I could get my hands on Rick, I'd--"

"Solomon," Jeremy warned his brother. "What happened next, Steph?" Jeremy asked, urging her to continue.

Eyeing Jeremy for a moment, Steph answered, "A lady saw me running, crying, with tears streaming down my face. She called out to me, so I stopped and looked at her. I turned around to see if Rick had followed me. He hadn't." She took a deep swallow.

The only sound in the room was the clock on the wall.

Her senses were alert. It was her survival instincts kicking in. She knew that. "She indicated to a bench seat nearby where we both sat. First, she asked if I was all right, and then she saw the bruises on my arms and the cuts on my body from the splintered timber chair. Surprisingly, she didn't ask me any questions. Instead, she stated that she was taking me to the hospital. I rejected her offer. I didn't want the hospital asking questions. I didn't want them to know I was pregnant either."

"Why?" Jeremy interrupted, his tone gentle.

Settling into the floor and crossing her legs, Steph leaned sideways against Liz's warmth for comfort as she joined her. "If it's in their system, then anyone with some power could have access to that information."

She glanced at Jeremy, who had briefly looked in Solomon's direction. She hadn't missed their subtle communication. She guessed that was exactly what Solomon had done. He had checked with the hospital to see if Steph had any record of a pregnancy. Why would he not? He worked for Child Safety.

"Yes, I didn't want child services to access it or the police." She directed her sentence to Jeremy, not Solomon. She couldn't handle his gaze. Not yet. "I hadn't one hundred percent decided on what I was going to do with the pregnancy, so the least number of people who knew, the better. Instead of going to the hospital, I decided to wait for Rick to get out. I knew he would eventually leave the unit to get a hit from somewhere, and I also knew from that hit I'd have a few days before he'd start coming down from it."

"So, Liz's timing seemed perfect," Solomon finished.

"Yes," answered Liz. "After waking up at Steph's the next morning and seeing her beaten again, I virtually forced her to leave Rick. She was afraid, but I knew if we didn't leave that day, she'd back out. It wasn't until she arrived at my place that she told me she was pregnant. We decided she would do the remainder of her pregnancy secluded at my house. No one would know. I don't have neighbours, and it was easy not to have visitors. I would just turn them away if they knocked on the door because I was still in grief myself."

"So, in a way, you helped each other through your own individual painful experiences?" proposed Alex.

"Yeah." Steph looked at Liz with a noticeable heartfelt smile. "Liz helped me see domestic violence was not okay."

"Steph, what happened to your baby?" Jeremy's no-nonsense question was the only way she figured he would ask and she smiled at his directness.

"It came about four weeks early." Her fidgeting increased, so Steph focused on Liz for support.

The next bit came out rushed but she didn't want to stop because she wanted her babies back, and the only way to get them back was to admit she let them go in the first place. She feared what might come legally, but she'd deal with it.

A strength stirred within her. She moved across the room to sit down in the lounge chair beside Solomon, then looked at him ever so briefly. He and his brother held power over her admission.

"Jeremy, I will spare you the details of the labour, as I don't think that is what interests you," she said with a forced smile, turning her head in his direction.

A brief nod of his head indicated she had assumed right.

Again, she took a deep breath to still her nerves and tremors. "I gave birth to a girl at 10:05 pm, shortly followed by what Liz said was going to be my afterbirth and placenta, but wasn't. Instead, I gave birth to another girl. I think I nearly fainted when the second baby came out. It was a complete shock."

The silence in the room was palpable for a moment, then the sound of a mother mourning echoed through the room. Her sob began soft at first and turned into a loud wail as she rocked back and forth on the chair beside Solomon.

No one moved.

The moment given to her was sacred.

She held her head in her hands and wept.

She hoped Liz would pick up from where she left off.

"We looked after them together. Steph was a good mum. She fed them and cared for them like any other new mum. The problem was registering their birth and hiding them from Rick." Looking at Steph, Liz stopped. "Steph, you need to tell them the rest."

Wiping her tears and taking another gulp of air, Steph composed herself. She knew Jeremy and Solomon would take the irresponsible actions of her abandoning her twin girls seriously. Speaking in a hushed manner and with a despondency etched no doubt on her face, she launched into her plea of guilt. "I knew raising two babies with Rick wasn't possible. When I knew I was pregnant, I stopped using drugs, drinking and smoking. I went cold turkey and haven't touched anything since. It's been over a year since I've been clean, and I don't want to go back to that life. I was hit by Rick often, and I knew I couldn't protect the girls. I didn't want Rick to know I'd had a baby, let alone two. That's why I couldn't go forward to hand them over. Instead, I etched out a plan."

A vision of them both being handcuffed and taken to the police station flashed before her eyes.

She couldn't do that to Liz. Panic crashed over her yet again as her eyes tore to her friend.

Instead of seeing fear, Liz smiled back at her, a sad smile of assurance. Steph had her answer to go on despite the outcome ahead.

"I chose to leave them at The Coomera Marketplace." Covered in shame, she bowed her head, letting her hair fall to cover her face.

A sound escaped from Alex's lips.

"You've lived under my roof this whole time…" His words trailed off. Alex couldn't finish his sentence.

"Sorry, Alex. I had no one else, no family, nothing." Steph couldn't look at the man. Plus, she knew her mumbled apology was pathetic.

"It's torn us apart being here. When Jeremy suggested it, we didn't want to come." Liz's voice was determined, almost blaming, when she swung her head to pin Jeremy with a look. "But Detective Jeremy made us." Each word punctuated and calculated, hitting its mark. "How were we to know the man we left the babies with was going to be the man whose house we were to stay at?"

Jeremy's shocked look at the words Liz threw at him was not lost on Steph. She tilted her head to the other two men, absorbing their take of Liz's cutting words.

"What about you, Liz? Why couldn't you take the twin girls?" Solomon challenged.

Liz met his contest. "I couldn't take them on, even if it was done legally," Liz admitted. "I was grieving. You tell me how I was to go forward and say I found the babies?" Her words dared him. The months of tension aimed at him in one swoop. When Solomon didn't answer, Liz continued. "I would have to tell them how I found them or where they came from, and Steph didn't want Rick's family to know anything about the babies. They hated her, and the thought of them rejecting her babies or of them being given to Rick frightened her." Liz's voice began to wobble. She paused as she swallowed to gain composure.

Steph watched on, wondering what her fiery friend would say next.

"Steph was convinced Alex would do the right thing. I knew at the time it was the wrong choice. But for Steph, it seemed the only way out."

"So, Steph, you left them at a door where anything could have happened to them?" Jeremy questioned, his eyebrows headed to his hairline.

Defending her actions, Steph answered, "I was afraid and desperate. Liz tried to talk me out of it, but the afternoon I rode off with the first baby occurred when Liz was out shopping. She didn't know I did it until she came home."

"But she could have come forward," accused Jeremy.

"I asked her not to. The second night, when I left the second baby, Liz followed me and hid, convinced it wasn't going to work a second time. That was when a pregnant woman found my little girl."

Both brothers looked at each other, and Steph noticed neither of them said anything. Instead, she watched Jeremy stand for the first time and pace back and forth while Solomon stayed seated beside her.

From the corner of her eye, she could see Solomon's gaze upon her. The truth was out. As bad as it now seemed, there was relief inside her, and no doubt inside Liz, too.

"Where to now?" Alex asked after some time of silence.

"What I want to know is, how and why you ended back with Rick? Didn't all that time away from him show you anything?" Solomon asked Steph.

She angled her body on the couch to answer him. Her eyes fixed on his. "That's quite the accusation without knowing anything, don't you think? I went back to clean out the unit so I could get my bond back. It had nothing to do with going back to Rick." Steph could feel the heat rising in her chest and up her neck. She stood and stormed a few steps away from the couch to spin back around to face Solomon. "See, the thing is, Rick has accessed my bank account the entire time we have been together. He would take all the money from my Centrelink payments and only ever leave fifty to a hundred bucks to use on food."

"Per fortnight?" Solomon answered.

Fidgeting with her fingers but remaining fixed on Solomon, she added. "Yes. A lot of the time, I was hungry. That's why I went to the church thing, and that's where I got the basket filled with food."

"Oh," Alex murmured.

Not being distracted by Alex, Steph pinned Solomon with her fury. "One part of me wanted to stay with Rick, hoping he would change."

Solomon slowly blinked and swallowed.

She didn't know what he was thinking, but she figured he wasn't happy with that answer.

Going deeper into her story would give him an understanding of the way women thought when dealing with his own caseloads of domestic violence victims.

The question was, did she reveal that now or privately with him? She knew she had some sort of feelings for him, but she couldn't figure out if they were feelings of gratitude or something deeper.

Alex cleared his throat, and Steph realised she had been staring into Solomon's eyes, trying to read what she saw.

Embarrassed, she looked away.

"I do need to figure out where to go from here." Jeremy sat, taking in the girls. "You will both need to repeat this, giving an official statement." Looking at Liz, Jeremy concluded with a question. "Can you finish off your version of what happened the night Rick turned up at Steph's place?"

Nodding, her face twisted into sorrow. "Remember, this is my version, and Steph, you can interrupt me if I get it wrong, okay. He had rocked up wanting her and saw she wasn't pregnant. Steph told me he was angry first, but then happy he could have her…"

Interrupting, Steph added, "I didn't love him that way anymore. He was once loving and kind to me, but drugs, particularly ice, changed him, and that was my fault. I introduced him to it, and I wanted to save him from it. He was angry and violent when he was coming down, and he was always home at those times." Looking down in shame, she said quietly, "I became his possession to do with as he pleased. Intimacy wasn't love, it was abuse, and I eventually saw that as it truly was." Steph felt Solomon stiffen, and from the corner of her eye she saw his hand curl into a fist. Cortisol flooded her body, and Steph fled the chair.

Liz grabbed her at the doorway and bear-hugged her, preventing her from leaving. "Shh, Solomon's not going to hurt you." Liz stepped back, and the glare she threw Solomon could have frozen water. "He's angry, but not at you, Steph. None of these men here are like Rick, are you?" The growl in her voice was fierce. She warred for Steph and took all three men on at once, defending her.

Something no one had ever done for her.

She had never felt worthy of being defended.

She had been cast aside by her parents. Cast aside by her foster carers. Cast aside by society. She had never felt good enough. And here was Liz standing up for her, saying she was worth fighting for.

Steph relaxed in her arms and caught Solomon raking an unclenched hand through his hair.

"We'll call it a night. Solomon, you and I will leave and allow the girls to get some rest." Jeremy targeted his brother with a look Steph couldn't decipher as he stepped out of the lounge room. Pivoting on his heel, he swung back around. "But one more thing, Steph, what did you name your babies?"

"I didn't. I wanted nothing tethered to me." She paused a moment before adding, "I am one withered Rose."

"Excuse me?" Jeremy asked, looking confused.

She had said everything she needed to say. There was nothing left, so she turned and walked out of the room, leaving the men to themselves. Relieved it was over, Steph collapsed onto her bed a few moments later. Sleep would probably elude her, but that was okay.

Finally, she and Liz had come clean. The weight of the lies had lifted, but the guilt for her actions pressed upon her.

CHAPTER 18

Steph sighed as she lifted her pen from the page and looked out the window beyond the garden to the cattle past the creek in the far paddocks. Journalling her thoughts every day was meant to be healing, or so they said. She had yet to find that. So far, she'd only got a cramp in her hand.

She shook the discomfort out as she watched a bee humming close to a flower by the windowsill. If she were honest, baring her soul last Friday night was unlike any fear she had experienced before.

It was the terror of the unknown. Owning up to her faults meant she could land herself in jail, and that had her terrified, day in and day out, for the past week.

Doodling on the page, she reread the last few sentences she'd written.

Solomon turning up is something I look forward to. He makes me laugh, and I know he would not hurt me. Yet, the response to run from him is there, like on autopilot.

She sighed. What could she do about that?

A knock at the front door startled her. No one had knocked on the front door during the three weeks she and Liz had been there. Who could it be? Just as they knocked again, Alex appeared, signalling for Steph to go to her room.

Opening the door, Steph heard Alex greet the person as their voices drifted down the hallway.

She stood just inside her bedroom so she could hear the exchange take place. She needed to know who it was.

"Howdy, Alex, we've had a break-in. Sue and I just wanted to let you know to keep a lookout for anyone lurking around and to keep your place locked up."

"Thanks, Dave, for the heads up. Sorry to hear that. Did you have anything taken?"

"Not much that I can tell. A mobile phone and some loose change on the bench. I must have disturbed them coming in from the farm. The back door had been jimmied open, so I called Sheila, our cattle dog, to go in. She growled near the front door and barked. Then I heard the front door bang shut. Thankfully, neither Sue nor I walked in on them, and Sheila scared them off. The police are looking around, but I wanted to let you know."

"Thanks again," Steph heard Alex reply from her bedroom. "I'll let the police know if I see anyone."

Steph peeked around her door frame to see Alex reach out to shake hands with his neighbour before closing the door. Stepping into view, Steph commented. "Great, that's all we need. Someone snooping around."

"We'll let Jeremy know, but I think it's wise for you to stay inside for the next couple of days. Hopefully, this was a one-off break-in in the area."

OJ sat sipping a cold Coke, watching the waves break on a secluded section of one of the beaches along the Gold Coast strip. He'd taken the weekend off and was enjoying a mental break the only way he knew how, surfing.

It kept him fit. It kept him alert, and it gave him time away from everyone and everything. He could sit out in the ocean and just be, without anyone telling him where to go or what to do.

It was his time. God's time.

Shaking his head as he scrunched the empty can, if he were honest with himself, he needed more than a weekend away. He needed to permanently get away from Rick and the caught-up mess he'd entangled himself in. But that would have to wait, now that he'd seen Steph and Liz enter that café early one morning during the week.

Rick had been adamant that someone should watch the café that Liz and her husband owned together. OJ had volunteered.

Rick had paid people to go in asking for her. He had become as obsessed with Liz as he was with Steph. The thing Rick didn't know, though, was that both women had resurfaced. OJ hadn't told him, and he wasn't planning on saying anything, either.

When OJ offered to watch the café, it was to protect them, not to be an informant. The ladies' early morning visit had surprised him because he had been out jogging and had to back up and hide behind a tree to observe them being hustled inside by a man about his size, dark-haired and Samoan in appearance.

It had been purely by chance that he'd come across them. He rubbed a hand down his face as he thought back to it.

No. He had to believe God had given him that moment because he didn't believe in coincidences. However, he'd jogged the same route each day since, and there'd been no second visit.

Should he jog past the café just before opening time each morning until he recognised a pattern? He had to. He had no choice.

In the meantime, he slipped from his bench seat, grabbed his surfboard and tossed his crushed can in the bin beside him.

He threw his surfboard in the back of the vehicle he'd hire, jumped into the driver's seat and closed his eyes, taking a moment before he headed to his Airbnb.

The smell of the freshly cooked pizza made Solomon's stomach growl. He'd been asked to be the 'Uber' driver for dinner at Alex's house. He hadn't complained, but his stomach was protesting.

He was looking forward to the evening since he'd blown it last week with Steph. He hoped a relaxed night would quieten his pounding nerves. Years of training in how to remain calm and not react around domestic violence victims were blown in one uncontrolled moment.

His clenched fist had sent Steph scurrying out the door in two seconds flat.

Why?

Because he had let his heart get in the way.

It was as simple as that, and now he had to get his heart out of the way. She was out of bounds, and he had spent the week telling his brain and his heart she was a no-go zone.

He had realised during the week that Steph had inched her way into his heart. That was the only explanation Solomon had come up with that seemed to fit his reaction.

It had become personal.

Both he and Jeremy had filed reports about the women's confessions. The fact that they were hiding from an abuser and had acted to protect the babies was in their favour, but a judge would decide in the weeks ahead. Jeremy had asked for it to be kept under wraps because of the possible danger the women were still in, so for now, life went on as it had been for the past three weeks.

Arriving at Alex's house, Solomon walked in without knocking. Country music was playing in the background, giving the atmosphere a relaxed vibe. The lights were dim.

Solomon felt his nerves drop, and he let out a deep breath right when Alex rounded the corner.

"Howdy, Solo." Alex's eye narrowed on his, but he didn't say anything.

Solomon could see he was debating whether to ask if everything was alright, but he let it go with a clamp on his shoulder instead.

He gave him a ginger beer in exchange for the pizza boxes.

Solomon broke eye contact and looked around the lounge room.

"The girls shouldn't be long, but first, I want to mention there's been a break-in at my neighbour's place not long ago. The culprits are still roaming around, so we need to keep an eye out tonight." Alex's voice was not alarmed but low and steady.

"Sure, bro. I have some energy to burn, so I'll be ready."

"Yum, smells good in here," Liz stated as she walked towards the kitchen table.

"Yeah, it does," Alex added, but Solomon knew his friend wasn't talking about the pizza because from all his senses, Liz had come from a recent shower. Her hair was damp, a sweet peachy smell hung in the air around her, and her cheeks were still slightly pink. Alex's gaze settled on his visitor.

Amused, Solomon realised he wasn't the only one becoming attached to the girls.

Steph stepped into the kitchen, catching his smirk at Alex, and she queried him with her eyes. He shook his head with a brief close of the eyes, as if to say, 'Don't worry'.

"Let's eat. I'll pray," Solomon said.

The foursome were finishing up dinner when Alex's Border Collie, Skipper, began growling and barking in the backyard. Both men exchanged a look, and Alex rose.

"We may have some unwanted guests trying to steal my stuff, and Skipper just alerted us. You girls stay inside and keep the doors locked. Solomon and I will go and check it out."

Liz put a hand on Alex's arm. "Don't. Can't you call the police?"

Alex's gaze travelled from her hand to her eyes as he replied in a slow drawl. "By the time the police get here, my stuff will be lifted from here and gone." His eyes remained unbroken on hers until she looked away and touched her cheeks.

"We're calling them anyway," Liz replied as she tried to remove the pink from her cheeks by rubbing them. "You're not being heroes."

Giving Alex a smirk, who replied with a grin, Solomon rose and followed him to the front door. They left, locking it behind them. The men circled towards the backyard when a flash of light to the side of the house caught their attention.

"Let's hang back in the shadows and see how many are sneaking around in my yard," Alex whispered over the noise of Skipper going berserk.

"Will you let Skipper out to go after them?" Solomon suggested.

"I had thought of that, but I don't want them running off. Plus, keeping her fenced in the backyard means no one will try to enter through the back doors to get inside."

"Good idea." So far, Solomon could only make out two shapes moving. They didn't seem bothered by the barking, which meant one thing: They knew she was contained. "I only see two shadows. What's your plan?"

"To sneak up on them and take 'em down." Alex was not kidding. From the light shining through the curtains, Solomon could see the determination in the man's steely face. "You ready?"

Solomon gave the affirmative with a strong nod. Dangerous manoeuvre, yes, since they didn't know if the intruders had weapons, but it was necessary if they didn't want them coming back.

Alex signalled Solomon to follow, and together, they crept into the shadows towards the flashlight.

"You see anything of use?" Solomon heard one of the assailants ask. He and Alex had made it inside the tractor shed without being seen or heard, their forms hidden behind the large tyre wheel of one of the Massey-Ferguson tractors.

"Yeah, lots of stuff. But to get out of here on foot means we're limited," the other replied in a gruff tone.

"We can always come back again," the first one suggested.

Solomon followed Alex's lead to creep closer. His heart pounded in his ears. Their soft footfall was covered by the verbal exchange of the intruders.

"As long as that dog is in the backyard, we'll be right. I haven't heard or seen anyone come outside either."

"True." Alex towered behind the one with the flashlight.

Both men swung around in the shadows. They pivoted to run, but Solomon struck the one closest, and he hit the ground with a thud, throwing up a cloud of dust.

Solomon jumped him, and the cloud plume increased, but he wasn't letting him get away. He coughed and spluttered, eating dirt, but he was sure the other guy was no better off.

From his shrouded halo of earth, Solomon saw the man with the flashlight swing it at Alex, who ducked the torch but was hit by a left hook to the face. Alex fell backwards with a thump, hitting something metallic as the sound rang out in the night.

Solomon heard a grunt come from Alex's direction. He hoped it was the other man and not Alex.

The man thumped Solomon with a fist to the eye that he couldn't see coming. They were flying blind. Arms flinging everywhere, hoping to connect.

Solomon's fist connected with flesh, and he heard the man spit out a curse. Good, at least one connected. He pounded him again in the same direction.

Solomon yelled in Samoan without thinking.

"In English!" Alex roared.

A flashlight and car lights shone into the shed as the four men rolled on the ground in the dirt. Solomon was just about to repay his foe with his fist when he heard the words, "Police! Hands up!"

Drawing back, Solomon sat back on his heels and raised his hands in the air. Looking towards Alex, he said in English, "Bro, we need to teach you some Samoan. I yelled, 'Police are here.'"

Crawling off the top of the other guy, Alex answered. "How did you know? I didn't hear them until they hollered."

Solomon shrugged. "Dad was a cop. He taught us to listen to everything. I heard the cars coming down the driveway, saw the flashing of lights and took a wild guess."

"I was too much in the zone, mate."

Solomon was too sore to laugh, but he let one chuckle escape before he collapsed forward, exhausted, onto his hands and knees.

Alex stared at him, gasping for air, as he raised his hands and folded them behind his head for a breather.

"You know, bro, you need to not only learn Samoan, but you need to get your ears and eyes checked and get to the gym," he said, turning to Alex, laughing.

"Give me a break. I'm a simple farming man. Give me a steer to wrestle any day."

"You look a sorry sight, Alex. Wait until the girls see your lip." Solomon couldn't help digging the man as he dusted the dirt from his clothes and stood. "They'll be fussing over you."

"You're not much better yourself, mate. I think you need to get to the gym more. You're puffing a bit too much over there."

Solomon raised his brows upwards and chuckled.

The police officers cuffed the two men and put them in the back of the police car, then one of the officers walked over to where he and Alex were catching their breath. "Are you boys, right? You should have waited. They could have had a weapon."

"Yeah," was all Alex could say as he nursed his bruised jaw and busted lip, rising to his feet a bit slower than he wished.

Solomon only shrugged.

"Are you okay if we go inside and take your report?"

Thinking of the girls, Solomon intervened. "Can we do it here, where we are? I'm happy to do it right now, Officer. But first, can you flash the torch around on the ground? I want to see what that guy hit me with."

Solomon saw a wrench lying on the patch of dirt where he'd been and figured that was why his side hurt so much. The man had hit him with a wrench. Geesh. He'll be feeling that for a week. The police came a second too soon. Solomon wished he could've reassembled the man's face. "Thanks, Officer." He picked up the wrench with his shirt and handed it over. "You can take this as evidence of his fingerprints if you like."

"I want that back," Alex said.

"It's only a wrench. I'll buy you another one. It's evidence of them using a weapon against me, bro," Solomon said, taking a deep breath in.

Twenty minutes later, and with the excitement of the night's events behind them and the police gone, the two men sat nursing their bruises with ice. Solomon was stretched out on the couch in the lounge room with his shirt up, ice draped over his lower torso and hip, while Alex was in the kitchen sporting ice packs to his face and shoulder.

"Solomon, you're lucky he didn't hit higher; otherwise, your ribs could have been cracked." Steph crouched on the floor near his face. Her perfume wafted to his nostrils.

He needed to get away from her, but where could he go? He was held captive in a lounge chair, with her as his nurse. He winced as he pushed himself farther into the back of the chair and away from her face. "That's a positive way to look at it." He grimaced when she touched it.

"I think you need to see a doctor to make sure there's no internal damage." Steph's eyes travelled up his body to search his eyes. The concern was tangible.

Alex hobbled into the lounge room with no shirt on, displaying an icepack over his shoulder and a phone to his ear. Handing it to Solomon, he mouthed, 'It's your brother'.

Not knowing which one, he greeted with ease. "Hey, bro."

"What in the world do you think you're doing wrestling a thief?"

No more guessing. "And how are you, Jeremy?"

Not being put off by his brother's sarcasm, Jeremy launched into his big brother mode. "I'm serious, bro. What were you and Alex thinking, taking them on? They could have had a weapon?"

"They did—"

Jeremy interrupted, "What? The report doesn't say they did."

"No, but does a fist and an old farm wrench count?" Trying to lighten the mood but failing miserably by the sound of his brother's huff on the other end, Solomon laughed.

"I'm sending Jay out to have a look at you. And no arguments. Otherwise, I'm sending Mum out."

"Okay, okay." Not wanting his mum's lecture, too, he agreed. "Send Jay out." Solomon hung up the phone and gave it back to Alex. "Looks like we'll have a personal medic in a bit."

"I heard," Alex said, waving a hand over his shoulder as he retreated to the kitchen.

Solomon remained on the couch to wait for his brother. With just him and Steph in the room, he took the opportunity to ask her some questions. Questions he wanted answers to.

Were they for personal reasons or to help her? He wasn't sure, but they were questions that still needed answering.

"Steph, what would you like to do about your baby girls?"

He saw the shock of the question hit her, but she recovered with a few rapid blinks to her eyes. She had shifted to sit at the end of the couch near his feet, and he watched her twirl her hair between her fingers. Would she fight to get her babies back or leave them in the system? He hoped it wasn't the latter. Whatever the answer, he wanted the truth.

She turned to face him and gathered courage, her lips parted as she licked them. "I want them back. Now that I've been clean for so long, I can think clearly. I also thank Liz for teaching me my worth, that I don't have to settle for what Rick gives out." Her eyes darted down to his bruised side. "I have sported too many of those," she whispered, pointing at his bruises. She stood up and moved to the bookshelf.

Solomon traced her movements with his eyes.

Turning to face him, she said, "I didn't have a good upbringing. I was rejected by the very ones who were supposed to love me. I was abused by the ones who were meant to protect me. As a result, I had a very warped view of love, so I constantly sought it through men." She gulped like she was trying to swallow a lump of chewed food.

His heart ached for her. How easy had it been to take one's own upbringing for granted?

Steph's eyes misted over. She swiped at them.

Thankfully, he couldn't move, as he would have wanted to comfort her. Solomon gave her time to battle her inner turmoil. Not wanting to push her for answers, he stayed quiet.

"You see, my own dad didn't show me how a girl should be loved or cared for, so I accepted anything. Although, deep down, I knew those things couldn't be right, I wasn't shown another way. I did what I had to, to survive. Liz says God brought her into my life. I'm still trying to understand that. Part of that now is to free myself from Rick and that abusive lifestyle, but honestly, I don't know how." Walking back to sit down beside him, her eyes revealed desperation. "How does a woman get free from a man who thinks she's his and no one else's?"

Solomon studied her for a few moments before answering. "One thing I know is that my family assist women suffering domestic violence, and I know they would want to help you. That is, if you want it. My training through my work gives me a perspective on the fear you must be living with. However, I can't begin to comprehend what you have suffered."

Thinking about his behaviour the other Friday night, of a clenched fist and her reaction to run, made his heart pound. He knew he had to apologise and work through this with her. "Steph, I'm sorry about last week when I clenched my fist and made you panic. That's the last thing I wanted to do. I never want to make a woman fear me. I don't want you to fear me. Forgive me, please." He turned her now downward face to look at him.

Steph cupped his hand that had held her face. "I forgave you the night you did it. I knew I had reacted in fear. Liz didn't react to it. I talked with her about it later. I could see how my experiences have shaped my perceptions. That's what I am working through."

He reached forward to hug her, muffling the groan of pain that escaped his lips. His ribs hurt something bad, but a hug from her was worth it. As they sat embraced in each other's arms, the front door opened, and Solomon heard his brother's voice.

Good timing, bro.

CHAPTER 19

Wednesday had come around again, and Liz and Steph arrived at the café early. Steph had brought more of her new treats for the customers to try. She was in the back kitchen when Liz walked out of the office.

"Jeremy just rang and said we could stay a little longer today if we want to. He doesn't see a threat happening here, but he reminded us that we should stay vigilant."

Smiling, Steph replied, "Some sort of normality would be good. It's not like Rick would try anything at this location anyway, even if word does get back to him."

"True." Liz turned and walked towards the front shop, eager to greet customers and catch up with the regulars.

OJ sat across the road at an eatery, watching the door for when the women left. So far, they hadn't. Last time, they were only fifteen minutes or so in the shop. Today, they'd been more than forty, and the café was opening in a minute or two. Today was the first time OJ had seen them since last Wednesday morning.

It seemed Wednesdays were their day at the café, but where were they for the rest of the week? He had to find out. Maybe he should stay around for a bit. His business with Rick was nearly complete, but that mission had been planned before Liz came on the scene. Now it seemed he needed to change his mission, or at least talk to his boss. Liz possibly needed protection, and he wanted to be the one to provide it.

So far, he and Rick had remained hidden. For how long that continued remained to be seen.

In the police building in the city, Jeremy looked up from his computer screen to his partner across the room. “Do you reckon this is a good idea, letting Liz and Steph stay during opening hours today? So far, no one knows they’ve visited except Liz’s sister-in-law. Now, staff will know, and word will get out.”

“Yep, I do reckon we’ve chosen the right thing to do. It’ll flush Rick out of hiding, and we’ll be there when he makes contact. A step ahead this time would be better,” replied Brendan as he tapped his foot on the floor.

Jeremy and Brendan had wrestled back and forth with the idea. They both wanted to catch Rick and this unknown OJ. Catching the men was what satisfied them. Up until now, Rick and OJ had remained elusive.

“In the next day or week, our life might just get a bit more interesting,” Jeremy concluded.

“I hate doing nothing, OJ.” Rick mulled over a plan on paper for his next pickup. “You know, since Liz and Steph got away, our lives have changed for the worse, and that makes me mad. I don’t want revenge. I just want the women back and then to go into hiding.”

"How, Rick? How will you hide?" OJ sat with his legs up, resting on the desk, ankles crossed. "I'm done with hiding. What's going to happen when the days go back to summer? It's easy now while it's cold. We can wear hoodies and beanies, but come summer, we'll need to change our plans."

"Precisely, bro." Rick swivelled in his chair to face his cousin. "When I find out where the women are, we will grab them again and go interstate."

"And how do you propose pulling that off?"

"It won't be us who get them. They won't connect us to the women. I'll pay someone else to do it." OJ watched as a slow, cunning smirk formed on his cousin's lips. "You know, bro, there are people who will do that sort of thing for money."

OJ leaned forward and plonked his feet on the floor. "Count me out. If I'm out, that means you can leave Liz out of it. She's been my girl since the start. I'm not doing this anymore." OJ glared at his cousin as Rick sat back, rocking on his chair, looking smug. He wanted to wipe that arrogant look right off his face. "I'm leaving town. And if I hear you touch Liz, I will come back personally and take you down. Find someone else to do your dirty work."

"Whoa, bro." Rick rose from his chair, tipping it back as he stood.

A challenge. OJ saw the look in his eye.

"I'm trying to get you to leave this life behind and keep you out of prison," OJ growled. "But you won't listen. Instead, you want to make it worse by kidnapping these women again." OJ's voice rose a decibel.

"No can do, my brother."

"What? Why?" OJ was getting more agitated at his irrational cousin.

"I'm not leaving Liz out of it. She's already too far in it."

After taking a mouthful of soft drink from his Coke can, OJ listened to his elaborate plan.

"While Liz was with us, she was spotted by some Sydney men, who…how do I put it…want her." Rick grinned broadly.

OJ's fist clenched beside him, and he slammed it down on the kitchen bench. "What!" His anger needed to escape, and his cousin shouldn't cop the brunt of it, although OJ reasoned he deserved it. "Tell me how we went from kidnapping Liz for you to get Steph, to her being wanted by men in Sydney."

He wanted, no, needed to punch something, and Rick's body came to mind. No. He needed a punching bag or some unending stretch of beach where he could pound the sand and get his adrenaline under control.

He glared at Rick.

"Tell me," he demanded, "how this got worse, and you had better tell me everything you know because your head is going to roll between my hands if you don't. And I mean it, Rick. You have brought an innocent woman into this pathetic life of yours."

"Calm down, OJ. I need to think."

OJ thumped his hand against the wall. "You better start talking."

"Stop." Rick thrust a hand through his hair. "I need you to let me think." Rick turned away and stared out the window as he drummed his fingers on the table and continuously ran a hand over his head.

OJ had to calm down. His training demanded it. He had the elite training behind him. He needed to draw on it now. It didn't matter family were involved. Emotions had no play in it. He had to think professionally. Taking some deep breaths, he stared at his cousin.

Spinning back around, Rick narrowed his eyes. "This is the plan I'm trying to hash out, and the reason I said our lives have changed for the worse. It's because the girls got away. I've tried to figure it out, but I'm coming up empty other than to kidnap them again."

"No, Rick."

Rick paced the small space, picking up a pen and clicking it on and off.

Hah, the same action he did when he was thinking. Funny, they had never really known each other, and they did the same little trait.

Rick was nervous, and that meant one thing. He was running scared from someone, and he had now dragged the girls into it.

OJ stopped an irritated sigh from escaping his lips.

"Believe me when I tell you this," Rick said, spinning to face his cousin. "I knew nothing about the Sydney men when we took Liz from her house that day. I wanted Steph, and figured Liz would be the bait to get her back. These men were the ones who devised the plan to initiate her the night she got away. I thought they were just like every other male who wanted a woman, but these men had different plans."

"How different and what plans?" OJ roared. He needed everything Rick knew. He was now forming his own plan and would only tell Rick the bits he needed to know.

"They were up visiting the top drug dealer in our area and heard about how Liz and her husband, Jeff, had been helping drug dealers get free from ice and other drugs. The Agiuses were not doing much to put a dent in their business until a major drug lord got free from his life of dealing drugs and started following Jesus," Rick accentuated with air quotes. "Apparently, the ex-drug lord totally transformed his life and began helping others get free from that scene. They took him out, and it was only mentioned on the news as a fight induced by drugs, and the media didn't run with it very long. Word on the street was that this ex-drug guy was walking to church, and they knifed him, leaving him to die. The guy who died was known by the police, and they figured it was a revenge death, but no one pushed for an inquiry either. He was the one Jeff and Liz Agius had been working with."

"And how do you know this?"

"They told me." Rick paced the small space again.

"So let me get this right." OJ spun on his heels and interrupted Rick's path. "They want Liz because we put her in their path. Not because of the drug guy they killed?"

"Pretty much."

"But why are you interested in saving Liz, if that's what you call it, from these men by kidnapping her yourself, again?"

"If you haven't noticed, I'm not using ice anymore. And that enables me to think clearly." Rick punctuated his words to make a point. "The problem is, I owe them money, and they're after me."

OJ ran a hand down his face. "Are you for real?"

"But why do they want Liz and not Steph? Steph is your girl. The way the rules work is, if you owe them money, they take your girl." OJ strode inches from Rick's face. He knew the veins in his neck would be protruding because he could feel the tension in his body coiled, ready to break.

"They want both of them," Rick spat out, "because they saw Liz and, let's face it, she's beautiful, and they want her for their classy gentleman's nightclub in Sydney."

"Their gentleman's club in Sydney?" OJ slammed his fist down again. His fists were getting a good workout, and he was beginning to sound like a parrot repeating everything his cousin said. He let out a heated sigh and glared at Rick. He would store that information for later, to research online. For now, he had to keep Rick talking. "Go on. They want her for her beauty, and so, you plan to take both women and hide with them yourself?" OJ couldn't believe the sheer stupidity of his cousin.

"Yep."

"How do you expect to pull that off? You know these people have ears and eyes everywhere, and they'll eventually catch up with you. What you need is professional help, and you need to pay them the money you owe them, my brother." He spat the last word out as if it were bitter herbs on his lips.

"No way!"

"It's the only way. If they want something you didn't deliver on, what do you expect they will do to you that isn't any different to the drug lord who crossed them?"

Reality hit Rick like a ton of bricks. The look on his face said it all. He plonked down on his chair. Defeated. Rick put his head in his hands and murmured. "Until those men crossed my path, I didn't see the mess my life had become. When they wanted Steph, I stopped using."

"I don't believe you. You don't stop just like that." OJ added a click of his fingers to emphasise it.

"It's only been a month, but I must fight to keep her, and getting clean was the only way I knew how to do that. Yep, I may end with the same fate as that man if I want to turn my life around, too."

OJ knew very well that the chance of Steph going back to Rick was slim, but while Rick thought it was still possible and he was clean from ice, he figured he'd keep his mouth shut. He preferred the clean Rick. He was predictable.

Could he walk away from Rick? He was his cousin, and he needed someone to get him out of this mess. Added to that, two women were now in more danger because of Rick's actions. Not to mention his own. "I've got to go for a jog. I need to process the information you just dumped on me and come up with a plan. My own plan."

Solomon arrived to take the girls home from the café just before lunch, and as he turned in the seat of his car, Steph plonked herself down beside him in the front passenger seat. She was exhausted from her morning's activities, and she hadn't realised café kitchen duties could be so taxing.

"Jeremy and I have been talking, and we believe it's time for both of you to meet our family. You've already met Jay, the paramedic, and we want you to meet the rest of the family, as we believe they can help you."

Steph noticed his eyes hadn't left hers, and her heart rate amped up. What were the men up to? And was she ready for it? "Steph, my nephews are about the age of your girls, and I realise that it could be difficult for you to meet them. Any thoughts or questions?" Raising his eyebrows in her direction, Solomon waited for her to reply.

"That's fine with me." It wasn't really, but what else could she say? 'No, I hate the idea. I don't want to go.' Stomp her feet. She could do and say all the above, but what would it prove? That she was a no-good, unfit parent.

Liz squeezed her shoulder from the back seat, and it bolstered her courage.

She had heard, and her friend knew it would be hard. Steph took courage in that.

They rode along in silence, and she stared out the window, wondering how she would handle seeing little ones who were her girls' age. Would she break down and cry? And could she risk being rude and disappear from the room if it got too much?

Arriving at a beautiful two-story brick home in a quiet cul-de-sac about twenty minutes later, Solomon spoke, breaking the otherwise quiet trip. "Welcome to my childhood home. Are you ready?"

"No, I'm not." At least she had voiced her honesty.

Solomon turned in his seat, and compassion filled his eyes.

She was sure she was not doing a good job at hiding any emotion etched on her face. All her fears ruminating around in her head were no doubt parading themselves across it for the man to read.

Who was she fooling? She knew she didn't deserve this family's support or kindness.

Her heart was pounding. She was nervous. Her family hadn't wanted her, and now this family were opening their home to her. It was too much. In the past, before Liz had told her there was a God who cared, she would have lied to get herself out of an awkward situation like this.

Now all she could do was hope.

She still wasn't sure of all the God stuff yet. He was supposed to be a father, yet her earthly one hadn't shown her a very good example. How could she trust one she couldn't see, touch or hear?

She pushed the thoughts aside.

Sensing her trepidation, Liz had already removed herself from the car and waited for Steph at her side door.

Looking through the window at her friend, Steph took a deep breath in, inhaling Solomon's woody scent and calming her nerves. It reminded her of being in nature.

Her favourite place.

She took another deep breath of his earthy scent and pushed the car door open.

Liz helped her out and walked with her to the front door.

Before walking in, Solomon stopped them and rumbled, "Jeremy and I haven't shared anything with them. They only know the bits that have been shown on the news, so if you want to tell them things, you can. They can be trusted." He turned back to the door. "Here goes."

Solomon did the introductions, and Liz remembered Cheriece and Mrs Niko from when they'd dropped the meal off. Liz couldn't believe they were the same family. God had brought them across her path again. Tears sprang to her eyes as the ladies embraced her.

Everyone in his family was present except for Jay and Jeremy, who would both come after work. As Solomon was leaving after lunch to go back to work, he turned to Steph, who had followed him to the door.

"Are you sure you're okay here?" he asked, eyes thoughtful, studying hers.

"Yes. Is there a place I can hide if I need some space?"

"There's a swing in a private courtyard out the back, and there's also my old room, which Mum has converted into a library. Either space will provide the quiet you need. Here, let me show you my room before I leave," Solomon said before he hustled out the door.

The truth was, there was a long, hard road ahead of her, and she was hoping the Niko family would put their hands up to help her because she had no clue how to go forward. She had no family to teach her how to be a mum or teach her how to get her children back.

Partway through the afternoon, Steph had retreated to Solomon's old room. She was absorbed in an action fiction novel when a slight knock on the door grabbed her attention. Relief flooded her when she looked up seeing Solomon standing there watching her.

He entered his old room with an ease of familiarity.

Steph straightened herself in the chair as Solomon reached absently for a book near her. He was smiling.

"What are you smiling at?" Steph asked, intrigued.

"You."

She smoothed her hair down and tucked a stray invisible hair behind her ear. "Why?" She ventured out on a limb with that question.

"Because you're relaxed in my house, in my room, tucked up in a chair, fully absorbed and unaware I'd been at the door."

"You were watching me?" Steph asked, full of nerves suddenly.

"Yep."

A little butterfly flew around in her gut at his honest answer. Trying to stop it, she placed a hand on her stomach.

Changing the topic, Solomon spoke, "Mum said dinner will be ready at six-thirty, so we have about an hour. You want to come downstairs to the swing seat? It will be dark soon, and it's nice out there at this time of night."

"Sure." Getting up, Steph kept the throw rug around her shoulders to keep her warm and followed Solomon down the stairs.

Dinner plates clanked as family members carried them to the sink and prepped them for the dishwasher. Light laughter and chatter filled the family home. Looking around, Steph watched as Jeremy organised the family to get the conversation going.

"Dad and Mum, thanks for having us all around for dinner. Can we leave the dishes for now and gather in the lounge? It's been a while since our rosters have worked in sync with each other. I want to talk about something that I think our family could help with." Jeremy stood with his back to the wall, near the entrance, waiting for everyone to settle.

Steph considered how he observed the room. Not that there was a threat present, but his police training was forever being outworked.

She smiled at his protective nature.

He turned to look at Jaymond and Jules and began with the obvious. "Around five and a half months ago, you were ready to have your own babies. Jules, you had gone out for a walk to gather your thoughts on the surprising news of carrying twins when you came across a baby in a basket outside The Coomera Marketplace."

Curiosity flickered across the mother's mind as her husband glanced at his wife, no doubt wondering where Jeremy was going.

Only Solomon and Alex knew about the girls' confession.

"At the time, you weren't aware that the little girl had a sister until you and Alex took her to the hospital. You were eventually able to meet with the carers as well. Tonight, I want you to know Solomon and I have spoken with the birth mother, and she wants to meet her babies and, if possible, work at getting them back."

The room went silent. Jules was the first to speak. "I have been praying for the parents every day. Can I meet her?"

"You already have," a soft voice spoke across the room.

All eyes turned to her.

Steph's eyes darted to Jeremy, who gave her a small, reassuring nod. His eyes almost undid her resolve to share the hidden truth. The depth of their compassion and warmth oozed their way into her heart.

There was a long pause. "I'm the birth mother of the twin girls."

The room went still, like the air had been sucked from it. Not even the twins fussed on their mother's lap.

Hearing her own voice admit to being the mother who had abandoned her own flesh and blood on the street was too much. Steph jumped up and fled out the door.

"Steph, wait." Solomon's voice trailed after her, but she didn't wait. She kept running.

She had reached the road by the time Solomon grasped her and pulled her out of the way of a vehicle coming towards her. She turned and sobbed, tears streaming down her face, "How could I do that to my babies? What kind of mother does that?"

"A mother who saw no other option. My family want to help you. I want to help you."

Sobbing, she pushed him away.

"Come inside," he whispered. "Let us help you work this out and keep you safe. Let us help you get your babies back."

She didn't want to trust him. She looked up at him. The light from the streetlamp cast a shadow on his eyes so she couldn't read them. Her hands were shaking, so she grasped them together. "You know, Solomon, I have a major hurdle. My trust in men is like zero, and I fear I will hurt you and your family because of it. My dad and mum left me, and Rick abused me, so I don't have a good history with family."

"Let us help you begin a good history, then. Being around my brothers and sisters, and my mum and dad, will help, and I'm sure Alex has been quite the gentleman."

"Yeah, I think he has." She smiled.

"What's that smile for?"

"Oh, nothing, a girl's secret." She wouldn't share what she thought was going on between Alex and Liz. The pair of them had said nothing. They didn't need to. It was what they weren't saying that was obvious.

They were shy around each other. It was so cute.

Solomon was watching her.

She gazed back at the house she had just exited, and with a strength she didn't think she possessed, she indicated with a hand gesture, pointing at it. "I suppose I need to go back in there."

He stepped back, allowing her to walk past him to face whatever lay ahead.

CHAPTER 20

Rick was getting antsy. No news had come through about the women, and OJ had no clue how that had occurred, considering the girls were there for a couple of hours on a Wednesday.

Rick had obviously not sent his scouts there that day at that time, and OJ was making himself scarce. Things were beginning to get thrown around the little unit they had rented out.

It was a Saturday morning, and Rick's phone rang.

"Hello… You're kidding me? Where? What…no. I'll send OJ because my face is too well-known." Rick hung up the phone and bellowed, "OJ, I need you here, now."

It wasn't like OJ couldn't hear the rantings going on in the small unit. Nonetheless, he strolled into the kitchen at his own pace, observing under a ball cap his scowling cousin. "What's up?"

Rick threw him a dark glare. Okay, so he wasn't up for casual.

"Liz is at the café right now. One of the boys watching the place just spotted her. You need to get down there and go get her."

"What the heck, Rick?" OJ backpedalled in thought and steps. "How do you suppose I do that?" He splayed his arms by his side. The gesture he hoped his cousin read as shock and unbelief, because if he didn't, he would be flinging his arms in circles around his cousin's head to knock some sense into him. "What, you think I can just walk in there and say to her, 'G'day Liz. I'm back. Remember me? I kidnapped you. Would you like to come with me again?' She would scream, and the cops would be there in no time." OJ pulled his ball cap from his head, rubbed a rough hand through his short hair and messed up what was already tousled. "I wouldn't even get her out the door, bro. There's probably an undercover cop watching somewhere from the sidelines for all we know."

"You're forgetting something. If I know where she is, then who's to say the other guys don't?"

"I haven't forgotten," he growled back. "I will figure something out." And with that, OJ turned and left the apartment, grabbing a small notepad and pen. He arrived at the café shortly after sprinting most of the way there. What was Liz doing there on a Saturday?

He watched her through the window, taking coffee to customers. He couldn't go inside. That would corner him. He couldn't afford to get busted.

Sitting and watching her smile and laugh with customers made him more determined to protect her. He had advised his people of Rick's new information, and they told him to sit tight. So that was what he was going to do.

But somehow, he had to get a message to her.

OJ saw a kid riding a skateboard towards him. Thinking quickly, he signalled for the boy to come over. Fortunately, the kid didn't think twice about gliding over on his board.

He guessed no one taught him about stranger danger.

OJ paid the lad five dollars to take a note to Liz. He'd watch from across the street, and if she looked in his direction, he'd leave immediately.

The boy entered the store and walked towards Liz. OJ waited and waited. Liz didn't come to the window to look out. He watched the boy walk out of the shop, chuck his skateboard to the ground and skate off.

OJ sprinted off after him and pulled him from his skateboard. "Boy, did you give the lady the note?"

"Ahh, yeah, dude. I did. She took it and looked embarrassed, then shoved it in the pocket of her apron. I asked her if she was going to read it, to look at who it was from."

Getting impatient, OJ demanded, "And?"

"And...she said, 'later when it's not so busy'."

Nodding his thanks, OJ paced back to his previous spot. He had nothing else to do, so he sat and waited. A half hour later, OJ's phone rang. Answering it, he looked across the street to a dark sedan that had just pulled in. He hung up his phone and took out the notepad from his back pocket for the second time. He scribbled words on another piece of paper and strode across the street, past the car and into the café. With his head down and his hoodie pulled up, he stepped behind Liz. "Excuse me, ma'am. I think you dropped this."

Liz turned around and looked up into his eyes.

She gasped and then began to shake.

OJ watched as she tried to speak but didn't. Her mouth opened a second time and then shut. She even looked like she tried to move, but her brain hadn't received the message. OJ looked into her hazel eyes rimmed with a blue line. They were so unique that he could be mesmerised by them, but now was not the time or the place. Those beautiful eyes were now filled with absolute terror.

Terror he had caused.

He held out the paper towards her.

Her eyes stared into his as her fingers reached forward, trembling, taking the note from him.

He closed her hand over it and nodded. Her fingers felt warm and fragile.

She should have screamed, hit him, defended herself or run, but the fright was too much, and she had gone into freeze mode.

"I know you did defence lessons so you need to work on them so you can react in time," he whispered but hated himself for saying it because he knew he was the cause of the trauma.

He wished she had reacted to him. He wished he could train her to respond to threats, but that wasn't his job. His job had been done. He had delivered the note. He turned and walked out, then hopped into the waiting black sedan.

"Liz, are you alright?" Steph asked, coming up behind her a few seconds later.

Liz's eyes were wide and on the door.

Steph followed her gaze. "What happened?"

"We've got to leave. OJ was here." Her voice shook as she spoke.

Steph dragged her all the way to the kitchen and rang Jeremy. No answer, only voicemail. She didn't leave a message. "I'm ringing Solomon. What happened?"

"OJ was here."

"I know that much. But what else?"

Solomon answered on the second ring. "Hey Steph, how's your day going?" he asked, sounding relaxed and chirpy.

"OJ was here. Come now." Steph cut over the phone, no pleasantries in her voice. Nothing. Total fear, but she didn't care. Rick had found her.

"I'll be there in ten minutes. Stay on the line. Is he still there?"

"I don't know."

A bang happened in the kitchen.

"Steph, are you okay?" Solomon asked.

"Yes, that was just a baking tin falling to the ground. Liz and I have moved into the office and locked the door."

"Good. Talk to me. Tell me what happened."

"Liz said OJ handed her a piece of paper, then turned and walked out the door."

"Did he get into a car?"

"I don't know. Hang on while I ask Liz… She said she didn't see anything. She just stood there, shocked, rooted to the floor."

"Okay, Jeremy and I need to work on her flight and fight skills. I'm driving to you now, and we'll take you straight to the police station."

"How far away are you?" Steph didn't wait for a reply. "Scrap that, I don't care how far away you are, listen to me in case something happens to us."

"Steph, don't say that."

"Just listen," Steph demanded. "Rick knows I'm here, right? Otherwise, OJ wouldn't have walked in. He gave Liz a note—"

"Yes. You said a piece of paper earlier. What did it say?"

"I don't know. Do you want me to ask her?"

"Later. But what did you want to say?"

She inhaled a deep breath and exhaled calmly. "Take care of my babies if anything happens to me. Make sure my babies know

I loved them and that I didn't abandon them because I didn't care. Tell them I loved them. Promise me." She choked on the last words.

"Steph."

"Solomon, promise me." Her voice heightened as her emotions rose. She was sobbing. "Tell them I loved them."

"Yes, Steph, I promise I will, but we will get you out of this, and you'll tell them yourself, okay."

"Thank you."

"What's more important right now is your safety, so while I talk to you, get Liz to ring Jeremy on her work phone, and if she can't reach him, ask for Brendan."

They kept talking on the phone until Solomon arrived at the café.

"Are you both okay?" he asked as Steph opened the office door.

She rushed into his arms, relieved without answering. She shocked herself by hugging him, but she didn't give a rip at that point. She was glad someone else was there to protect them.

He pushed her back and looked into her eyes. "Steph, are you okay?"

She nodded.

Looking at Liz, he asked the same question. He waited for her to reply. She gave a brief nod but kept staring out the one-way mirror, her eyes glued to the front door.

"Did you get a hold of Jeremy?" Solomon asked.

Shaking her head, Steph sat down.

"Brendan?"

"No. He and Jeremy are on a job," Steph answered.

"Right. I'll ring Jeremy's private number myself and leave a message. What I'm amazed at is OJ's confidence to walk in," Solomon commented.

Remembering the note, Steph turned to Liz. "Liz, where's the note?"

Liz handed her the piece of paper she still held. Without speaking, Liz reached into her pocket and pulled out a second note.

"You never said anything about a second note," Steph exclaimed with a little too much force. Taking it from her and handing both notes to Solomon, Steph watched his face as he read them, searching for clues of danger.

He tried to cover his concerned look by rubbing his hand down his face. He read the second note, then looked back to the first. "We need Jeremy. If I can't get him, I'll ring Dad because he was in the police force, too. I don't know what to do. Do we leave here to go to the police station and risk being tailed, or stay and risk them coming back? I'm thinking if Rick knows you're here, I'll be outnumbered whichever way we go." Solomon tapped his knuckles on the office wall, concern etched on his face, as he waited for Jeremy to pick up.

After leaving a message on Jeremy's personal phone, he rang his father.

"Dad, it's Solomon. I'm at the café, and I need your advice. OJ, the man who was involved in Liz's kidnapping, walked into the café, gave Liz a note and walked back out. Do I ring the police to come here or take the girls to the station myself? I can't get a hold of Jeremy or Brendan."

Steph watched Solomon pace the small office as his father spoke to him on the phone. He remained focused on the floor as he listened. Steph flicked a gaze towards Liz. She had left her lookout of the front door to cradle her head in her hands, rocking back and forth on the chair.

Steph couldn't comprehend the audacity of the man to walk into the café and walk back out. How long had they been stalked for? A slight tremor rolled through her body. They were safe for now, at least with Solomon present. She trusted him. For the first time in her life, she trusted someone not to take advantage of her.

"Ok, thanks, Dad. I'll ring them now." He hung up.

She shifted her eyes to Solomon, absorbed in what he had to say.

"Dad said to ring the police to come here. They'll transport you to the police station in their vehicles to wait for Jeremy, who'll have to reassess the dangers and see if it's safe to go back to Alex's farm."

From the back of the black sedan, OJ watched the police car arrive. He hadn't expected that reaction, but then again, he was wanted for kidnapping, so they'd screen the area. It had been about twenty minutes since he'd given Liz the note.

Surely, they'd think he'd be long gone, but instead, there he sat in the back of a dark-tinted car, talking with his boss, watching the scene unfold before him.

"What's next, OJ?" his boss asked. "You know Rick better than all of us."

"Well, he'll be wondering where I am. Word would have gotten back to him already that the police have rocked up. His scout would have rung him for sure. We need to take care of this Sydney drug lord who's responsible for one ex-drug dealer's death and possibly more."

The black sedan drove away from the scene with OJ watching comfortably from the back seat.

❋

Jeremy hit his steering wheel with the palm of his hand as he slumped into the driver's side of his car and pushed the start button. At that moment, he wished he were driving any old car he could crank its engine over with a bit of force. Pressing a button on these new cars did nothing for pent-up emotion.

He was angry he'd been held up in an interview. Leaving his partner to tie up the ends, Jeremy sped through the city towards the Surfers Paradise Police Station, hitting speed dial as the city lights blurred past. "Bro, where are you?"

"Following the police car that contains Steph and Liz. We're headed back to the station now."

"Do you have the two notes you mentioned?"

"Yes, in my pocket."

"What did the notes say, and who else has touched the paper?"

"The first one said, Rick knows where you are. He wants you and Steph back. I'm giving you a warning that he's not the only one after you."

"Great! That's all we need." Jeremy spat the words as he drove at top speed. "What else, Solomon?"

"Liz said the first note was handed to her by a boy with a skateboard who said a man gave it to him outside. She said she didn't think anything of it. She thought it may have been a man's phone number, so she shoved it in her pocket."

"Okay, and the second note?"

"The second one said, 'Liz, you need to trust me. I didn't hurt you before when we shared a room and a bed. Someone worse than Rick is looking for you and Steph. I will be in touch. I had to warn you.' That was the note OJ hand delivered, so only Liz, Steph, and

I handled that one, but the first one will have the boy's prints on it, too."

"Man, I want to talk to this OJ," growled Jeremy through the phone. "But he remains elusive. Maybe we can draw him out?"

"You mean you're going to use Liz and Steph as bait to lure all these men out?" Solomon bit back.

"Yes, maybe." There was a long pause on the phone as Jeremy thought it through. "They will know the dangers. I'll ask Liz since Steph is trying to get her babies back. It won't be set up without her knowledge and full cooperation. I'm hanging up now. I'll see you soon."

Liz's heart had not settled. It was still pounding at a hundred beats a minute as she and Steph strode through the police building, flanked by two officers. Solomon trailed behind their little group on his phone, talking to Alex, she guessed by the intermittent bits she could pick up from her side of the conversation.

"Thanks, officers, you may leave and shut the door on your way out. Solomon, the notes?"

She turned and saw Jeremy at the front of an interview room with a whiteboard filled with writing.

Liz sat hesitantly as Jeremy greeted her, and Steph pulled up a chair beside her. The usual friendliness and banter were gone. It was all business, and although she was glad, she hated the reason it had to be that way.

Solomon gave a quick bro shake to his brother and Brendan before drawing out a chair and straddling it opposite the girls.

Looking at Liz, Jeremy directed the first question at her. "Do you know what the notes say?"

She shook her head.

"Solomon, can I have the notes?"

"Oh, yeah." Solomon tilted and retrieved them from the back pocket of his jeans, handing them to his elder brother.

"Liz, are you ready to know what the notes say?"

For a long moment, she stared at the detective with a fear she hated feeling. Every bit of those four harrowing days resurfaced. The initial kidnap, the terror of OJ's pounding feet after her, his football tackle as he wrestled her to the ground, the rough thrust of her into the car that started it all rushed through her mind in a matter of seconds.

Her heart raced as she remembered it all. The whole traumatic ordeal. Like it had just happened.

She supposed that was what psychologists called retraumatising the victim.

Gathering resolve, she realised if she was going to stop what was happening to her, she needed to know what the notes said. She was not going to play the victim anymore. With a slow nod of her head, she answered with a strength she didn't feel. "Yes."

As Jeremy read the notes aloud, her mouth dropped open and all the blood drained from her face. She turned to Steph and witnessed the same reaction.

"I'm sorry, ladies. I wish I could make this go away easily. There's one option to bring this to an end, but it will involve your active participation and cooperation," Jeremy said with confidence, but Liz noticed his eyes were on hers.

He was speaking to her.

Stepping over his chair, Solomon objected. "Jeremy, isn't there another way, like talk to OJ and get information from him instead of risking the lives of the women?"

"Possibly, however, to get to OJ, we need Liz to go back to work." Focusing his attention back on Liz, his eyes washed over her. He observed her posture and vulnerability. She could tell he knew she had gone through so much, and none of it was from her own doing. His eyes bore into hers. "Liz, it'll mean putting you out there for these 'others' to find you, too."

She visibly shuddered.

She dropped her head in her hands as Jeremy continued to speak, with more compassion than before. "The plan is for you to go back to work and wait for OJ's next move. Hopefully, it will be him who moves first and not the other person or persons of interest." Jeremy paused to let what he had said sink in. When neither of the women responded, he continued.

A warm hand rested on Liz's back. Steph brought her comfort, and it was her undoing. She wept. She tried to hold it together, but she couldn't. She wanted to be strong, but why was crying seen as a weakness? She'd asked herself that question over the last few weeks.

She had grown up being told not to cry, not to show any form of weakness, and now that she had cried almost nonstop over the last few weeks, that was all she appeared to be, weak.

She hadn't even cried that much when she'd lost Jeff. She had held herself together to be strong. Yes, she had cried, but not like this. Same with the babies. She had initially cried, but she hadn't continued mourning.

But now, all she felt like she was doing in her secret place was crying.

What was wrong with her? Was she a waterfall?

Jeremy's voice drew her from her thoughts, and she looked up and gathered Steph's hand in hers. With water-filled eyes, she held Jeremy's gaze, not ashamed to be seen with tears.

"For some reason, I trust OJ not to take you from the café. Our rules will stay the same. You and Steph will be dropped off at work and go home to the farm. You will now have a full-time undercover police officer with you at work and at Alex's house. To flush 'em out, the ones who wish to do you harm, is to keep to the regular pattern. If you girls want your life back, then we need those people caught. Any questions?"

"Yes." Liz had found her voice. "What do I do if I recognise a person? I could freeze again."

"We'll help you with that. We'll do some self-defence lessons with you and Steph. These will start straight away."

"Yes, I've done that before and it hasn't seemed to help me," she replied.

"We will have you do it again and again, until it sinks in," he said with a genuine smile as he slid his hands in his slacks, ending her argument.

"When this is all over, can I see my babies?" Steph whispered.

That question threw both men off guard. Jeremy looked to his brother to answer. "Steph, child services have assessed your case and considered the facts presented. They've acknowledged your thirteen or so months of being drug-free and have approved an hour of visitation each week. Depending on the magistrate's ruling, that may change. However, while this is happening, you cannot see them."

Liz heard Steph exhale the breath she'd been holding in with a whoosh and felt arms wrap around her, pulling her into a little dance on her chair.

Liz stiffened. She didn't feel the same excitement and knew she should have. Pangs of guilt rushed over her.

"Sorry, Liz. I know this was bad timing, but I couldn't hold that in."

Liz chewed on her lip, releasing a slight shoulder shrug. "I'm happy for you, Steph. I really am." Liz linked her fingers with Steph's and gave them a light squeeze to show her solidarity.

Jeremy cut in. "Back to the topic at hand. Remember, you won't be able to see the girls until this is well and truly over. You can't afford to put them or their carers at risk. So, no contact will be made until these men are behind bars, and we know no one else is after you."

Steph nodded.

Steph's news was a blessing amidst a nightmare they could all look forward to.

CHAPTER 21

The next day was bitterly cold, and neither of the women slept much. Getting up to go to work proved extra hard. Alex had been caught up with the new information and had been asked to be another set of eyes at the café.

Liz had barely started her shift when the door chimed, and in waltzed her friendly host, Alex, whistling a tune. She caught her frown and turned it into a smile.

Heat flowed into her cheeks as he gave her the money and briefly held her fingers in the exchange. "Relax," he comforted before letting her fingers go.

She took a deep breath in and let it out.

Looking into his eyes, she replied barely above a whisper, "Thank you, Alex." Liz made his coffee and was taking it to him when a man walked in the front entrance. He wore a baseball cap pulled low over his eyes, baggy jeans and a green pullover. When his eyes fell on her, he looked down. Her heartbeat clipped to a runner's speed.

Did she recognise him, or was she paranoid?

The man moved towards the counter, and the girl stationed there took his order.

Liz stayed by Alex as she discreetly watched the transaction take place.

"Do you recognise him, Liz?"

"I don't think so, but then again, I tried not to make eye contact with the men when I was kidnapped." Her fingers were shaking, and Alex reached out and briefly held them in his hand. Whoa, that connectivity hit her with a whole lot of new sensations. Like she'd been thrown a curveball. Now her heart was not just beating fast because of the customer, but because a man held her hand.

Good grief.

As the man at the counter received his drink, he said something to her colleague, then handed her a piece of paper and left.

Moving the short distance back to the counter, Liz retrieved the note from her work colleague. Shaking, she unfolded it and read it.

Liz, meet me here tomorrow at 7 am. Bring Steph. No police.

OJ

Gayle was already out the door before Liz had to signal her.

"Ouch, couldn't you have used less force?" Steph complained as she lay on the ground panting to catch her breath later that afternoon.

Jeremy had not been kidding when he'd said they were starting self-defence. He had sent the coach out to Alex's farm, and they had just finished their first session.

"Well, the coach said to do it like I was being attacked, so that is what I did. I had to get in the role."

"Fair enough." Steph stared up at the afternoon pink and orange hues of the sky for a minute longer before rolling over to face her friend.

"Do you think you can do this? I mean, what they're asking you to do is to put yourself out there?" Absently, Steph picked up a piece of grass and began rolling it between her fingers and thumb. Liz was the closest person she had to family. She wasn't just her friend anymore. She was her sister. She didn't want anything to happen to her.

"I'll do what needs to be done." Liz rolled over to face her and intertwined her fingers with hers. "Like I said from the very beginning, when you came to my house that first day, we are in this together and in it for the long haul, wherever the path leads us."

The smile Liz gave her brought tears to her eyes. How did she deserve a friend like that? She sure knew she hadn't done anything special to make her stay. If anything, Steph had done the complete opposite.

She had turned her life into hell on earth.

Staring at her friend and listening to the sounds of Alex's farm surrounding them, she wished the goats bleating around her, the chickens clucking and the smell of fresh hay could bring about the peace her soul longed for.

She looked past Liz and saw a horse in the background.

She remembered what Alex had said one afternoon that horses were present and in the moment of life. If she could learn to appreciate the moments she was in, life was doable, one step at a time.

Steph tuned back to Liz. With her as her friend, right by her side, she could take baby steps wherever they led, one step at a time, one day at a time.

Later that night, after Liz had gone to bed and Alex was in the lounge watching a movie, Steph sat down at the kitchen table with the man she'd come to appreciate. Solomon was sipping his coffee, watching her.

"What are you thinking?" Steph asked.

"Thinking that I can't wait for this to be over. It seems every time we talk, it's about the case."

"True. What would you like to know that is not about the case?" Steph asked.

"It relates to the case, but it's more about you." Taking a deep breath and letting it out in a slow exhale, he asked, "If Rick turns up tomorrow and asks if you still love him, what's your answer?"

Staring into her hot tea, she shifted in her seat and sighed. She couldn't look at him because she knew she couldn't give him the answer he wanted. What a child safety officer wanted to hear. "I don't know what I'll say to him. That's the truth, Solo." Steph swirled around the remaining contents of her cup, mesmerised by their movements.

What were her feelings for Rick?

Solomon didn't say anything. He sat silent in the chair beside her, with only the sound of his breathing as her companion.

His curiosity got to her. She tilted her head to find him watching her. He didn't look away when she caught him. He kept studying her, and she saw something in his gaze but she didn't know what.

Was it intrigue, interest or confusion? She wished she could discern his thoughts. Should she ask him? Heck, she would ask him. "What do you think I should say?"

He flicked a look down at his cup and back up to her eyes. She could see he was wrestling with what he needed to say, and she would give him the time to say it.

A beat or two passed until he spoke.

"I can't tell you what to do or say, but one thing I do know is that men like Rick will promise that they'll change, and generally they don't. Once you go back to them, everything goes back to normal. For them to change, they must do it without you around, and even then, if you go back to them, the risk you take in trusting them not to flip the lid and go back to violence when under pressure is dangerous."

"The question is, how will I know he has truly changed?" Steph's question was the one she had been wrestling with the entire time she had walked away from him.

Solomon's eyes blinked slowly closed as he squeezed his lips shut, and as he re-opened his eyes to focus on her, she could sense he was uncomfortable as he exhaled a breath of air. She was testing his patience.

"You don't want me going back to him at all, do you?"

"It's not that. I believe in second chances. I believe people can change given the right circumstances and the right environments. But you must give him time to heal. Give Rick time to work on himself, and then watch and listen to how he behaves around others and family. Don't go rushing back to him."

She knew what he was saying was true. How many times had Rick promised to change, and he hadn't? How many times had she promised to change, and she hadn't until she fell pregnant and was forced to change because of two little beings growing inside of her?

But she had changed. So Rick could change. That was her dilemma.

"The thing is, Steph, are you willing to go through that journey with him and wait, and hope. He might change, or he might not. You know him better than all of us. But he now has a rap sheet, so you need to think of that, too."

She could only nod her head. Her head ached from the stress of it all. She rubbed her temples where a headache was beginning to form.

"You head to bed and get some sleep."

"Thanks. I'll see you in the morning." She took their cups to the sink and rinsed them. She doubted she'd be getting any shut-eye soon, but she'd be thankful for her cosy bed to sink into.

It was ten minutes to seven o'clock, and Liz's heart raced as she paced inside the front door.

Brendan was across the road in an unmarked police car while Jeremy busied himself in the café office. Liz was surrounded by people who cared for her. Her sister-in-law was the chef in the back, and Gayle posed as a waitress.

The shop cameras were rolling, and Steph and Liz were to sit at a table that would give Jeremy a clear view of what was happening. The only thing they didn't have on was a microphone, but one was hidden at the counter to pick up the conversation.

At seven o'clock, Liz placed her hand on the front door and unlocked it at the same time a man in a hoodie and jeans strode across the road, relaxed, towards the entrance of the café and stood facing her, just outside the door.

OJ's eyes traced her up and down before he took a step inside. She gulped past the lump in her throat as her fingers trembled to lock the door behind him. She knew Jeremy could see everything from where he sat and, at a moment's notice, would step in if OJ even hinted at taking her with him.

Liz should feel safe knowing two men and one woman had her back, but try as she might, she couldn't stop her body from shaking.

She should have had a deep peace that God was with her, but she was scared witless.

And she supposed that should be normal since she was staring down the man who'd kidnapped her.

With a trembling hand, Liz indicated where she wanted OJ to sit, and surprisingly, he conformed. He waited for her to sit before he took up the chair beside her. Being this close to the man who had captured her made her want to bolt, but she remembered he hadn't added any extra hurt before, and for some reason, she sensed he wouldn't this time either.

He had a message for her, and she wanted to know what it was. He appeared to be genuinely concerned for her, so, for now, she would trust him.

They sat for a moment, staring at each other, and Liz couldn't discern what she saw in his eyes. Steph was on her other side and felt her hand embrace hers under the table.

The smell of freshly brewed coffee filled the air. Liz wished it were a friendly chat over coffee with her favourite grilled cheese and bacon croissant. But it wasn't. Her stomach churned with anxiety instead of hunger.

OJ cleared his throat and leaned forward on the table with his hands clasped together in a relaxed hold.

He wasn't nervous.

Why?

"Thank you for meeting with me, Liz. I thought you might not turn up, and you had every right not to trust me. After all, I put you both in the hospital." He glanced at both women.

Liz thought he looked like he struggled for a moment to spit out what he wanted to say as he dropped his eyes to the table. He moved slightly in his chair.

Yep, he was fidgety.

But why?

"I had to stop both of you from being put into that car, and the only way I knew how was to make it look like a struggle." His eyes locked on Steph's. "Steph, you put up a good fight, but truth be told, if Rick had gotten out of his car that night, both your lives would have ended very differently." His eyes bounced from Steph to Liz.

Steph raised an eyebrow at the last comment and huffed. "What? Rick would have hurt me. That's nothing different to what I have lived."

"No, he wouldn't have. Other men would have." His words were as cold as his stare.

Liz shivered, shocked at OJ's admission. She had thought about what could have happened that night and had forced the thoughts away, but to hear it verbalised again, was another thing altogether. It was now her turn to confront the man who had kidnapped her. "What is wrong with you?" Liz blurted out. A boldness flooded her. Maybe it was because she had the backing of some men and women in blue, but the situation infuriated her. "You're confusing me, OJ. Why would a man like you be mixed up in this mess? I asked you when you snatched me, and you didn't answer, and I guess you won't answer me now either." Liz paused to study the man before her.

Those dark, almost black-coloured eyes that had shown her kindness in that house of hell were peering back at her with a depth of trust that shocked her. Was she reading him, right?

“I mean, why kidnap me and then save us girls by letting us escape?”

His eyes shifted subtly, locking onto hers like a predator homing in on its prey.

She shifted under his gaze, suddenly feeling exposed.

“I can’t discuss it. I’ll say what I need to say and then leave without being followed.” He broke eye contact, shattering her discomfort.

She breathed again. There was something about OJ she couldn’t put her finger on. He was alluring, dangerous and charming, all at the same time.

“I know you would not be here unprotected. Even though I said no cops, I also know you are not that dumb. So, to those who are listening, if you want me to keep cooperating with information, you need to let me leave. I don’t want Steph or Liz hurt, which is why I’ve come forward.”

Both women nodded. Liz hoped Jeremy got the message loud and clear.

“Rick knows I’m here,” OJ continued. “He asked me to come forward to protect Steph mainly.” Apologetically, he looked at Liz. She saw sincerity in his eyes. “I’m sorry, Liz. Rick knows he’s a wanted man, but he has information that will save both of your lives from a worse hell.” OJ leaned back in the chair and looked directly past Liz into the one-way office window.

Pivoting around on her chair for a moment to look at his reflection, Liz pondered OJ’s body language. He looked way too at ease. She kept rolling the same question around in her head: why? If OJ was wanted for kidnapping, why did he not look nervous? It was like he knew there was a cop behind that window, and he was toying with them.

He was untouchable for now, and he knew it.

Turning back around to face him directly, Liz went straight to the point. "Okay, OJ, tell me why you're here. I need to open the café." Liz was trying to act and sound normal, but she was far from it.

Staring straight at her, OJ leaned forward in his chair and placed his arms on the table. His head was a foot from hers.

She felt uncomfortable under his scrutiny and dropped her eyes to the table.

"Liz, I've been watching you for a couple of weeks now."

Her eyes flew upwards to land on his as her hand covered her mouth. "You mean…you could have… You could have." She shook her head and looked away to gather her composure and turned back more determined, with more tenacity, and growled the words with a force that even shocked her, "Taken me, and you didn't?"

His deep, dark brown eyes didn't recoil from hers as she glared him down. She mightn't have been able to take in all his body language, but he certainly didn't flinch at her comment.

"Yes, but I don't want to take you. That's my point. I didn't tell Rick where you were until he was alerted on Saturday by one of his lookouts. I'm here today because of what he has told me." He pulled his bottom lip in with his tongue and chewed on it with his top teeth as he studied her again. He folded his arms in front of his chest as he settled his back against the chair.

"What is with you looking at me like that?" She looked away, awkward and uncomfortable for the umpteenth time. She wished she had whatever he had, but she didn't. She retreated under his watchful eye.

He oozed the confidence she didn't possess. He was so comfortable studying her, keeping his eyes on her.

Steph took charge. "OJ, why are you here? What message have you got?"

Liz heard his chair scrape against the floorboards. He must have squared his chair to face Steph, and that gave her the courage to tune back in and turn her face around. He wouldn't be facing her directly.

Good.

"Rick didn't tell me until the morning of your escape that a group of men from Sydney were going to take Liz that night after getting acquainted with her," OJ said, looking at Steph. His eyes never left hers, but Liz thought she saw a tick in his jaw as he almost growled the words out like it pained him. "I let you girls get away in the car park. I knew men wanted you, but I had no idea they were from Sydney, with the intention to take you back there."

A shudder travelled down Liz's body that didn't stop. From the angle she was sitting, she could see the same eyes that showed concern for her in that frightening house. They revealed sincerity. "I believe you," she replied quietly.

OJ tilted his head to her and gave her a slight nod in recognition.

Steph's voice was not so forgiving. Her eyes pinned him as her fist slammed onto the café table, rattling the salt and pepper shakers in their spot. "You have got to be kidding me, Liz? You're going to believe a man who kidnapped you and took you to a drug house? An ice rape house, might I add. Not to mention, he was in cahoots with Rick?" Steph stood, and her chair toppled over as she stormed away from the table.

"Where were you when this happened? On a bus." Liz threw the accusation at her friend's back. She knew it would hurt, but it was the truth she'd been holding in.

Steph snapped her head back around. "How dare you?"

"You abandoned me." Like she'd abandoned her babies, she felt like saying, but didn't. "You cleared off, done a runner and left me to be harmed by Rick and OJ." She shook where she sat beside the man whose eyes tracked from her to Steph. Liz had forgotten there were others in the room. With adrenaline running through her veins, Liz dared Steph to speak with her piercing glare.

"How do you not know OJ didn't drug you and rape you, and you just don't remember?" Steph asked as she took two steps towards the table, towering over OJ, waving a hand in front of his face.

The man didn't flinch.

Liz saw Gayle move slightly at the coffee machine, ready to intervene for something.

Alex had shifted in his chair.

The whole atmosphere had shifted.

CHAPTER 22

Liz was confused. Was Steph trying to be her friend and her enemy at the same time?

Liz's heart hammered in her chest. Her friend did make sense. It was possible that she could have been drugged. But wouldn't she have known that? She had felt coherent the entire time. Add to that the side effects of being raped? She knew her own body.

The girls had been together for three weeks, and that accusation about OJ had never come up once and they were having it now, in front of him, in front of everyone.

Liz was furious.

"No, he didn't rape me." She punctuated the words loud and clear. "Don't you think I would have felt the aftereffects of it had he drugged me and forced himself on me?" Her cheeks heated at the thought of it, but she pushed on.

She couldn't look at him.

At that moment, her body began to shake at the thought of what could have happened, more than with the anger of Steph's accusation. "Yes, OJ kidnapped me, but that was to get you back. He didn't touch me in that house." Her voice rose inside the quiet café. She realised everyone was staring at her and Steph again. "I trust him, even if no one else does. He protected me, even if he kidnapped me. Warped? Yes, but he also beat men up to stop them from touching me."

"Sounds like his cousin," Steph scoffed.

Liz's eyes hardened. They were getting nowhere. "He's nothing like Rick. If you saw them together, Steph, you would see they are nothing alike."

"I can't believe you're defending him," Steph growled back from her spot where she had retreated, beside the window.

The verbal barrage had gone on for far too long, and it was not why they were there at the café.

Liz plonked down on the seat beside OJ. "I can't believe I'm defending you either," she said with resignation, "but I trust you. I can see it in your eyes." Her voice was quiet.

His liquid chocolate eyes drank her in, receiving her mercy, and he was grateful without saying a word.

She recognised the glint in his eye and responded with a nod.

"Okay, OJ, what do we have to do to keep these men away from us?" Steph took charge of the conversation, bringing it back to why they were there, as she folded her arms across her chest and leaned against the food bar attached to the window.

"Like I said," he answered, his eyes landing on Steph, "neither of you need to trust me, but if you seriously think about it, Steph, I could have done all of what you said while I slept in the same room, even on the same bed as Liz. I could have forced myself on her, but I didn't, did I?" He spoke his last sentence through clenched teeth. He was as ticked as Liz.

The silence that followed was loud. OJ's glare was fierce but controlled.

"I don't know anyone from Sydney. Why are Sydney people after me?" Liz's voice broke the stillness. The thought of being kidnapped by a drug ring petrified her.

OJ's attention went back to her. He folded his arms back against his chest as he settled into his chair. "Apparently, they heard through their contacts that Rick had you, and, seemingly, they wanted you. You were a bonus for them. They learnt that you were the one who had spoken with the drug lord who had changed his life to become a Christian. Word is, they weren't too bothered by you initially. They had settled their score."

Liz asked, "You mean they killed him?" She leaned back against the chair.

"What I know is, you affected the main drug lord of the area, who brought them lots of money. He was the one knifed as he went to church over eighteen months ago. What I've been told is the police did nothing, as they saw it as a drug fight and didn't want to get involved."

Gayle shifted behind the coffee machine, catching OJ's eye. Liz saw him shift in his chair. He was ready to move. He pushed his chair back from the table slightly, giving himself space to get up. He physically rubbed his face with both hands as he looked around the café. She guessed he was taking stock of who was around.

She noticed his gaze stop as he stared at the one-way office mirror for the second time. She wondered what message he was giving Jeremy through that intense look.

"But that doesn't answer why they're now interested in us when they didn't care before?"

His eyes flicked in her direction. "So, like I said, these men didn't care about you initially, and it would have continued that way if Rick had continued to lie low. But he was running in their circle and did a few things to draw their attention."

"Oh, typical Rick," sighed Steph. "He can't help but tick people off."

Liz shifted the conversation to her husband. No one had ever given her answers as to why he had died. Maybe the man before her knew the answers to them. He certainly knew a lot more than the cops did. "My husband. Was his death...an accident? I heard his brakes may have been tampered with, but the police report didn't indicate that?" She waited anxiously for his response. Looking down, she fiddled with her fingers on her lap.

"I don't know."

Not the answer she wanted, but it would have to do.

"But what has Rick done to bring attention to us?" Steph asked.

OJ blinked a couple of times. Liz watched as OJ played tennis with his head, flipping back and forth between her and Steph's questions. "Rick owes them money, and that's why they're after you. They know you're Rick's girl."

"Was Rick's girl," Steph corrected.

"It doesn't matter. To get you, Steph, means they get him."

"And me?" Liz asked.

He hesitated before continuing. "I'm told one of the headmen wanted you that night simply because you were in Rick's possession. He saw a photo of you and liked what he saw. He was going to take you to a gentlemen's bar in Sydney."

Liz blanched. "A what?"

"A gentleman's bar... A prostitution club, Liz."

Alex huffed from the table where he sat.

OJ cut him a glare.

He was meant to be a customer, but that didn't matter.

"Yes, I know what that is," she said, flustered, with a wave of a hand.

"It's how those men roll. I know I wouldn't have been able to stop them from getting either of you had we taken you both home in the car that night. That's why I had to make it look like I had fumbled the exchange, though I'm glad the other car turned up because I'm telling you—"

"Yes, yes, we know, otherwise Rick would have grabbed us, yada yada," Steph butted in. "I've heard enough of the same thing. What now?"

"Well, until I know for sure where these men are, you need to go back into hiding. If I could find you, then so could they."

Looking directly at her kidnapper, who had his face turned away, and at Steph, Liz couldn't help but realise that, ironically, he had become her protector. "Remember our prayer, OJ." Her voice sounded timid, even to her own ears, but it made him turn to face her. "God did protect me. He answered our prayer on that fateful evening. That is the comfort I take going forward from this meeting."

"Yes."

His baritone depth resounded inside her, matching his eyes that looked past her outer body and deep into her soul. It sent shivers down her spine. She ran her hands up and down her arms to chase the sudden chill away.

Standing up and stepping towards the door, he ended the conversation. "I have a vehicle waiting outside that'll not be followed. Tell your police buddies." His gaze bounced between the women, Alex and Gayle. "I want to protect you, but I have come to realise

God is better at protecting you than I am. If He chooses to use me again to save you, He will." He took the two steps towards the door and, in no hurry, twisted back around as he placed his hand on the doorknob. "I will get word to you if I hear anything. I know your in-laws work here; they'll get my message to you." With a smile, he turned around, unlocked the door and walked out to the waiting black sedan.

"Get those number plates on the system, now!" ordered Jeremy over the inner earpiece. "I want to know who that car belongs to." Jeremy rushed up behind the women to get to the front door. He needed to see the car for himself. Seeing its taillights turn the corner, he slammed the door shut.

He had to get himself under control. The women in the room needed that much from him. But the confidence of OJ irked him.

"Well done," Jeremy began. "I imagine that would have been very hard to sit through. We captured everything on camera, so now we can go back and analyse it. The fact that he didn't hide his identity has me wondering about something I need to check up on."

"Like, he is an undercover cop and doesn't want a bullet in his head or you barging in and raining in on his parade," smirked Steph.

Jeremy appreciated her insight but didn't reply. He instead rang his partner. "We need to get Steph and Liz back to the farm and get to the station as soon as possible to start going back over the video and everything that was revealed." He turned to face Liz. "Let your staff go back to their routines. Let them open as normal, but you won't be coming back until we get a handle on what's going on."

Together, Steph and Liz walked arm in arm through the kitchen as Jeremy watched from behind in admiration. He shook his head at how she'd held herself together with what she'd just heard.

Stepping up behind them, he urged them forwards with a gentle hand on each of the curves of their backs towards the door where Brendan waited in his unmarked police car.

"To the farm, Brendan," he spoke over the roof as he shut the door behind the women. "We need to take extra care to make sure we aren't being tailed. From what I gathered, I don't think it will be OJ. But it might be Rick. His desire for Steph is still strong; plus he organised this morning's meeting, so no doubt his people will be out watching and willing to follow us to our hidden location." Jeremy slid into the seat beside Brendan and pulled his visor down to study the women in the back seat.

Liz had her head lolled back, her eyes closed. Probably pondering the morning's events. A shudder flew over her.

He turned his eyes to take in the second woman. Maybe she had less of a role today, but the glaze over her eyes was hard.

The war of words between the two girls had been heated, and they would have to work through what had been said.

Steph stared out the window and twirled a brown lock of hair.

He smiled to himself at how a little action such as that probably calmed her soul.

The drive back to the farm took longer than usual. Jeremy had been right. A car had tailed them from the café, and they had to lose it before they could head in the direction of the farm.

Solomon and Alex were waiting at the farm when they arrived, and Jeremy briefed them on the basics, keeping his opinion of OJ's possible identity to himself.

The fewer people who knew, the better.

Alex spoke first. "Is my place going to be secure enough, and are we safe staying here?"

"Yes, for now, anyway. We may have to move Steph and Liz depending on what we learn. Gayle will continue to stay here. We won't be able to tell you everything, obviously, but we will tell you enough."

"Good. So, I can go about my business and keep farming. Is Kelly still allowed to come out?"

"I don't see why not. If anything changes to place this farm and its occupants in danger, you'll be the first to know, and we will go into shutdown. We cannot afford to take any chances, either with Rick or this new threat from Sydney."

A mobile phone rang, and Brendan stepped aside to answer it as the girls excused themselves to go inside the farmhouse.

Jeremy continued with his briefing. "One last thing, if you notice anyone or anything unusual, do not check it out yourselves. Ring us immediately." He stood front-on to his brother, directing his next comment directly at him. "No more He-Man antics. Leave the wrestling of the bad guys to us."

Defending himself, Solomon argued, "But what if you cannot be contacted?"

"Ring the police. Period."

Getting the hint, Solomon dropped it.

Jeremy knew his brother would protect the women at all costs, and he was pretty sure Alex would, too. He just hoped they wouldn't do anything stupid.

Brendan walked back and signalled to his partner. "Jeremy, we've got to go."

Nodding to Brendan, Jeremy turned to Gayle. "You look after everyone, and we'll be in touch. If you hear one whisper of danger, ring us. Don't wait. You'll most likely be outnumbered if they rock up here. Let's hope it won't come to that."

Solomon followed his brother to the car. "Jeremy, how serious is this threat to the women? I get Rick is still after them, but these Sydney men, do you think they're serious?"

"We take all threats seriously until proven otherwise. They may have moved on from Liz by now. Let's hope that's the case for Liz's sake. However, Steph is in danger until Rick pays his dues. If he delays, the stakes will go higher as they push harder on him. That could push him to do something desperate. He'll want to find her before they do. That would be my guess. And if he's smart, he'll pay them what he owes and some."

"Okay, thanks, bro."

Leaning on the open car door, Jeremy followed his brother's gaze out across the paddock. "Solomon, we'll do our best to catch these guys. In the meantime, don't make it harder for Steph by getting close to her."

His brother cut him a look that Jeremy understood.

Hands up in surrender, Jeremy turned and sat down in the car. With a wave and a toot of the horn, the detectives drove off down the road.

With Gayle on watch, Steph felt like she could relax a little. Having a police detective in the house was the best idea Jeremy had come up with. They could rely on Gayle to keep watch while they tried to switch off from the threat to their lives. Gayle laughed and enjoyed herself, but she also walked the perimeter and kept a constant scan of their surroundings.

A few days after seeing OJ, as they finished eating lunch, Alex's house phone rang. The look on Alex's face and concerned gaze in Steph's direction had Solomon up off his chair, striding towards Alex, and intercepting him before she could move.

He ushered Alex away but wasn't fast enough because she caught the last of his words. "Thanks, Jeremy. I'll pass on the news to Steph."

Steph watched the men disappear inside as her heart skipped a beat or two.

"I wonder what that was all about?" Liz murmured beside her.

"Me too," Steph replied.

It wasn't long after the men returned Gayle approached the table from the corner of the house. She, too, had received a call, as she was slipping her phone into her back pocket. "I'll tell the girls. It's my job." She directed the comment to the men. Gayle's focus was on Steph as she came to stand by her side. "I've just had a phone call from Brendan. This afternoon, Rick was found injured in his apartment. His wounds are life-threatening, and as we speak, he's being operated on at the hospital." Gayle paused, her eyes never leaving Steph's eyes, but Steph couldn't hold the focus.

She had to look away. She had to get away. She had to get to Rick. He needed her. It was because of her that he had been injured. Her head swung upwards. "How? What happened?"

"A stab wound to his chest that missed his heart but pierced his left lung."

Steph let out a loud wail. She couldn't hold the sorrow in.

When would the pain stop?

He may have been her abuser. He may have almost killed her, but that was when he had taken drugs. But she had known him when he wasn't like that and…and now he lay on an operating table fighting for her life.

"I need to go to him." She scrambled to her feet, pushed back her chair, and Liz's arms were around her in seconds. She pushed her away. She needed air. "No, no, he can't die. I brought him into this mess. He can't die." She wouldn't forgive herself if he died. At one time, she had hated him. She had been scared for her life, but now he was helpless, and it was all her fault.

"I need to get to him. I need to tell him I'm sorry for everything I've done to him. For…for bringing his life to ruin. It's my fault, I led him into the drug scene," she blurted out.

She was breaking apart in front of all of them.

She collapsed. "He can't die… He's the father of my babies, and he doesn't even know it…" Her voice trailed off as her body shook with sobs.

Steph felt arms around her but had no idea whose they were. She was cradled until her legs were numb. By the scent of the perfume that eventually reached her blocked nostrils, she guessed Liz had rocked her back and forth, lulling her to stillness.

Tissues had been shoved into her hands at some point. Her eyes felt puffy and swollen. She would look a mess, and she had no idea how long she and Liz had sat like that.

Time seemed irrelevant.

"I want to see him. Can I see him?" Through her tears, she could see Gayle's concerned eyes a foot from hers as she crouched on her knees by her side, with Alex and Solomon looking on behind her.

She didn't dare study their faces. She didn't want to see what they showed.

"The attacker is in police custody. The good news is Rick is in good hands and under police watch," said Gayle.

Gayle waited as she absorbed the information, but Steph noticed she had also avoided her question.

Liz was the first to speak. "Do you think that's his payback? Are we safe now? Has the threat to us gone?"

"They're good questions, Liz. We cannot confirm anything right now. Jeremy is looking into it. We guess that it is payback. That they won't be after you girls. We think Rick has paid the penalty for owing them money. Other than the attack, a substantial amount of money has been transferred out of his bank account today."

"Can I see him?" asked Steph again, and this time her voice was stronger and louder. "I know he wronged me in almost every way possible." She ducked her head, knowing she did not want to look at the man behind Gayle.

His look would be smouldering. He had warned her that Child Safety would take it very seriously if she had anything to do with him. But didn't his life count? Didn't his life hanging by a thread mean something different?

"We'll have to ask Jeremy about that. He'll ring once they have finished operating. His family are at the hospital now, so I think you shouldn't be there when they are," Gayle suggested.

"I suppose you're right about that. If you'll excuse me, I need to go to my room." Steph got up from the floor and headed inside.

CHAPTER 23

Steph was not in her room. Solomon had knocked, and the door stood open. She was not in the lounge room either, so he ventured outside to look for her. He found her sitting alone on the front porch with her knees pulled up and her forehead resting on them, sobbing quietly.

Solomon squatted down beside her and placed one hand on her shoulder. He waited until she looked at his face. "Are you up for company?"

"I suppose."

Solomon stayed crouched beside her, watching her stare out across the front lawn to the trees beyond. He didn't try to say anything. He didn't need to fill the gap. Being with her and showing her that she was not alone was all he needed to do.

"I don't know what I want," Steph began as she remained focused beyond the trees. "I suppose I was getting used to choosing not to be with Rick because he was mean and cruel, but now, because he lies in a hospital bed, vulnerable and in pain, I want to run to him and make sure he's okay." She turned to focus on Solomon and searched his eyes, trying to read him.

He let her read the sadness they showed. He didn't cover the disappointment he felt from her words. She had to see that her way of thinking concerned him.

"As a child safety officer, I know that's not what you want to hear" she said. "Maybe it's not how I really feel. I don't know." Rubbing her eyes roughly in frustration, Steph looked at him more earnestly.

"It's fine, Steph, really. I'm here to bounce things off. I may not like what I hear, but you need to get it out of here." He placed his hand on his heart region. "And to here." He placed his hand on his forehead. "Or maybe it's the other way around."

"What do you mean?" She looked at him, confusion reigning in her brown eyes.

"That you have believed in your mind and in your thoughts for a long time that you're not good enough or worthy of anything better than what you've been dealt, but you have come to learn over the last several months that inside of you there's someone worthy of being loved and cherished, and that's what you must now believe to be true."

She looked at him, and a new gloss misted over her eyes and spilled down her cheeks. "I think you're right. Liz has been helping me see I'm not the lies I believed about myself."

"I am glad you have each other."

But he couldn't have her. Solomon breathed in the farm air around him. He had to focus on the smell of the dirt, the mowed lawn, the distant sound of cows mooing, anything but the woman beside him. He intrinsically knew he had to put himself last. His feelings and desires had to be squashed for the overall health of the woman who sat a foot from him.

Putting her head back down onto her pulled-up knees, she sat silent for a moment. Eventually, she looked up as Solomon shifted from a crouched position to sit beside her. She searched his face and his deep brown eyes. "Is it wrong to feel sad for him and relieved at the same time? I mean, I'm sorry he's hurt, but I'm equally glad he's been placed under police watch. That way, I don't have to live in fear of being kidnapped or hurt by him anymore."

The sincerity and fear he saw reflected in her eyes had his heart skip a beat. He wanted to protect this woman, but he also needed to protect his own heart. "I think that's normal. If you didn't feel relieved, I'd be concerned. Likewise, if you want to run to him like you said, then I'm equally concerned that you don't understand the extent of the nature of domestic violence."

"I know what you say makes sense. The thing is, I know what kind of guy he was before drugs and alcohol took over his life, and I was the one who did that to him. I know he can be a different man. I changed. He can, too." She chewed her bottom lip.

It took all of Solomon's focus not to want to reach out and touch her lip from the attack her teeth were giving it. Fidgeting with his hands, he chose instead to stare at the ground when he spoke. "From my training at work, the less contact you have with him, the better it is for you. That is, if you want your children back, the department will look at how often you contact Rick, thinking that if you do, you're more likely to go back to him in the future. Child Safety would be less likely to reunite you with your children if that were a possibility."

"Okaaay." She dragged the word out. "So, what now?"

"Why don't we focus on the here and now, like getting you doing what Child Safety needs to see so you can have visits with your girls? Knowing the carers are on board and Jules and Jay have made it clear to the department that they will be a support for you also will help this process begin."

"But first, we need to know these Sydney men aren't after us, right?"

"Yes, and Jeremy and Brendan will keep us up to date on that."

"Where do you think the other two are?" Liz asked Alex as she took in the view around him. The sun was setting, and it looked magnificent. She was glad for the months she'd spent on the farm. She had eventually let her guard down and allowed someone to see her dreams and failures.

"I don't know. My attention has been focused on the one person right beside me."

Liz's cheeks flushed. She was glad for the growing dimness. The angle of the sun setting cast a shadow on her face, and she hoped Alex couldn't see the heat that was no doubt on her cheeks. The thought caused her to duck her head involuntarily downwards.

Feeling a gentle touch to her chin, Alex lifted it. His light brown eyes were intense as the sun set. "Why does that make you feel shy? Me saying that."

Her eyes flicked away, embarrassed again.

He was turning her insides into mush, and she didn't know what to do about it. He was studying her. She could sense it. She risked a glance at him, and there he was, reading her, taking her in.

His liquid honey-brown eyes roamed over her cheeks, her hair, her eyes, and down to her lips, then, very quickly, as if he caught himself, his eyes travelled back to land on her hazel eyes.

Her heart thundered in her chest.

During the afternoon, Liz learned again that life was often unpredictable. She thought about how, over the last couple of months, Alex had begun to help her see that her responses were more important than what she faced.

Her kidnapping was traumatic, and it couldn't be changed and her husband's death was still painful and raw, but with Alex's help, she'd begun to move through those events instead of keeping them constantly before her.

She was seeing them not as focal points but rather as intricately woven parts of her life.

She took a deep breath in, held it for a couple of seconds and breathed it out slowly. In the orange hue that silhouetted the kind farmer beside her, she would go forward and embrace her future.

Her past would not define her.

Should she tell him of her thoughts on how he was becoming more than a carer of animals to her? That somehow, she had begun to care about him.

Could love happen twice?

"Can you pass me the salt and pepper, bro?" asked Jay as he held out his hand to Solomon.

The brothers had gathered again for their breakfast around Jay and Julia's kitchen table. Life had settled a little since Rick's attack, and Jeremy had kept his finger on the pulse since Rick was still under police guard. It had only been a week, but his wounds were healing slowly.

"What have the girls decided to do now that OJ has passed word that the Sydney men have moved on?" Jeremy asked Alex as he reached for a piece of bacon to add to the growing mound of food on his plate.

"Liz has decided to sell her place and find somewhere smaller."

Turning to Solomon, Jeremy asked, "What about Steph?"

"She hinted she wants to live with Liz, saying she found living under the same roof not lonely. So, who knows what they will eventually decide? But one thing's for sure, they'll be calling on us to help them shift. Who's up for that?"

Smirking at Solomon's sarcasm, Alex raised his hand, adding himself and his truck to the move when it took place. "Those girls are like family now."

"I would say you're leaning more towards a spouse, my man," Jeremy snickered.

"Hey, come on..." Alex defended himself.

"Yeah, I reckon you boys have been captured by those girls. What do you say, my brother?" Jay lovingly slapped his younger brother on the back to get his attention. "Hey, I know you heard me. Don't go acting all deaf on me."

"Whatever..." mumbled Solomon. "Like Alex and I have any chance of defending ourselves anyway."

"Ha, so, it is true?" burst out Julia. "You just agreed. I knew it."

"You ready to go, Alex?" suggested Solomon. "Let's get out of here and let these three dribble on with their rot while they clean up breakfast."

"Good idea." Alex rose and took his plate to the sink. "Thanks, Julia and Jay, for breakfast again. I'll see you next time. Are you coming with me, Solomon?"

"And where would you two be going together? Liz's house?" teased Julia.

"See ya," tossed Solomon over his shoulder as he walked out the door with a wave over his head.

"Not answering means it's a yes," roared Jay with laughter as he watched them both leave the kitchen. "Brother banter is good for the soul," he chuckled, patting his heart.

"Well, if that's what I'm in for, I ain't letting you know when I like a girl, bro." Jeremy stood and helped clear the table.

"You won't be able to hide it from us, my brother. We have receptors, you know, that pick up on your behaviour."

"Well, I'll not visit."

"And that'll give you away, too."

"All right, I have no more to say, so I'm going, too. I'll leave you two to carry on this conversation by yourselves. Thanks for breakfast." Jeremy walked to the door as his phone rang. "Yep, Niko here."

"It's Brendan. You need to get to the station ASAP."

"What's up now?" he withheld a groan.

Solomon hit the doorbell, and the delight he witnessed on Liz's face couldn't be denied when she opened it and saw their two familiar faces. Her smile radiated from her eyes and her lips as she swung her ponytail over her shoulder absently with her hand.

Holding the door open, Liz invited them in. "I just boiled the kettle."

Alex stepped from Solomon's shielded body to reveal a takeaway tray with four cups. "Thought we would buy one on our way over."

"You're wonderful. Thank you. Please come in. Steph is out the back. I'll go get her."

"Nah. How about we all go out there? It's a nice day to be outside."

As they walked to the back garden, Solomon caught a view of the front window and the memory of the girls being attacked and Liz being kidnapped flooded back. He tried to shake off the odd feeling of being on edge. He put it down to probably being back in the house where the girls had gone through so much. Trying to shake it off, he followed the others through the house.

It had only been a week since Rick had been attacked, and although it was considered safe for the girls to be back at home, Solomon found himself keeping a lookout and signalled Alex to hold up when he got to the back door.

Unaware, Liz kept going through to the patio table. "Do you feel anything odd, or is it me being back here and knowing what went down that puts me on edge?"

"Nah, mate. I felt it too when I got out of the car, like I was being watched. The girls have only been back one night. Let's keep a lookout, but don't say anything to them."

"Okay, I'll ring Jeremy before we leave and see what he has to say."

The next hour of the beautiful sunny Saturday went by without a hitch. Solomon had laughed at his mate's farm stories to the point tears had rolled down his cheeks. How could one man get up to so many crazy stunts?

Despite the laughter, the same feeling hadn't left him. He excused himself to do a perimeter walk to the front garden to ring his brother in privacy. When he reached the front and saw a man crouched behind the bushes peering over the other side gate, where Alex and the girls were situated, his heart spiked.

Knowing there was only a small gate that reached waist high, he rang Alex.

❁

"Yep, what is it?" Getting up casually from the table, he smiled at the girls, not wanting to alert them yet to his call. "Where are you, mate?" Alex whispered. "What? I can hardly hear you."

"Get to the opposite side of the house from where I went. There's someone on that side looking over the fence. I can't see anyone else yet, but I'm checking as we speak."

Alex's long strides caught the attention of the girls, and they leapt to their feet. His breath hitched as he spoke rapid-fire sentences. "Girls, get inside. We have a visitor or two. Ring the police."

Fear gripped their faces immediately, and Alex hated seeing it. They moved quickly to the back door and shut it behind them without hesitation or questions.

He moved off the porch and around to the other side with one prayer from his lips.

Okay, Lord, I need You to intervene.

Alex crept around the side of the house with a confidence he hadn't felt before. He knew God was with Him.

Alex ducked down behind some rose bushes, hiding himself from the view of the front yard. Their perfume was the opposite of the prettiness of the scene he had found himself in yet again.

He could see a man peering around the corner of the house. With his phone on silent, he rang Solomon. "How many do you see? Do we ring Jeremy or take them down ourselves?"

He whispered back, "I have rung him, and he's on his way. He reminded me of no He-Man antics and to move only if they move."

"Fine. Anything else?"

"I see the one looking over the fence to the backyard and another one across the road pretending to pick up rubbish in an orange

T-shirt. I think another one is farther down the road, across from the lake, in a car they came in."

"Okay. I'll hold my spot, but if he jumps over the fence, I'm taking him down." Alex hung up the phone and pocketed it in his jeans. His heartbeat increased as his adrenaline kicked in. His body was pumped, ready for action. All his attention on the man around the corner. He blocked out every other sound.

Not even thirty seconds later, Alex's phone vibrated in his pocket. Pulling it out, he saw it was Jeremy. Keeping his eye on the intruder, he answered with a whisper, "Yep, Alex here."

"How many can you see?"

"Just the one."

"Okay, we're on our way, but ETA is ten minutes. If you must act, do it, but don't be a hero. Be smart."

"Yes, boss." Alex hung up and waited.

He could see the man growing impatient. He kept looking back over his shoulder and then into the backyard. Whoever they were, they obviously knew that was where he and Solomon had been sitting with the girls and assumed they were all still out back.

Alex hated the thought of being watched, and he was getting prepared to take on the intruder. He preferred this reversal of roles. The hunter stalking his prey.

Alex stayed in his hiding place, blanketed by bushes, waiting for the man to make his move.

He didn't need to wait long for the man to slip quietly over the side gate.

Alex's heart pumped as the adrenaline urged him forwards, but he paused his reaction time, waiting for the man to get closer. He was ready like a tiger watching its prey.

The man edged closer, unaware that Alex crouched hidden in the shadows.

One more metre, and he would make his move. Alex couldn't see any weapons on him, but that didn't mean there weren't any.

The man took another two steps and Alex jumped. He hit the man from behind, knocking him to the ground with a thud. A gun fell from his back pants, and Alex kicked it out of reach as the man recovered and sprang to his feet.

Alex stood, braced, ready to fight.

The man laid a quick punch into Alex's gut then his head. The lad was quick. Alex gave him credit for that, but he knew how to fight, so at least it would be fair.

Bring it on, Alex thought.

Alex laid into his foe, remembering his boxing combinations. A crosscut punch first, then an upper cut with his left, back to a quick jab with his right. One, two, three, Alex counted his punches as he hit the man. He didn't want to knock him out, but if he had to, he would use all his former skills to his advantage.

The man steadied himself and reached to his ankle, pulling out a knife.

Now Alex had to think quicker. What did he know about taking someone down with a knife other than not getting cut? He blocked a punch, then he saw the knife-wielding hand come his way. He bobbed and weaved, keeping his eyes trained on the man.

The hit he had taken was now forming a welt over his eye. He could feel it, throbbing.

How had his morning turned from laughter at the Niko household, and having a pleasant coffee with the girls, to having a knife fight in a backyard?

"Remember your prayer, my son. Keep Me in this," echoed in his head.

The man launched himself, knife extended towards Alex.

Alex jumped back as the man swung his arm in a wide arc.

I could use some help about now…

"POLICE!"

"Thank you, Jesus." Alex vented his prayer out loud.

"I said police, so drop your weapon," roared a familiar voice. Jeremy stepped through the side gate, his weapon raised. "Drop it now, or you'll get one through the leg."

The man threw his weapon.

"Raise your hands in the air and keep 'em there." Jeremy was not suggesting anything.

Alex was impressed and relieved at the power he carried.

Brendan felt the man down for any more hidden weapons, then cuffed him and led him to the police car waiting out front.

"You right?" Jeremy stood before Alex while he leaned over and sucked in a deep breath.

"Yep. You came at the right time. I was trying to remember how to take down a guy with a knife." He winced in pain when he laughed, then added, "Thankfully, I didn't have to try out any more moves."

"He got you a good one on the eye, but I see you levelled with him. Well done. No hero moves. So, what happened? And go from the start."

"He was watching over this side gate. Solomon saw him and rang for me to intercept him before he got into the backyard. I hid in the shadows while we waited for you, and he made a move to climb over the gate. I waited for him to get just past me, and then I rushed him from behind, knocking him to the ground and knocking his gun from his back pants."

"Where is the gun now?"

Alex spun around to where he had kicked it. "Look around. We were near the bushes," he suggested to Jeremy. "Stop looking. I found it," Alex spoke seconds later. He bent to pick it up, but Jeremy stopped him, knocking his hand away.

"Don't touch it. I need to finger-proof it to see what's on our system. You'll add another set I have to remove." Jeremy side-eyed his friend, who backed off, hands in the air. "So go on with the running of events. You were up to knocking him over, and his gun fell out."

"Yes, so I kicked it away before we laid into each other. You see, I used to train in boxing and didn't want to just lay into the guy, but I was prepared to do it if he wouldn't stop. Then he pulled the knife from his shoe, and that's when you guys decided to turn up."

"What made Solomon go around the front?"

"Well, when we rocked up at the house over an hour ago, I felt like we were being watched. Solomon sensed the same thing, then, I guess, after an hour had passed, he went to investigate and found our little friend here, looking over the side gate. Solomon said there was another one over the road and a car down near the lake. Did you get anyone else?"

"Yeah, we did. Solomon took out the guy who came across the road when the first one entered the backyard. I'm guessing that was their signal of the all-clear."

Turning serious, Alex squared with Jeremy. "My question is, why were they here?"

"That is for me to find out."

Alex replied with a curt nod. "I need to get some ice on this eye, if you don't mind. I need to head into the girls."

"Look out, you're becoming a bit of a hero to the ladies, don't you think?" Jeremy called after him as he walked towards the house.

Alex laughed and waved his hand over his head as he kept walking. "They dote over me."

Jeremy was already in the car and Brendan was settling into the driver's seat when Alex yelled from the front door as he held an icepack to his eye.

Signalling Alex over, Jeremy climbed back out of the car and waited by his door for his busted-up mate to approach. "The girls talked and wondered if they knew them. They want to see their faces."

Jeremy looked across to the squad cars with the men in the back before answering. "If they're up to driving into the police station, they can view them from behind the one-way glass. That way, the men won't know they're there. I'm not giving them the satisfaction of seeing the girls."

Alex's jaw hardened at the thought of the men getting some sick pleasure from it. "If I had it my way, I wouldn't let the girls get within cooee of those fellas. In saying that, I also understand why Liz and Steph want to see who they are."

Jeremy nodded his head.

Alex was ticked off. His adrenaline still pumped through his veins. He bounced on the balls of his feet as his fist curled by his side. "You know, Jeremy, if Solomon and I hadn't been there—"

"Bro, don't even go there. You were, and thank God you were." Jeremy didn't let him finish the sentence. The detective slapped him on the back before stepping back into the vehicle.

"I couldn't agree more," Brendan added from his driver's seat. "Get the girls to go with you in your car and have them pack a bag. For the third time, they will be staying at your place until we know what this is all about."

CHAPTER 24

A week later, the farmhouse phone rang.

"Steph," Alex bellowed through the back window. "Solomon is on the phone for you."

She walked in from the back patio with her breakfast bowl, followed closely by Liz.

Liz stayed planted where she was, watching her face. The girls hadn't heard from Jeremy since they'd stood behind the one-way glass outside the interview room. Liz had recognised the men from the drug house but Steph hadn't. The girls had been waiting to hear more from Jeremy, but this was Solomon. So what could he want?

Steph watched her friend curl her feet up under her bottom and sink into the lounge chair beside her. She didn't care about Liz hearing her discussion. They'd gone through so much together, and they had worked out their verbal brawl from the café the other week.

Now she watched as Liz closed her eyes and let sleep take over her body.

She smiled at the peace on her friend's face.

Steph knew that the last week had been tough on Liz. She'd been waking up screaming again from dreams of her kidnapping. Either she or Alex would stumble into each other in the hallway to get to Liz's room at odd hours to sit with her, brushing her hair with their fingers or rubbing her back until she went back to sleep.

The men from last weekend had been reminders of what she'd gone through. Surely, the drama would end soon.

"Steph, are you listening to me? Did you hear anything I just said?"

"Nope, sorry. My mind was on Liz."

"You get to start seeing the girls this week."

"What? Are you serious?" she squealed.

"Of course I'm serious," he answered into the phone as Liz's eyes flew open and landed on Steph.

"I can't believe it. Are you sure, Solomon?"

Liz sat up and mouthed 'What's happened?'

"Solomon says I get to see the girls this week."

"What? Wow." Liz echoed in the background.

Steph plugged her ear with her finger so she could hear what else Solomon said while her eyes danced at Liz with excitement. "Thanks, for calling with this wonderful news. I'll see you tonight for dinner." She ended the call.

"Okay. Spit out the details." Liz grabbed her hands.

"Child Safety has given Jay and Julia permission for them to parent coach me, and my sessions start this week…with the twins!" shrilled Steph.

"No way. I'm so happy for you. That is awesome." Liz got up, dragging her friend upwards in a tight hug. She whispered in her ear, "I have been praying for this day. And it has come. Thank you, Jesus." Liz released her hold and stepped back, her eyes filled with tears.

"Thank you. Months ago, I never thought that this day would come." Steph hugged her middle and swayed side to side. "Thank you for standing with me and not giving up on me." It was Steph's turn to go teary.

Liz took Steph's arm and led her outside to the bench seat where they had often sat during their stay at Alex's farm. The Jacaranda tree covered the ground with a layer of purple flowers.

It represented Steph's life.

A life full of colour, thanks to the Life-Giver.

"You know, Steph, I will be here to help you the whole way. You won't walk this alone."

Gazing out over the green paddock, Steph took in her surroundings as she chewed her bottom lip. "Do you know there has been one question I've never been able to bring myself to ask Solomon? What are their names?"

"I suppose that's something we will find out soon enough."

Jay and Jules sat with the twin girls' carers at the Department of Child Safety. They were meeting to plan the next steps to assist Steph on her journey. The first coaching visit would take place in four days at the Niko house.

Jules nearly couldn't contain her excitement as she sat listening to the words going back and forth between the carers and Child Safety. She had trusted God would bring this about because she was convinced her Heavenly Father had brought her across the second baby's basket for a reason, and that reason was now coming to pass.

She and Jay would play an instrumental role in helping a mother reconcile with her babies.

❋

Jeremy sat at his desk, dialling Alex's mobile phone number. He needed to tell Liz what he'd learnt, but it was Alex he was worried about. He picked up his stress ball and squeezed it.

The phone rang a few times before Alex picked up.

"Hello, Jeremy. How can I help you?"

Settling back in his chair, Jeremy pondered how to start. Squeezing the ball, he briefed his notes. "Apparently, the men had "by chance" seen Liz leave the café the day before they had their run-in with you and Solomon. They had followed her to her home and hatched a plan to repeat what was planned for Liz." An outburst of anger that Jeremy expected erupted over the phone, but he kept talking over the top of it. "So, since that first opportunity had been foiled, they thought they had a moment to claim it back."

Alex growled across the phone. "I wish I had hit him harder."

Jeremy ignored him and kept going. "According to them, they acted alone. Rick did not know of it." Jeremy paused as Alex grunted his disgust again, followed by what Jeremy guessed was a closed fist slamming down hard on the patio table.

"Is she safe, though? That's all I want to know," Alex asked in a controlled manner into the phone.

"Yes, well, I've said that before, I know. And I hope so, is all I can say. As far as those men go, they will be sentenced due to outstanding warrants against them, as well as trespassing onto Liz's land and attacking you. They shouldn't be bothering Liz or Steph again. I need to talk to Liz, too, though. Is she close by?"

"Sure, but before you go, one last question. Any news on who the mystery man, OJ, is?"

"That I cannot tell you. But what I do know is he has moved on and left the state."

"I figured as much. I'll go get Liz for you."

Liz jumped to her feet from the seat under the Jacaranda tree and ran to retrieve Alex's phone. She was more than ready to talk to Jeremy. She had heard the sudden outburst of anger from Alex and had swung her head just in time to glimpse his fist slam against the patio table.

It was at that moment the pair had locked eyes. He hadn't shifted his gaze from her even as she ran to him. A protective shield had risen in his eyes. She understood that look. Jeff had given her that look numerous times, and now Alex had.

Her insides had turned warm and fuzzy. What was this man doing to her? She couldn't tell him. She was not ready to admit anything to herself, let alone to him.

Holding her breath, Liz tore her eyes from Alex's intense expression to stare at the phone in her hand. She wanted to hear what Jeremy had to say, but she was equally scared. Liz's hand trembled as she cradled the phone to her ear. Her eyes locked on Alex for a second time as he remained right beside her. How was it possible that she had found a strong, stable man a second time around who might be willing to walk alongside her, if that smouldering look was anything to go by?

But her huge secret that only Steph knew would no doubt stop him from looking at her like that.

As she hung up the phone, she collapsed. The news Jeremy had told her was too much to take in. The strong arms of the man whom she had begun to lean on were waiting for her. With tears of relief, she wept, not holding back.

She was no longer afraid to show them.

She was secure in who she was, and because of this, her heart had healed.

She now knew she could stand strong against the winds and storms of life.

She was no longer afraid to love again.

"They're beautiful." Steph choked back sobs. She could barely control herself. She didn't want to scare her girls, but she stood there cradling both in her arms. She couldn't believe it. With Solomon standing nearby and Liz watching, the Child Safety Officer left them alone.

Steph couldn't bring herself to ask the question that had haunted her since the first day she had abandoned them in the baskets unnamed. With tears streaming down her face, she looked at Jay and Jules, and the carers seated beside them. Her heart pounded almost out of her chest. "What are their names?" she choked between sobs.

The carers spoke first. "We call them Princess and Honey-girl."

"Steph, they haven't been named legally." Solomon stepped forward and stood beside her. His eyes were intense, looking into her face.

"What?" Steph was confused. She looked from him to the carers, to her babies. "How could they not have names?"

"They do not have birth certificates as their births were not registered."

Her eyes locked onto his. She could hear his words, but they were not registering. "What do you mean?"

"Child Safety can give interim birth certificates, but if the parents do not register their children's births, then children grow up without birth certificates."

"So, I get to do that?"

"Yes, you do," Solomon answered.

"I get to name my babies and register their births?" Steph wrapped her babies in a hug. She couldn't believe it. Her dream was becoming a reality. She was being given a second chance. She was allowed to name her babies.

Looking around the room, and with tears in her eyes, she motioned for Liz to come forward. "I want to introduce you to your niece." Steph handed one little girl to Liz.

"This is Primrose. She's my firstborn, and her name means first rose, new beginnings and hope. She has a little birthmark in the shape of a leaf on her ankle, that's how I remember her as my firstborn," she said through a sheen of tears.

"Steph, she's beautiful."

"And this is Lilly, meaning purity, innocence and rebirth."

Solomon stepped forward and wrapped his arms around her. "I'm proud of you," he whispered.

Steph's heart was full.

She had been given a second chance at life.

A second chance at being a mum, and she had named her babies.

THE END

BONUS

The Shadowed Files: Every Truth is Hidden in Darkness

For a sneak peek of Shadowed Lives - Book 2 of The Shadowed Files, read on -

Chapter 1

Two Samoan men, both six foot two, bodies rippling with muscles, stormed into the Australian Federal Police Headquarters in Brisbane, sending office staff scurrying to get out of the way. Papers fluttered to the air when one woman caught the heel of her shoe on the mat, scampering to clear the path as her morning coffee sloshed over its rim.

OJ hadn't intended for such an entrance, but as his gaze landed on the woman, he reached for her waist, securing her against himself before she hit the floor. A whirl of white papers settled around them when his eyes spotted the coffee about to tilt its contents to the floor. He clasped her hand in his, and he felt her chest breathe in as she gulped.

He lost his previous scowl, looking down at the woman he had flustered. Her blue eyes were wide, staring up at him, and her blonde hair was dishevelled, as her petite form rested in his arms. "Sorry," OJ said as he released his hold and took a step back.

Her cheeks flushed as she took another step back and squatted to pick up the papers, placing her paper cup to the side as she rearranged the scattered papers. OJ saw in his peripheral vision the floor staff peering around pot plants and leaning against walls to see the commotion he had caused when he crouched to assist.

The pretty, petite blonde didn't say a word, but her fingers spoke plenty as they trembled, collecting the papers from his hand. She rose to her feet and gave him a slight smile as she left, looking back over her shoulder once before going out of sight.

At his shiny black army boots sat her coffee, abandoned. He rose, holding her cup, scanning the empty hall where she had disappeared.

"That was mighty chivalrous of you. Are you going to apologise to the whole staff for frightening them, too?" crooned his partner, Josefa Richards, who stood beside him with a wide grin and his hands on his belt.

"I don't think I'm the only one who needs to apologise. Look at you, standing there with your hands on your tactical belt, looking intimidating."

"Whatever," Richards said with a wave of his hand. "Do you seriously think she's coming back for that coffee?"

"Not if she sees your smug face," OJ said, dumping the coffee in the trash bin as the elevator dinged. "Come on, let's get out of here and leave these people in peace." OJ noticed the stolen glances from women wearing badges and raised brows of men with concealed weapons as he turned and stepped inside the elevator. OJ leaned against the cool glass and sighed, hitting the button to the top floor of the building. "What an entrance to our first day here."

He and his long-term police partner, Richards, had flown into the Sunshine State, aka Queensland, less than two hours ago, and at this point, he'd rather be lying by the pool unwinding and settling into his new compound along the Brisbane River. But no, here he was riding an elevator to the top floor to meet his new boss. "We couldn't even unpack our bags, bro," OJ growled through clenched teeth as the elevator came to a stop and they exited, making their way around to the room marked 'Sergeant'.

"Welcome to the same rat race but in a new and sunnier state," Josefa laughed, slapping him on the back, easing some of the tension snaking along his spine.

He could always trust Richards to do that for him - ease tension. The man marked with scars faced death and the gun barrel too many times for OJ to count, but he always smiled and laughed his way through life.

"Come in." They heard from the other side.

Richards opened the door, and OJ stepped in behind his partner, coming to a complete halt when he saw the man by the window.

Their eyes locked and narrowed on one another.

"You." They said in unison.

OJ side-stepped his baffled partner as Richards swung his head from side to side.

The room fell silent.

Scenes flashed before OJ. The kind of ones that woke him in cold sweats at night flew through his mind's eye, quick and fast. Liz Agius's screams and hazel eyes with her blue-rimmed irises that he somehow couldn't seem to shake even now, as he stood before the man who took him back to the place he had tried to forget about.

Shaking his head to dislodge memories, OJ pivoted on his heel and stormed out of the room, slamming the door behind him.

He needed to get away, and his shadow, Richards, was on his heels, grabbing his bicep and reefing him around in no time. "Get a grip, man. Tell me what is going on. What just happened inside that room?"

OJ stared at his partner and shook his arm free. He ran a hand through his short-cropped hair, tussling it, not caring that it messed up his image. Who cared about looking schmick for the new boss?

He heard a door open and saw Richards' body straighten beside him. "The man signalled us to come back in. I think we'd better go."

OJ refused to look at Richards as he moved past him, but Richards grabbed his arm. His long black lashes framed his honey-coloured eyes. "Are you alright, bro?"

OJ was not alright. Nothing was alright. He had avoided anyone reminding him of his last sting, but here was a living, breathing thorn in his flesh, come to torment him. OJ shook his head to dislodge the terrible visual before him.

Nope.

The man remained standing in the doorway, staring at him. Dragging his feet as though trudging through mud, OJ followed Richards back into the room.

Jeremy couldn't believe it. That man had glared him down through the one-way mirror in Liz's cafe several months back, and now he stood staring him down one foot away. The confirmation of his identity and what he did glared before him. "It can't be," Jeremy said, gathering his composure, as he sized the man up and down. He couldn't believe it. He was about to get cozy with the man who'd caused him grief for several months.

OJ had been working as an undercover officer for the Australian Federal Police while posing as Rick's man, and that was why Liz felt safe with him.

Jeremy rubbed a hand down the back of his neck as the two men stepped at ease and rested their eyes on him and onto the Boss seated behind the desk. Interesting times ahead, no doubt. But did the other man he entered with know about the last assignment?

The Boss rose from behind his desk to stand at his window and look out over the city at the high-rise buildings. "Good evening, gentlemen. Thank you for agreeing to meet with me on such short notice," he began as he turned to face them, bouncing his gaze between them. "My name is Timothy Walker, and you can call me Boss, Sir or Sergeant Walker. This here is Senior Constable Jeremy Niko, who has recently returned after serving some time as a Detective at the Surfers Paradise Police Department."

Jeremy's gaze landed on OJ, using his skill as a human profiler to read his discomfort and annoyance at being thrown in the deep end.

To his credit, OJ did not avert his eyes. They read anger, red and boiling. But since they were all agents, and Jeremy knew they could not bring up past assignments unless current missions depended upon them, he stayed silent, glaring at the man.

"First Class Constable Olioli Lese Taito, welcome," Boss Walker stepped forward to greet them. "And First Class Constable, Josefa Richards, I would like to welcome you to our lovely state of Queensland. I hope the two of you find this a lot sunnier and more pleasant than the one you left." Sergeant Walker smiled, relieving the tension building in the room. "Josefa, what would you like our team to call you going forward?"

"Richards, Sir."

"Fair enough. Richards, it is. And you Olioli. What about you?"

"OJ, Sir." The man's gaze returned to Jeremy, staring him down.

He knew OJ cited him his rights by the glare alone, even if Jeremy outranked him. Jeremy was glad he had the man on his side. He liked him straightaway by the look he threw. Jeremy nodded his head as OJ's eyes stayed fixed on him.

"And Jeremy, what about you? Do you have a preference from the team?"

Jeremy wondered what the Boss thought of the undercurrent in the room as his eyes roamed back to the leader of the pack. He knew it wouldn't have escaped him.

"Niko or Jeremy is fine, Sir."

"The two southerners will be Senior Constables at the end of this year, so no outdoing each other. I want you working as a team," said the Boss. "Do you hear me?"

So, the undercurrent had been picked up by their Boss.

"Yes, Sir," they chorused.

"And I am aware you two know each other from a previous mission. Don't let that become a problem here. Do you understand?" The boss's eyes travelled from OJ to land on Jeremy, pinning them until they answered.

"Yes, Sir," OJ answered first, followed by Jeremy.

Jeremy noticed Richards' slight shift to his partner, but OJ didn't move his gaze off their Boss.

"You will all have two days off and begin on Monday at 0800 hours back here. Any questions?"

"No, sir," the men answered together.

❋

OJ's brows knitted together at the sudden interruption to the thumping reggae music in his ears as he jogged along the beach Saturday morning. He should have left his phone in the car, but as an AFP agent, that was just something you didn't do. He glanced at his pocket as he continued to jog. The phone continued to vibrate, and he groaned as he dragged it out, eyeing the number on the screen. Why would his old boss from Sydney ring him? He hit the answer button. "Yes, Boss."

"Your cousin took to being a target again, and we need you back in that ring. We need to know whether it is the same drug lords back in Brisbane circling to finish off what they didn't complete last time, or whether it is a rumour of a new human trafficking syndicate."

OJ kept his rhythm going. He would not stop his feet from pounding the sand. "Didn't the investigation record his previous attack and money transfer equal the drug score?"

"Yes, but Rick Limo has been attacked in prison, and you're going in."

That had OJ stop in his tracks. A cold chill ran down his spine. "Do I have to remind you what happened the last time I went undercover in prison?" The words were spat with such force that his old boss would have recoiled in his seat had OJ been sitting opposite him.

"That guy is gone. Killed by someone else." His old boss showed no emotion and no recognition of OJ's near-death encounter.

"Kill or be killed."

"Something like that. Plus, you're the only one no one suspects of being a cop. They think you're one of them."

"And how do you know that I'm not posted on an assignment now? How can you ring me up and direct me to go back to them like you're still my boss?" OJ was ticked. To be more accurate. He was more than ticked.

He was raging inside.

He'd left the undercover drug life behind. He wanted nothing more to do with it. "I did you a favour the last time, and that sting went wrong. Are you forgetting I was involved in kidnapping an innocent woman?"

And her face still tormented him in his dreams because he knew he had affected her for life, but there was no way he was telling his old boss that.

"I swore to protect innocent citizens, not victimise them. I'm not doing it. I am under Sergeant Timothy Walker's directives now, in Brisbane," OJ said, reminding his old boss of where he was newly located.

"I've already spoken with him, and he has given me the go-ahead because this is of interest to him, too. You and Richards will work together as we think they're after Stephanie Sefo."

"Excuse me?"

This had just gone from bad to worse.

"What did you say?" OJ spoke louder over the phone. Flashes of Steph and Liz flew through his mind like a video on fast forward. Images of him watching their movements, cataloguing their daily routines, Liz's hospital visit and him following her to her car all flashed through his mind. She was beautiful, and it was true what he had whispered to her that day. He'd played his role well, jamming fear into her, and he'd hated himself for it ever since.

He needed oxygen.

"We think the group you slipped into in Brisbane during your undercover work several months back are connected to a human trafficking syndicate in Sydney." The familiar voice on the phone broke through his brain fog. "Isn't that your specialty now, OJ?" His old boss never even gave him time to reply before he continued. "Rick got word to his lawyer that a human trafficking ring was organising hits out of his Brisbane prison, and the next day he ended up knifed."

"So, someone leaked it." He knew what his old boss was doing. Calling his bluff. "Where do I need to be and what time?"

"Sergeant Walker said you are meeting him on Monday at 0800 hours, so that is to remain the same at the Headquarters. Walker will update you and Richards on the work. As usual, stay alive and--"

"Stay fluid," OJ said along with his Boss, and they ended the call.

OJ turned and stared out to sea as the waves crashed onto the beach. He jogged towards them, ditched his shirt, keys, earphones and phone and dove under the waves. He needed to restore his thoughts, and jogging wasn't cutting it. He'd have preferred a board, but body surfing would have to do. Anything to focus his mind upon and away from the phone call. At least he hadn't been dragged back to Sydney or Melbourne. That was one positive.

Stop thinking about it and surf.

The waves felt good. It was summertime, his favourite season.

It was a Saturday, his day off, and he'd driven up to the Sunshine Coast to jog and swim for the day, chill at a coffee shop and meet up with his old friend from Samoa.

A girl from Samoa.

The ebony-haired beauty had strolled past him a few months back, kicking sand with her feet, laughing with a friend. Her face had been hidden behind large sunglasses and a big floppy white hat. The girls hadn't seen him, and that had given him the advantage of doing what he did best.

His undercover work.

Creepy even for his standards. Yes. But what guy in his right mind would let a girl from his island home get away without talking to her? He'd impressed himself with his discretion as he hung back, watching them walk from the beach to the shops, arm in arm, laughing at a man who lost his beloved ice cream to the ground from a swooping magpie. He smiled at the memory as he ducked under the next wave. He was glad he'd plucked up the nerve to approach the pretty-eyed, Samoan beauty because he'd learnt they'd come from the same village.

OJ watched an ocean bird dive down to land on the water. It could dive and land wherever it wanted. Could he? His job didn't offer that. But the discipline on the job and the synchronised, fluid movements as a unit were what he liked. Maybe that was what drew him to Lani, a mixture of freedom and familiarity. But somehow, they had landed together.

How could he have stumbled across a girl from his own village, living in Australia, up the road from him? Could you call the Sunshine Coast an hour and a half 'up the road' from Brisbane? He was not letting her go without at least a conversation and a catch-up. He wanted to know more about who she was and where her family lived. Maybe they knew each other as kids?

❀

Steph eyed the blue door that led to Rick's hospital bed. She'd had to abandon her own babies for the man not more than ten metres away from her.

The police officer standing guard outside the door stared straight through her, and while she shook one hand out to relieve the tension in her fingers and then the other, she knew she was doing the right thing by her babies, being there.

Rick was the father of her children, and they deserved to have at least one photo with their father. That's what she'd tell anyone who dared to ask her why she was there. But most of all, there was an underlying reason why she was there, but would she come out and ask Rick what she wanted to know? She'd get in and get out. But the problem was getting in with that officer staring her down.

The hospital elevator door pinged, and out stepped a familiar face - Detective Jeremy, the detective from Surfers Paradise Police Station who had discovered she was the mother of the newsworthy story of the abandoned babies on the doorstep of The Coomera Marketplace twelve months back.

He looked in her direction, and she dropped her head, pulling her long, brown, wavy hair over her shoulder to cover her face, hoping against all hope that he hadn't seen her. His footfall sounded close as he moved towards the nurse's station.

"Well, well, who do we have here?" He stopped behind her frame.

A NOTE FROM THE AUTHOR-

As a previous career to children in the foster care system and a kindred career, I witnessed and experienced first-hand the importance of empathy, kindness and compassion toward those who were experiencing violence, whether it was male or female.

If you need help and support of any kind, reach out to your local community. I know there are people out there who want to help, because I was one of those who desired to see children reconciled with parents, grandparents, aunts and uncles.

THIS BOOK IS DEDICATED TO -

-those who have experienced intimate partner violence or domestic family violence

-those who have gone through the processes of the Child Protection System, the Department of Child Safety or the Foster Care System in any of its many forms

-those who have loved ones or who have personally been affected by addictive substances

AUTHOR BIO

Vikki lives in a rural country town in the beautiful Sunshine State of Queensland, Australia, where she enjoys farm life with her husband and their adult children. When she's not writing, you'll often find her outdoors with her two miniature horses, Dippy and Chester, reading or watching Turkish TV.

Much of Vikki's married life has been spent as a stay-at-home mum, homeschooling her three children, fostering, and serving her local community. She now works alongside her husband in their family-run business, Reconcile Life, as a qualified counsellor and facilitator in supporting men and women through behavioural change, identity development, and spiritual growth. Together, they help individuals heal, rebuild, and step into a hope-filled future.

www.ingramcontent.com/pod-product-compliance
Lightning Source LLC
LaVergne TN
LVHW100515110826
845146LV00002B/643

* 9 7 9 8 9 0 0 5 7 1 4 0 9 *